DRIP

Drip
(a gothic bromance)

Andrew
Montlack

Book design by Design for Writers
Author photo by Ted Waitt

www.AndrewMontlack.com

Library of Congress Control Number: 2017902057
CreateSpace Independent Publishing Platform, North
Charleston, SC

ISBN-13: 978-1541102125
ISBN-10: 1541102126

Printed in the United States of America.

Dedicated to:

My Parents and Stepparents, for grounding me
(both definitions).
My Sister and Ben, for laughing.
Jean, Tom and Cara, for taking me in.
David Friedman, for bursting bubbles.
Peter Wonsowski, for illustrating.
Peter Scott, for asking "So what?"
Fernando Soldevilla, para sumergir
los puros en brandy.
Ron Kalish, for teaching me alchemy.
Mike & Carol, for making Something happen.
Josh Lox, Kevin Goldstein, Adam Altman,
Joe Waldman, and Thom Bowers, for letting me shoot.
Tony Horton, George Papadopoulos, and
Dan Schaedle for spotting vampires.
Kate and Hannah,
for the only thing that really matters.

And remembering:
Ethel Calvert

PROLOGUE

ONE CRISP BUT SUNNY autumn Friday, two minutes after the 3:30 p.m. bell rang, two 8-year-old boys, J.D. and George, bounded out of Roosevelt Elementary, followed by a third boy, Rich.

As long as there have been days of the week, Friday has meant freedom for boys and girls in school, and as long as there are Fridays, there will be boys and girls running excitedly out at last bell, filled with adventure and nervous happiness and hope that the weekend will bring something new and exciting into the world.

As J.D. ran across the schoolyard, smiling his mischievous smile, he put on his well-worn Middlestop Mosquitos cap (sports caps were not allowed to be worn in class, and J.D. always had his at the ready for the moment when the last bell sounded).

"Hey, J.D., slow down!" Rich demanded, but it was George who fell, quietly, behind. Rich was pudgy and brutish, and he would throw his weight around when he ran; this allowed him to go a great distance, knocking down any bushes or small branches or squirrels that might be in his way. George was skinny and scrawny, and he needed his asthma inhaler in order to run any distance at all; he had a hard time navigating obstacles even with his thick glasses on.

J.D. did not slow down but instead ran faster, leading the boys across the baseball field and into a thicket of tall shrubs and evergreen trees. Rich reached the thicket and barreled his way through the bushes, followed by George; every time the larger boy pushed his way past a branch, it would snap back and hit the smaller one in the face.

George, after enduring many scratches, wrestled the last, unyielding branch out of his way and came out into a wood of tall, silver maple trees that seemed to go on forever. J.D. and Rich were nowhere in sight, and George felt certain that he would never find his way out.

From somewhere just ahead, George heard J.D. shout "Wow!" He went towards the sound and came upon a grove filled with piles of abandoned furniture and old appliances. Some of the hardware, such as the portable, black and white television set, or the yellow, full-size refrigerator, were common household items; others, like the cracked, black and blue lava lamp and second-generation videogame console, were unfamiliar; although drawn first to the latter, the three boys delighted in examining every forgotten relic that providence had left them.

Within ten minutes, J.D. grew bored and, joined by Rich, he began arranging a dilapidated, brown couch over a half-unrolled, indoor carpet. George picked up a textured lazyboy (mid-70's, wooden lever hanging off the side, stuffing bursting out of orange cushions) and placed it next to the couch, and all three together rolled a thick, fallen tree trunk opposite the couch and chair.

Rich produced from his back jeans pocket a dog-eared deck of playing cards, along with a wad of crumpled dollar bills and an empty candy wrapper. He handed the deck to J.D., who had just produced from his own back pocket a similar, though neatly clipped, wad of ones. Rich and J.D. turned and stared at George. "Show me the money," J.D. said.

George fished through each of his windbreaker pockets, while J.D. shuffled Rich's cards and Rich fidgeted with his money. Eventually, George pulled out three dollar bills and a handful of coins, which fell onto the ground. George scrambled to pick up the change.

"Ten dollar buy-in, man!" Rich said, getting red in the face. "Ten dollar buy-in!" He turned to J.D. "He doesn't have the money!"

"I'm spotting him," J.D. replied. J.D. dealt out three hands of cards onto the carpeting. "Have a seat."

For the rest of the afternoon, under rustling oak leaves and a hot, shaded breeze, the boys sat and played poker (J.D. expertly, because that was his nature, Rich impatiently, because that was *his* nature, and George uncertainly, because that was *his* nature).

George, who when the game started refused to let J.D. cover his bets, had been losing steadily, and he put his last 75 cents into the ante. Rich met George's 75 cents and smacked a quarter on top, raising the bet to a dollar. J.D. glanced at his cards and without hesitation tossed ten ones into the pot.

A tense silence descended on the group because J.D. had just made the biggest possible bet. Rich glared at him, but he met Rich's gaze with a mischievous grin.

George, who had been puzzling over the five cards in his hand, asked, "Can I exchange four cards?"

When he said this, whatever was building in the air between J.D. and Rich got turned back onto George. Rich shouted, "Are you retarded?"

J.D. snapped, "You can't exchange anything until next hand, and it's not your turn anyway! Pay attention!"

"I know it's not my turn," George replied. "I'm just trying to understand the rules."

"Retard!" Rich spat, and George looked down so that he would not have to look anyone in the eye.

J.D. softened. "George, you can exchange up to three cards, 'kay?"

George quietly nodded, and as he did he happened to notice, hidden up one of J.D.'s shirt sleeves, a pair of cards with just the tops sticking out. Rich could not see them because he was sitting across from J.D., but George was sitting midway between the two boys, and he could see the white tops of the hidden cards just fine.

George opened his mouth to say something, but he stopped himself and instead looked J.D. in the eye. Rich was busy searching through his pocket for more money, but J.D. saw that George saw, and he gave George a wink.

Rich slapped a ten-dollar bill onto the pile of coins and bills. "Show me," he said, turning over his cards. He had a ten of clubs, a jack of spades, a queen of spades, a king of spades, and an ace of clubs. "Royal straight," he said, leaning forward proudly, for a royal straight is one of the best hands in poker.

George had to fold. He did not have to show his hand, and he was glad of it, for all he had was a pair of twos.

J.D. threw down his cards: a ten of hearts, a jack of hearts, a queen of hearts, a king of hearts and an ace of hearts. This was a royal flush, which was *the* best hand in poker and beat a royal straight.

Rich stared down at J.D.'s cards. He tilted his head. "Those aren't from my deck."

"They're the same cards we've been using all afternoon," J.D. said.

Rich pointed to the dog-eared ten of hearts, jack of hearts

and queen of hearts. "Those three are mine," Rich said. "My cards are all bent at the top left corner." He then pointed to the unblemished king of hearts and ace of hearts. "Those two are brand new."

"They all look the same to me," J.D. said. He leaned forward to examine the cards, and when he did, George noticed that the back of his shirt had ridden up, revealing two new decks of cards; they were lodged between the back of his pants and his bare skin.

George let out a chuckle. He wished he had been able to keep it to himself, and it is too bad that he did not; Rich stood up and glared down at him, pointing a pudgy finger. "You. You're the cheat."

"Relax," J.D. said. "I'm sure it's an honest mistake."

But Rich grabbed George by the shoulders and plunged a knee into his stomach. George doubled over, unable to breathe.

"Hey!" J.D. shouted. He grabbed Rich and pulled him off of George. He got between them, bracing Rich with his arm. "Ok, take a walk, man."

"Make me," Rich replied.

"Make yourself," J.D. countered.

"Make me make myself."

"In about two seconds I will."

Then Rich grinned at J.D. in a nasty way and said, "What, you gonna go get your mom? Oh wait, I forgot! You don't have one: she's dead."

J.D.'s face went white, and his arm slackened; then he slammed his fist into Rich's nose.

Rich screamed, and J.D. swung at him with both hands, knocking his head left and right, left and right, left and right. Rich fell to the ground, and J.D. lept on top of him. Rich tried to wrestle him off, but it was like trying to shake off a pit bull.

J.D. landed punch after punch until Rich's nose and mouth were bloody and swollen.

He pinned Rich down by one shoulder, drew back his free fist and paused. "Apologize."

"I'm sorry," Rich wimpered.

"Not to me; to him."

Rich squirmed around to face George. "I'm sorry! I'm sorry!"

J.D. climbed off of Rich; Rich got up as fast as he could and ran out of the grove, making outraged cries all along the way.

J.D. went over to George, who was still doubled over, with the wind knocked out of him, and helped him to his feet. "Just breathe."

George let out a wheeze and a series of coughs, and then he was able to straighten up. He took a breath from his inhaler. "Is your mom really dead?"

J.D. did not answer.

"I'm sorry," George said.

Another of Rich's anguished yells came from the woods beyond, and J.D. laughed proudly. "He's twice my size, and I got him crying like a little girl."

"How come you get away with everything?"

"I don't know. It's easy."

George frowned, puzzled. Earlier that week, during history, he and J.D., who sat next to each other, were drawing dialogue bubbles into their textbook illustrations and secretly showing them to each other (George had the Continental Congress gathered around the Declaration of Independence saying "I shall have the fried pork dumplings," and "I am allergic to MSG," and so on; J.D. had a portrait of George Washington proclaiming, "I feel horny. Find me an intern"). J.D. snickered audibly, but it was George's silent, tight-lipped expression that somehow drew Ms. Feldstein's attention and ire, and George wound up having to stay after school for detention.

"You saw my decks, didn't you?" J.D. said.

George nodded.

"Thanks for not saying anything." J.D. reached into his back pocket and pulled out a 2-inch brass pocket knife. Digging into the small slot in the curved, wood and metal handle, he pulled open the blade. "Give me your hand."

"What are you gonna do?"

"I'm making you my blood brother."

George looked uncertainly from the knife to J.D. "Does it hurt?"

"No idea." J.D., seeing the doubt in George's eyes, flicked the blade across his own forefinger; a red bead appeared. "It's nothing," he reported. He handed the pocket knife to George. "Just do it quick, like you're pulling off a bandage."

George took several practice swipes across his finger. Satisfied, he touched the blade to his skin and held his breath.

The boys sat like this for several minutes: with George trying to cut his finger and J.D. trying, through his laughter, to encourage him, but George could not bring himself to do it. Finally, J.D. stopped grinning and chuckling; he took the knife out of George's hand and reached for his other hand. George recoiled instinctively.

"Close your eyes," J.D. said. "Trust me."

George squeezed his eyes shut and held his breath, puffing out his cheeks. J.D. gently but firmly grasped George's hand and slowly drew it toward him. Seeing George's ridiculous face, he could not help but let out one more, small laugh.

J.D. held George's forefinger firmly and said, "On the count of three, ok?"

George gave a small nod.

"One." he snapped the blade across George's finger.

George let out a shout, his eyes popping open, but his startled look quickly changed—first to open-mouthed awe, then to a proud grin at the red that was now oozing down his hand.

It is impossible to say who let out the first laugh, since each was giddy at having passed the test of bravery, but the result was that both boys fell into a long, exhausting laughing fit, which only ended when one of them—neither would later remember which—held up his bleeding finger and pressed it into the other's.

CHAPTER 1

Two young men, wearing backpacks over black graduation gowns, strode through the thicket, guided around the branches by twelve years of practice. The one smiling an easy smile and wearing the red Middlestop Mosquitoes baseball cap (featuring the town's cartoonish, bloodsucking mascot) was the first to see the plastic fencing encompassing what was now a partially-missing wood. He looked past the barricade, past the grove—ignoring the blooming spectacle of orange and yellow foxgloves—and squinted at the small swarm of pneumatic shovels and bulldozers that was tearing up the field beyond.

A newly-installed billboard promised, "BrewMart Lifestyle Center Coming Soon. 'We're Taking Middlestop Out of the Red and Into the Black!'"

The young man with the cap quietly hopped the fencing and walked into the remaining semi-grove. The other fellow took a running jump at the fence, and *WHUMPF!* His gown caught on one of the support stakes, catapulting him face-first into the ground. Such a racket would normally have been masked by the sounds of the construction machinery, but as it happened this particular thud occurred in between pneumatic hisses, and the noise caught the attention of a mustachioed crew foreman.

"This is private property!" the foreman barked.

"Relax buddy," said a laidback voice. "He's with me." J.D. appeared from behind a tree. His gown was gone, and he looked very professional in his tie and slacks and brandishing his cell phone. "This is our intern." He pointed to George, who was struggling to untangle his grass-stained gown from the fence.

The foreman said nothing but stared at J.D., apparently unimpressed with either this piece of information or with J.D.'s performance, or with both.

"I'm John, from project management," J.D. continued. "John—the *other* John—says—Now this isn't me talking, this is *John*—he says to say, and I quote, 'Turn in those receipts you've been withholding by the end of the day or your subs can forget about final payment.'"

But the foreman just kept on staring.

J.D. held up his cell phone. "John asked me for pictures of any debris piles on the work site, so I'll be taking pictures."

The foreman crossed his arms. "You tell your 'Project Team-'" he started to say.

J.D. held up his hands. "I'm just the messenger, man."

The foreman looked away, directing a frown at one of the shovels. J.D.'s chuckle and warm, dimpled smile drew the foreman's attention back.

J.D. leaned in and spoke softly. "Look, this is bullshit. You know it; I know it. I've only been with the team for a few weeks—this is my first real job—but I can smell an adrenaline junky at work, and John? The guy reeks of it."

The foreman nodded.

"If John starts fighting with you guys over this piddly crap, guess who gets to spend an extra ten hours a week taking on the day-to-day stuff."

"For overtime," the foreman replied.

J.D. shook his head. "For salary," he said. "There's no overtime."

The foreman nodded again.

J.D. pointed to one of four garbage dumpsters—the only one not overflowing with mangled tree trunks and unused orange plastic. "There's lots of good angles to shoot from; I can make that one look like four different ones. I'm just going to walk my intern through the site first, then I'll take care of us."

"Next time, bring your hard hat," the foreman replied. He turned and walked back to his crew.

George shook his head. "You're the anti-Christ, you know that?"

J.D. grinned. "Lucky for us." He retrieved his robe and backpack; then the two young men, looking like a Wall Street trader and a medieval plague doctor out for a hike, headed for the obscurity of the grove.

The indoor carpeting was still there to greet them, even if it was a good deal more weather-beaten, but the spot was not entirely unchanged: the couch, chair and appliances had all been removed, and in addition to the fencing, which bounded the perimeter, there was a sign staked into the ground announcing "Property of BrewCorp, L.L.C. Report Any Suspicious Activity." A telephone number was provided below.

J.D. and George stopped at a pair of adjacent trees. J.D. took off his slacks, sliding them gracefully down over his shoes and revealing a pair of vintage, plaid shorts underneath. George, removing his backpack, produced from it a pair of scotch glasses, a travel-sized ice bucket, and a bottle of Usquebaugh (18 Yr.); he fixed a pair of proper doubles—one rock each—and handed one to J.D.

J.D. pulled from his backpack a pleather-bound certificate. He opened it and beamed proudly at his degree. It read, "University of Middlestop. Bachelors of Engineering. Summa Cum Laude."

George retrieved his own degree and examined it uncertainly. It read, "University of Middlestop. Bachelors of Arts in English."

J.D. raised his drink, and George raised his; the young men clinked glasses, and each downed his scotch in one smooth gulp. They sat quietly, enjoying the woody burning in their throats. George closed his eyes, savoring the experience.

When he opened them, he saw that J.D. had produced his silver Zippo lighter, along with a cigar cutter and a pair of cigars. He chopped the ends off and handed one over. Each dipped his cigar into his drink, lit one end, gradually working the flame around for an even smoke, and then took a series of short puffs.

"What can you do with an English degree?" J.D. asked his friend.

"Frame it."

J.D.'s exhalation took on a giggly quality. He rubbed a drop of scotch into his degree. "Should've stuck with engineering."

"Yeah." George closed his eyes again and massaged his forehead.

"Did you submit your teaching application?"

George shook his head slowly, mouthing a "No."

J.D. sat up. "Bro, we got rent, we got student loans," he insisted, his voice becoming edgy.

"Ok, ok."

"Well, let's go then. Did you talk to the career guidance office and the alumni association?"

"Yes. They're not going to be any help."

"What did they say?"

"They said," George started to say, but he hesitated, mustering his nerve. Then he began again, speaking slowly. "They said: I should have played a sport; then they could help me."

J.D. frowned. "You suck at sports."

"Yes."

"*All* sports."

"I know."

"You got asked to leave t-ball."

"That's true."

"Brett's dad was afraid you were going to get hit in the schnozzle."

"That's what he told coach Ryan."

"Did you hit up the English department?"

"That was the first thing I did!" George snapped.

"Did you flash them the honor society card they awarded you?"

"You know what that card is good for?" George asked, becoming increasingly agitated. "If they ever open a Middlestop University Sigma-Tau-Delta Flyers Club at airports, I'll be able to sit in a comfy chair while I wait for my flight."

Then he stammered, "I couldn't—I couldn't..." George took several breaths and another gulp of his drink. "I need to get out of this town," He said finally.

"It won't help. Wherever you go, *you'll* still be there."

"All that tutoring and summer school, and I was still just scraping by," George said. "*You* were there. *You* know: never went out, dropped theatre in 10th grade, spent *hours* trying not to fail out of honors trig."

J.D. deadpanned wiping imaginary tears from his eyes.

"All I am saying is that I was never interested in it, and by college I couldn't handle it." George took a puff from his cigar.

"I know your chosen field of study happens to be where the jobs are, but I'm better at presenting dissertations on Shelly and Hawthorne, and I love it, so kill me."

"You know what your problem is?"

"No, but will you please tell me all about it?"

J.D. flicked his cigar at George, causing its inch-long, burning ash stalk to fall into his lap. George convulsively beat at the ash; instead of putting out the ember, this caused a small flame to ignite on his gown. He made an involuntary, cartoonish gasp, jumping up and wrestling out of the burning robes. J.D. clutched his stomach, laughing so hard he could not make a sound.

"What is my problem, Bro?" George asked; J.D. responded with a vigorous fit of laughter. "What is my problem, Bro?" He repeated, this time kicking the burning gown into his friend's lap.

It was J.D.'s turn to leap up. He danced on the gown until the flames were out and his laughter had subsided. "Your problem, Bro," he answered, "is you're so damn negative. There's opportunity everywhere, but you don't see it."

"We grew up and live in a dying steel town. Where do you see this opportunity?"

J.D. pointed a thumb over his shoulder. "Right here."

George saw that he was pointing at the Property of Brew-Corp sign. J.D. pulled out his cell phone and dialed the printed telephone number.

CHAPTER 2

THE LED CLOCK DISPLAY changed from 6:29 to 6:30, and the automatic coffee maker housing it gargled to life.

The surrounding loft was sparsely furnished with curbside finds: an upholstered, wooden armchair from the late 1960's, a high-backed, quarter round bench (found by the entryway door when the bodega on the ground floor lost its liquor license and became a Chinese carry out), a 3-piece couch held together with twine, a plywood-and-cardboard entertainment center with peeling paneling, and a scattering of mismatched coffee tables, TV trays and decade-old, jerry rigged appliances.

Large cardboard boxes, opened but not unpacked, filled the apartment. The remaining free space, which was most of the common area, was riddled with wall cracks, peeling white paint, loose floor planks and water stains.

Next to the bathroom, from behind the nearest bedroom door, a distorted radio alarm began screeching, masking the angry horns of morning traffic with the angry opinions of a shock jock. The door to the farther bedroom opened, and George stumbled out, wearing a pair of boxers and a t-shirt ("Liberal Arts Graduate...'Would you like fries with that?'"). He walked towards the bathroom, but the nearby bedroom door whooshed open, raising the shock jock's volume, and J.D., in his crew-neck (holes worn into the yellowed armpits) and Middlestop Mosquitoes cap, obliviously strode into the bathroom, shutting the door in George's face.

George stood still, hoping to have his patience rewarded with the sounds of a brief morning pee and flushing toilet; instead, he heard the shower; he went to get his coffee.

George's bedroom was cracked and peeling, like the common areas, but it was more orderly, and the small amount of clutter that was there was his own: piles of academic papers, a wall shelf of carefully arranged literary tomes, and, never leaving his bedside reading table, a dog-eared copy of Goethe's *Faust*, atop a hardbound edition of Mary Shelly's *Frankenstein, or The Modern Prometheus* (though it never earned George any much-desired dates or invitations to poker games, he would regularly call out anyone who, even in a passing reference, shortened the title to *Frankenstein*).

One sorely-missed piece of furniture was a mirror, and as George sat at his rickety secretary desk (the cheap, plywood back panel had long ago fallen off), he squinted into his darkened CRT computer monitor, relying on its reflection in order to perfect his necktie.

J.D. walked into the room. He wore a short-sleeve Guayabera and gray, tapered chinos, over black leather, 1970's ankle boots; he was holding a paper resume and a USB stick. J.D. assessed George's outfit: a brass-buttoned navy blazer over an earth-toned argyle v-neck sweater. "Are we going to Emily Dickinson's funeral?"

"It's a job interview, isn't it?" George said defensively.

"Not in a time capsule." J.D. handed the memory stick to George. "Something's messed up with my margins, bro. They were fine two weeks ago. Thanks." He walked out.

George turned on his monitor. He had to try several USB ports before his computer would recognize the memory. After five minutes of searching through the volume, he located J.D.'s resume.

OVERHEAD FLUORESCENT LIGHTS CAST a bluish pall over the waiting room. George thought of his high school cafeteria, though not because of the lighting, nor because of its size—this room was much smaller; the reason George felt the familiar knot in his stomach was that most of his and J.D.'s schoolmates were there. The ones who were not seated in plastic chairs, using tablets or going over resumes, were huddled in small groups, chatting boisterously and giving the windowless room an obnoxious energy.

George found it unnerving to see classmates he had grown up with all dressed in suits and ties for the first time. It reminded him of a set of 19th century paintings of dog-headed gentlemen. He had seen them at the Middlestop Museum of Art, before it was forced to sell off its collection.

He turned to J.D., who was scanning the room, his eyes darting back and forth. "This is a cattle call; we're going to wind up wasting the entire day here for nothing."

J.D. stopped scanning the room and stared straight ahead. "Sheila Stylavitch."

George followed his gaze and saw the name on the Human Resources Manager's misaligned, temporary door placard:

"Sheila Stylavitch." George's stomach knot tightened, and he tensed as a wave of memories hit him: he was back there, trying once again not to drop his food tray as Sheila, with her braces and horse teeth and permanently crinkle-nosed smirk, stood two inches from his face and, in front of the whole snickering room, shouted, "Hi, Georgie, you gonna show me your tiny little dick? Show me your tiny dick Georgie! I know you got one!"

"Sheila," J.D. repeated, grinning. He pulled out his cell phone and thumbed his way through a phone directory search app.

George looked for a distraction. He recognized Brett, his former classmate and brief t-ball teammate, standing in a corner and drilling himself on some sort of recitation. He walked over.

"Weakest point?" Brett was saying, looking down to consult his business portfolio. "My weakest point is I'm a perfectionist, which is actually a real asset."

George overheard J.D. behind him, flirting over the phone ("Sheila? J.D. Yeah it has...All grown up...Well, why don't you teach me?"). He tried to ignore the rest of the conversation.

"I know it's a big workload," Brett was saying, trying to remain confident and calm under the increasing scrutiny of his imaginary interviewer. "I can *handle* it...I can *handle* it. I *said* I can handle it. Look I was getting an ulcer. What would *you* do? I had an *ulcer*? What the *fuck*, mother*fucker*?"

"Hey Brett," George interrupted.

Brett looked up from his notes; after a moment, recognition flashed across his face. "Oh, hey George."

"Am I interrupting?"

"Oh. No. I've got this all sewn up."

George quietly nodded.

DRIP

Perhaps aware that George had seen his performance, Brett looked away, then down at his watch. "I wish she'd hurry it up. I've been here since 7:30."

J.D. appeared next to George, pocketing his cell phone. "Let's go." From their blank looks, J.D. could see that George and Brett had no idea what he was talking about. "We're in," he told George.

Hearing the door open, all three turned to face the Human Resources Manager's office.

There emerged J.D.'s former debate team partner, Jim Adams ("Urea based fertilizer status quo is not a significant problem requiring regulation; it's not like people are going to smoke the stuff…"). Jim was walking out, clutching his overly polished black leather portfolio and sobbing.

In the doorway behind him, Sheila appeared. She had always been tall, but because she was two years ahead of them, none had witnessed her gradual transformation into a stunning, power-blouse-wearing professional. She leaned slightly to one side, bending one of her knees and creating two simultaneous impressions in George's mind: one, that she was busy—meaning that this stance would allow her to efficiently spring back from the doorway to resume her work—and two, that she was publicly making some sort of private communication to J.D., one that concerned supermodel legs.

George would not have recognized her at all but for her face-melting scowl. The horse teeth remained, but without braces they seemed to be in better proportion to the rest of her face. "Oh my God," he uttered under his breath.

"J.D.," Sheila said in a shrill voice that resonated throughout the room. Heads turned as conversation quieted. Brett looked from Sheila back to George and J.D., and with a growing realization, his look of confusion became a glare.

"Come on," J.D. said, but George did not move. "Walk." J.D. shoved him forward.

George, knowing that he would be pushed every step of the way if necessary, began to walk on his own. They crossed the waiting room, wading through a small sea of resentful faces. They reached Sheila, and George noticed that she was giving him a puzzled look; he could feel his stomach tightening.

"You know George, right?" J.D. said, but even as Sheila shut the door and gave him a peck on the lips, she kept staring at George.

"Sit down." She sat behind her gray, steelcase desk, something out of a county-building fire sale, and indicated the cushionless swivel stools opposite.

George and J.D. took their seats. J.D. placed his resume on the desk, and George did the same (his seat was missing a footrest and kept trying to turn; he had to hold onto the front of the desk to remain facing forward).

"Oh please." Without glancing at J.D.'s resume, Sheila pushed it back to him. "I can get you an internship with Brew-Corp. That's BrewMart's holding company. They're looking for engineering and accounting graduates; you'll be working on fire, electrical, HVAC systems for new retail spaces. Some construction site visits but mostly deskwork with their development department, at the headquarters building in Chippewa Falls."

"That's that new polygon-shaped building, isn't it?" J.D. remarked.

"It's a *sex*tagon," Sheila corrected. J.D. grinned at the misnomer, but Sheila's expression admitted nothing. "J.D., that's what the shape is: it's a *sex*tagon."

"Of course it is," J.D. agreed.

"It's fifty dollars a week, and they're looking to hire." Sheila placed an application packet in front of J.D.

"You're the best."

"That's right Baby Boy." She picked up George's resume, eyebrows furrowing as she examined it. She said, into the piece of paper, "They're not really looking for English teachers right now."

George nodded and was about to thank her for her time, when J.D. cut him off. "Oh, that's the wrong resume, Bro. Tell her."

George returned J.D.'s meaningful glance with a look of clueless confusion, and J.D. said to Sheila, "George majored in accounting too."

Sheila glanced up from the resume and looked George in the eye. "Double major?"

"Double major," J.D. repeated.

J.D. and Sheila both stared at George. He nodded his confirmation and returned the Human Resources Manager's look with an anemic smile that did little to mask the pleading in his eyes. Sheila pointed decisively at him. "No."

J.D. stood up. "Then I'm out too."

"Fine," Sheila said, expressionlessly.

J.D. inclined his head towards the door. "Looks pretty slow out there for engineers. Don't you get, like, a bonus for bringing in the smartest guy in the room?"

"Are you the smartest guy in the room, J.D.?" Sheila asked, seemingly bored.

"Sheila, don't even. Yeah: I'm the smartest *fucking* guy in the room, and I've got another interview in an hour, so-"

"Where have you got an interview?"

J.D. just stared at her in silence. He turned to George. "Let's go."

George stood as J.D. opened the door.

Sheila looked from one to the other; then she told George, "I'll need you to fill out some paperwork."

J.D. turned around. He made no wisecrack codifying his victory but simply returned to his seat as she typed a short sentence into her computer (obsolete workstation, secured to the floor with a steel cable).

She printed two copies, placing them in front of George, who had also sat back down; forgetting to steady his chair, he slowly rotated a quarter turn clockwise as he studied the top document.

It stated, simply, "I, Georgie Unger, have a tiny little dick." There was a blank signature line and a place for the date.

"I don't..." George stammered. He grabbed a hold of the desk and twisted himself around to face forward. "I don't have a pen."

J.D. handed his pen over.

George held it over the agreement, pausing as a homebuyer might do before signing a questionable mortgage. His seat completed another, lazy quarter turn. He signed his name on both pages and reoriented the stool. Averting his eyes, he offered the papers back to Sheila.

She only took one. "The other copy's for your records."

CHAPTER 3

THE MORNING UPTOWN M2 was five minutes late, but when they boarded, J.D. did not seem to George to be concerned. Public transportation had always made George nervous, but since he and J.D. lived within bicycling distance of their college, it was something that he had been able to avoid, previously. Now, however, as he squeezed through the crowd of haggard-looking riders, some coming from a night shift at the hospital to their second or third day jobs and others headed to the precious few machine jobs at Middlestop Tire, Inc., George found himself overwhelmed with a feeling of despair.

J.D., as he could be relied upon to do, had located an improbable oasis towards the back of the bus, where a pixyish young lady was humming Beethoven's *Ode to Joy*. The two riders in front of her got up, and as they moved to the nearest door, standing passengers made a path for them. J.D. moved quickly and precisely through the clearing and over to the empty seats. He slid in next to the window, and as he held the remaining seat for George, he turned to look at the girl.

She could not have been more than seventeen or eighteen. Next to her sat a cardboard box filled with red roses; they matched her beret. Her muffled voice radiated the controlled, high-pitched quality of a trained lyric soprano. She only held J.D.'s gaze for a split second, but when he winked at her she smiled with her whole face, and the dimpled, squinting openness of the moment fed his own smile. Then she looked down at her lap. Self-consciousness turned her grin inward, giving her humming the intimate quality, to J.D.'s ears at least, of a shared secret between them. The moment passed, as George stumbled over a standing passenger's foot and, turning to apologize, half-fell, half-slid, into the seat beside his friend. J.D. hummed the comical staccato notes of a circus tune (*"doot-doot-do-do-loo-do-doot-doot-do-doot..."*); several nearby riders chuckled.

"Thanks for that," George said, unsmiling. As the bus pulled away from the curb, he turned to look out the window; he was just in time to see a soft tomato flatten itself against the glass. From one of a pair of run-down projects next door, a 4th floor balcony artillery battery consisting of eight-to-twelve year old boys was launching rotten produce down at them. The effect of the vehicle's creeping, fitful cruising speed and the dry, hot weather were such that the tomato did not quickly peel away from the window but instead crawled slowly down, leaving a viscous seeded trail, like a giant orange and brown snail.

Waiting for the window to clear, George stole glances at his fellow commuters. One, a pale middle-aged woman with a green, short-sleeve hospital shirt and dark circles under her eyes, sipped coffee from a Styrofoam cup (clichéd birthday-balloon green and blue colors, half-mug-half-maple-tree logo, with a streamlined, 1950's-style font: "*BrewMart*"). A coughing fit interrupted her sipping—everyone in town got the annual summer throat tickle; the joke was that it was malaria: The Mosquitoes were once again biting Middlestop in the ass. George saw other green and blue cups peppered throughout the bus. He hoped that this meant that BrewCorp was not just

24

another local soft-goods startup, doomed to failure, but that it instead had some traction and growth potential. The thought lifted George's spirits, and he turned back to the window.

They were crossing Bends Bridge, a fifty-year-old, cantile-vered river span that connected their west side neighborhood to the east side. In the late 1980's, city council had approved a plan to remove aging truss work and widen it into a six-lane highway. They believed that the renovation would duplicate the effect of Robert Moses' mid-century New York City high-ways and bring more people to live in the city; it did just the opposite; the removal of the truss work offered migrating drivers, on their mass exodus to the newer suburbs, a view of the steel mills, train tracks and industrial docks that lined the Chippewa-Middlestop waterway, below. A few roiling, white plumes still emanated from one or two smoke stacks—but most of the manufacturing infrastructure was now a perma-nent museum exhibit.

The bus reached the first stop on the east side of the bridge, Society Circle, home to the statue of Middlestop's founding father, Ezra Middle. A bearded, bronze Middle stood with one foot atop a massive fallen tree and the other atop the mangled frame of his wagon. Under the tree trunk, a group of vagabonds (real, not bronze) was inspecting its shopping cart inventories.

One man in particular, an amputee whose half-pants were duct taped at both knees, gave the statue an uncomfortable irony: according to city legend, Middle was traveling to Cal-ifornia to prospect for gold in 1850 when the falling trunk crushed his wagon; seeing this as a sign from God, he founded the city on that very spot, but what most versions of the story tended to gloss over, or completely ignore, as in the case of the statue, was that Middle lost both of his legs in the accident, was pinned to that very spot against his will, and died two weeks later from gangrene and exposure.

The bus pulled in to a stop, and two more tired looking riders boarded. George and J.D. noticed that they were sitting across from a BrewMart store; unlike any other parking lot on the route, this one was full.

"Huh," George puzzled; he could see that J.D. was also interested. "Do you think they brought the shoppers in from somewhere? Like a paid promotion?"

"Look at the shape the cars are in," J.D. said.

None of the vehicles was new. There were temporary plates taped to the windows, and there were dents and scratches, as well as color-mismatched replacement doors. These were authentic Middlestop shoppers alright, and they were entering and exiting the glass-fronted building in decent numbers.

"Now how's he gonna get that home?" J.D. wondered, spotting a couple and two young children struggling to bungee what looked like a giant, boxed flat-screen television onto the roof of their 2001 sedan.

"Wind shear'll rip it right off," George guessed.

"No it won't, but when they get it out of the box, the LED matrix will be crushed; there'll be about two dozen darkened lines running through the picture."

George was grateful when his friend did not launch into a lengthy and impassioned lecture on television electrical theory. Often George enjoyed trying to keep up with J.D.'s technical rants, but not today. "I have no idea how to do accounting."

J.D. was half listening as he smiled at the passing store. "It's a piece of cake."

"It's not a piece of cake!"

"We're interns." J.D. turned to give his friend an annoyed look.

"But...look, if they're looking to hire...I mean if I want to get hired-"

"I'm going to get us hired." J.D. turned back to the window.

"I'm sure you are, but I want to get hired on the merits of what I do."

"What do you do? You write about dead poets who no one reads once they're out of school. No one's gonna pay you to do that."

George blinked. He blinked again. Then he swallowed. Even though he knew that this was just J.D.'s way of ending the discussion, it did nothing to lessen the feeling of having been slapped in the face. He stared at the back of the seat in front of him.

"I'd like to see *you* earn second place in the English department paper competition," he mumbled. Then, to himself: "Who am I kidding? Prob'ly spends one night browsing *Faust* and takes the prize."

He glanced over, looking for any reaction, but J.D. gave none; what J.D. did do was make a fist and mime jerking himself off. For ten minutes after that, George kept quiet and stared off into space.

They passed street signs declaring, "Leaving Middlestop Heights," and "Chippewa Falls Village, Est. 1963." The homes here were newer and larger, with spacious yards. Mothers and fathers were loading children into SUV's for their morning school commute; lawn treatment crews were unpacking sprayers from vans.

Past the residential neighborhood, J.D. spotted the pink and tan stucco and Spanish colonial revival style architecture of a lifestyle shopping center. He pulled the overhead cable and got up. George did the same.

The bus stopped at the gas station, just past the shopping center, but it was forced to block the gas station's driveway because a yellow and black vehicle—extra wide, like an obese wasp on wheels—sat idling in the middle of the bus stop. Despite the bus driver's honking, the car did not budge.

J.D., George, and an older woman with a rain bonnet and callused hands got off.

The wasp's rear driver-side door opened, and J.D. and George were treated to a spontaneous bit of morning street theatre:

THE DRIVER WAS FILING her nails and balancing her cell phone between her head and left shoulder; she spoke loudly so as to be heard over the air conditioning and children's television. "I know. I *know*."

Two of three kindergarten-aged kids were slouching comfortably next to her, unimpressed with the permanently smiling, red and green amoebas that were singing and dancing on the TV, over the dashboard. The third child, the little girl who had just opened the back door, climbed down from the back seat and was walking around the car to join her siblings in the front.

"She's awful," continued the driver. "She's *awful*."

The old woman—she could have been 50; she could have been 70—climbed slowly into the vacated back seat, passing the little girl as she did. Settling in, she quietly grimaced at what could have been her arthritis, or the noise, or her driver's bright green nail polish, or a mixture of all three. Then she closed the back door.

The driver, who had not noticed her daughter walking around the front grill, reflexively put the wasp into drive. The little girl, apparently familiar with this behavior, banged hard on the hood two times with the expressionless, hostile precision of a Manhattan j-walker. Whatever experience had taught her to respond in this way was something that neither George nor J.D. could imagine; if on one or more occasions her mother had run her over, then she looked remarkably well.

"You'll dent it!" the driver warned her through the windshield.

Her daughter ignored her, opened the passenger front door and nudged her brother's thigh. He slid closer to his brother on the left and made room for her.

"That's what I told him," the driver said, resuming her phone call but now looking at her children. She added, "Hold on, Shan, hold on," and addressed her daughter and two sons. "What are you doing?"

"We want to be with you," the little girl replied.

"Ms. Betty rides up here," she said. "Get in the back, all of you."

"I'm fine," the old woman said from the back seat.

"She's fine, mom," the boy in the middle repeated.

"Never mind," the daughter decided. "I like riding with Ms. Betty." She climbed back down from the front seat.

"Ok, Shan," the driver said, returning to her call.

The little girl shut the front door and waited patiently for something to happen. The car began to lurch forward. She hit the door hard, twice; the car stopped, and she walked to the back door and climbed in.

The last thing that George and J.D. could hear was a sentence fragment from the driver: "not your car, and when you hit other people's things-," then the back door closed, and the bloated wasp pulled away.

FROM THE BUS STOP, the entrance to BrewCorp's headquarters was easy to find, even though there was no street sign. The protestors gave it away. There were dozens of them: men, women and children. Some were young, some old; some gothy, some business casual; some handicapped, some just clumsy, but all were angry.

The younger, healthier people marched in a circle, chanting, "What do we want? *BrewCorp, pay your fair share!* When do we want it? *Now!*"

Older protesters held up signs. One, an elderly man in a dilapidated wheelchair (rust and duct tape on the frame, torn rubber on the wheels), had a handwritten poster propped up in his lap; it read, "I can't afford a new wheelchair! How can I afford to pay BrewCorp's taxes?" Next to him, a middle-aged woman wore a sandwich-board sign that read, "Schools and Teachers, Not Corporate Leachers!"

Surveying the group, J.D. said to George, "You're worried about getting hired? This freak show is our town's workforce; they're your competition. This'll be like running in the special Olympics."

George snorted his disgust at the comment. "You're nasty, you know that?"

J.D. nodded, grinning proudly. He was chuckling, but something caught his eye and made him stop. Amidst a circle of celtic-cloaked youths stood a gnarled, quaking figure—her back was to J.D., so he could not see her face. She held up a burning, smokey sage leaf with one trembling hand, and with the other she made odd, repetitive gestures towards the nearby brick post with the BrewCorp Park placard. She was blocking the entryway.

J.D. frowned. "Hope you brought your twenty-sided dice," he said to George and then waded into the throng.

George crossed the picket line as well. He realized that a lot of his time with J.D. was spent ignoring angry looks. He could not understand why this did not bother his friend; all the upset faces made George feel ashamed, and feeling ashamed made him angry with himself.

J.D. and George emerged on the other side of the protest and found themselves right behind the shaking, old woman. Since there was no other way around, J.D. averted his eyes and pushed past her. She was uttering something, but it was inaudible over the chanting and shouting, and as J.D. strode down the driveway, he had the unsettling feeling that she was watching him.

BrewCorp's parking lot could have accommodated the weekend rush of a regional amusement park. It dwarfed the seventy or so cars parked in front of the faceted, tinted-glassed, five-story jewel that was the headquarters building. The best spots were taken by six, large, black, urban tanks on wheels, bearing the license plates "HALL-1," "SYTRY-1," "AMON-1," "BALLUM-1," "BUNET-1," and "FOURNEUS-1."

A giant, blue and green BrewCorp marquee, shaped like an angular coffee mug handle, protruded from what must have been the main entrance. George made a face. "Lovely. Atomic war chic, 1957, isn't it?

J.D. looked back over his shoulder; though he was snickering at the comment, he put up a shushing finger as he strode through the parting automatic doors.

CHAPTER 4

THE ONSITE HUMAN RESOURCES manager had prepared name tags for them—"J.D. Pence" and "George 'Little Richard' Unger" (Sheila had telephoned ahead). Within minutes of their arrival, J.D. and George had joined the eight new hires, as well as dozens of employees, in a cavernous, chandeliered conference hall.

George recognized the composition the 16-piece big band was performing (Duke Ellington's *Skin Deep*, with a faithful reproduction of Sam Woodyard's 1956 Newport Jazz Festival drum solo), but it was J.D. who embodied the rat-pack swagger of the tune when a redhead with stunning legs walked by: had most young men rubbernecked at her exposed knees, they would have received a hostile glare or simply been ignored, but when J.D. did it, something in his smile earned him a flattered return smile.

George was only vaguely aware of the flirtation, but he was painfully aware of being the only argyle-accoutered person in the room. Had the pattern taken the form of a button-down vest rather than a pullover, and had George not worn his navy blue, brass-buttoned blazer over it (and had he worn black, slim-fitting jeans with Etsy-purchased vintage ankle boots, as J.D. had done), he would have blended in with the hipster, business-casual dress code that the non-executive employees and interns had adopted; as it happened, he stood out like a sore thumb, and this hyperawareness was causing him to sweat profusely. He hastily walked to an unoccupied corner, where he pretended to examine an LCD screen presentation: Gilded Roast™ Cold Brewing Process (a Flash-rendered tank, filling with cold coffee, as animated red coils beneath, and a cartoon thermometer above, showed it getting heated).

J.D. came to his side. "Come on, man." He pushed George back into the middle of the room. George began to hyperventilate. "Hold your breath."

George did as he was told, being careful not to obviously inflate his cheeks.

"Now breathe out slow. It's just people." J.D. scanned the room. "*There's* someone for you."

A woman with short, wavy hair passed in front of J.D., who pointed her out with a half nod. If anyone stood out more than George, it was she: her polka dot v-neck blouse and matching floor-length skirt belonged in a Katherine Hepburn screwball comedy. She smiled and waved at select colleagues as she drifted to the front of the hall, and when she mouthed an indecipherable greeting at someone across the room, two rows of silver braces shined, making her look like a thirtysomething adolescent.

"Tell her you're Oscar Wilde," J.D. said. "She'll be into it."

"Oscar Wilde was gay."

"So much the better: turning you can be her project."

George stared at J.D. "Do you always develop a fully-realized alternate bio for yourself when you talk to women?"

"I'm whatever I need to be. That's..." J.D. trailed off, gaping across the room.

The woman had joined a pair of middle aged men, standing by the podium. From their perfectly cut gray suits, military postures and expressionless faces, J.D. could tell that they were executives; from his targeted research on the company's corporate governance webpage the night before, he could tell that the thick-necked man with bleached-blond hair and dull, pit bull eyes was Mark Amon and the other man, with the receding hair, close shaven beard, moustache, and small, perfectly round, wire-framed spectacles, was Richard Sytry—both senior vice presidents.

"That's what?" George prompted.

"The game." J.D. left his friend's side and swaggered across the room.

As George watched J.D. go, nervous sweat stung his eyes, forcing him to blink and squint and make all sorts of ridiculous faces. He fished a handkerchief from the oxford shirt pocket, under his argyle vest. Wiping the top half of his face, he cast about, frantically, searching the room for some quiet crevice or unfrequented section of wall where he might seek refuge.

He instinctively moved towards the corner with the LCD presentation, but there were now half a dozen co-workers gathered there, and they were lamenting the recent 3-game Mosquitoes shutout at the hands of a longtime rival.

A popping noise made George turn around.

The woman sitting at the nearby, round event table had pale skin, too much mascara, black hair with red streaks, and a small eyebrow stud; she was there by herself, marking up a thick legal document with her right hand while giving a sheet of bubble wrap a thorough going over with her left. George moved closer to the table and grasped the chair opposite her. "Excuse me, is this seat taken?"

She did not look up from her work but shook her head. George sat down and let out a sigh of relief. It was audible but did not break the woman's concentration. Atop the green tablecloth sat her black leather purse, designed to resemble a straightjacket. George had seen the style a few times on the MU campus. He studied the woman's face more closely and realized that he knew her.

J.D., meanwhile, reached the pair of executives in time to hear the end of their heated conversation. Amon was demanding a decision from Sytry about someone named G.L.

"We're not moving on G.L. until The Old Man tells us," Sytry replied.

"I just want to know who gets G.L.'s bowties," the woman with the polka dot blouse said. The men chuckled. "Especially that red one? With the green stripes?"

"Hi! J.D. Pence!"

The executives and the woman turned around. J.D. stood next to Sytry, offering his hand and smiling confidently. The three stared at him.

J.D. gave an involuntary shiver; he could not decide if the chill was because of the building's aggressive HVAC system or merely the shock of being rebuffed for the first time in his adult life, but he thrust his hand forward and smiled even more broadly. "I wanted you to get to know me because I'm going to become indispensable to BrewCorp."

Sytry fixed J.D. in his piercing, unblinking gaze. "Show me something indispensable."

J.D.'s smile evaporated. He recovered, giving Mr. Sytry a friendly chuckle. This was to stall for time as he thought up a witty retort. He was about to talk about his ability to hack interactive stuffed animals to DJ house music.

Sytry did not give him the chance. "No? Then don't waste my time."

"Yes, sir. Sorry to have bothered you." Shaken, J.D. quickly retreated across the room and looked for his friend. He spotted

George at a table, comically, spastically sliding his chair next to a beautiful, gothy-looking employee; she was putting a hand on his arm, saying something and smiling. *This looks interesting*, J.D. thought and walked over.

"We should get together for a coffee or-," George was telling her, when J.D. swept in, wedged a chair, which he had grabbed while crossing the room, into the tight space between them, and plopped down onto it.

"These guys must be pissing away a fortune on air conditioning," J.D. said, smiling at the woman as if she were an old acquaintance.

She rested her chin on one hand and furrowed her brow at him. "Now, that's an odd way to insinuate yourself into a conversation between two people." The sarcasm in her voice was so smooth that for a split second J.D. thought that she was genuinely intrigued. *This IS interesting*, he thought.

"J.D.," George said, "this is Cerri Morgan, from my graduate seminar on 19th century comparative lit-"

"J.D. Pence," J.D. interrupted, locking eyes with her. "Future C.E.O."

"Oh, how wonderful," she deadpanned and then looked at George. "I don't mean to be rude, but I have to submit this in twenty minutes." She returned to her proofreading.

Before J.D. could think of anything else to say, the lights dimmed, the music stopped, and a hush fell over the room.

A black and white still appeared on each of the two large projection screens that hung astride the podium: a tan, leathery face was winking out at the room over a cup of coffee; the bushy white eyebrows, high forehead, and tight-lipped grin could have belonged to a seventy-five-year-old Paul Newman. A title appeared below: "Billy Hall, BrewCorp Founder." The score accompanying the image began with a 3-note piano solo and slowly built up into a majestic symphonic piece—like something out of a positive political campaign ad or a Grand Canyon tourism video.

"Billy Hall started out with a dream," a voice over began (the narrator was a famous movie star with a naturalistic, soulful voice). "To improve lives by providing the best products at affordable prices. That dream is now a reality."

J.D. leaned in toward the woman. "What do you do?" he whispered.

"Work for BrewCorp," she whispered back.

"What do you *do*?"

"I'm a paralegal. Watch the pretty pictures."

J.D. returned his attention to the presentation and began to fabricate another zinger.

The next still in the video montage was of a pair of older men. They could have been farmers, or perhaps they worked together in an auto factory. They were hoisting a large HDTV box off of a store shelf and were sharing a laugh with half-a-dozen surrounding children.

"Today, BrewMart stores bring neighbors together," the narrator said, "and revitalize communities, with innovative programs..."

I got it, J.D. thought. He turned to the woman. "How fast do you type?"

"Excuse me?"

"I'm going to need an ace secretary when I get to the top. How fast do you type?"

She did not look up or smile. "The circus is in town."

J.D. glanced up at another still image: two construction workers, standing in front of a state-of-the-art playground (undulating, universally accessible benches and slides, plat-forms with big bubble windows, checkered mats, blue and green everything); a man in a gray suit standing next to them, smiling broadly and presenting the builders with a giant, photogenic coupon: 70% off ANY Purchase. A title appearing below, read, "BrewMart Citizen Discount Program."

"Like the citizen discount program," the narrator continued, "offering savings of up to 70% to our customers who are making the world a better place–"

J.D. looked back at the woman, searching for something to work off of; he noticed the straightjacket purse. "Do you have an insane, very small monkey?" He whispered.

This time, the woman looked up, puzzled. She followed his gaze. "It's a metaphor. George will explain what that word means." She removed a small metal case from her purse and stood up. Sliding her black, short thumbnail along the opening, she retrieved a business card and leaned over J.D. She handed it to George. "Give me a call and we'll set something up."

"Where's *my* card?" J.D. asked.

She stared at him. "I left it in the spokes." She could see that he was properly confused and added, "Of your unicycle?" Then, squeezing the bulb of an imaginary clown's horn and mouthing, "Ooh-gah, Ooh-gah," she left.

J.D. watched her receding rear. "I am gonna nail that."

George stared at his friend uneasily, but J.D., now fully recovered from the executive chastisement he had earlier gotten, turned obliviously to watch the rest of the video.

One of the construction workers was pushing a six-year-old girl on the new swing set. The still dissolved into an extreme close-up of the little girl's ecstatic face. "Welcome to the Brew-Corp family," the narrator concluded. "At BrewCorp, it pays to do good."

The screens darkened and the lights came up.

Billy Hall was standing at the podium. He wore the same

gray suit as the senior vice presidents, but unlike them, he wore no tie and kept the top of his collar shirt unbuttoned. His air of success, earned and enjoyed, was infectious; he was like some gray-haired bulldog who had managed to wind up in the possession of a professional barbeque rib chef. The room burst into applause.

J.D. happily joined in with the cheering. George did not follow suit but instead, as he typically did at sports events, drinking parties, and any such large, enthusiastic groups, massaged his forehead and stared at a fixed point located ten miles beneath the table in front of him.

The applause died down, and Hall spoke. "I'm Billy Hall, Chief Executive Officer of BrewCorp."

A new round broke out. The no-nonsense, bulldog eyes surveyed the room and waited for the sound to subside; it did not.

"Thank you. Thank you." He held up sun-spotted hands to calm the room. "Please...Okay... Welcome to..."

Taking the hint, the room settled.

"See?" the man chuckled. "Get something done, and the world stops complaining about you and starts clapping."

There was laughter from around the room, followed by more applause, which quickly abated.

"Welcome to the fastest growing startup in the Midwest," Hall bellowed proudly. "BrewCorp didn't become that by being mediocre: we expect hard, exceptional work from each of our employees. If you hit a road block, smash it; if you can't smash it, grow wings; and if you can't do either of those two things, then work someplace else."

Polite laughter.

"Work hard and fearlessly, and you *will* fly," Hall insisted. "I'm not just talking about ten years from now, either, and to prove it, I tender this offer to everyone in this room..." He paused, looking around, watching his audience, and letting the tension build. Then he sprang it: "The first of you to successfully pitch me a plan to surpass our current growth—and I don't care if you're an executive or an intern or a janitor—I'm making you a vice president."

Animated murmuring broke out. Even George had to look up and ponder the C.E.O.'s words.

"As an executive," Hall continued, "you'll have access to our private club, in the Blue Steak Grill."

He reached out and motioned at one of the projection screens; both of them lit up on cue. The photograph had been taken from outside of the restaurant. J.D. and George, and everyone else present, recognized the royal blue awning and walkway, as well as the large window, offering a street view of the soft, amber-lit interior. The Blue Steak was Middlestop's oldest restaurant, and it remained a world-class steakhouse, according to *The Middlestop People's Chronicle*.

"You know what that means?" Hall asked the room, motioning at the screen a second time. "You'll be playing with the big boys."

The image changed to a black and white photograph: the C.E.O., sitting in an art-deco booth (maroon leather, shaped like a voluptuous upper lip); he wore a double-breasted, six-button tuxedo with short lapels—a sharp style if one was able to find it (perhaps in an upscale Manhattan vintage clothing store). He was laughing heartily. Obviously it was Halloween: a jack-o-lantern grinned from beside the costumed man's tabletop martini, and the two vacantly smiling young ladies, one under each of his arms, were done up with feathered headbands and short hair with intricate, flattened curls.

J.D. looked from the photo to the live C.E.O.; he saw, in the old man's dimpled, open-mouthed smile, everything he expected of his future self, made flesh. George looked at the C.E.O. as well; he saw that his future self would never make it past this man's lobby.

CHAPTER 5

"THIS IS NOT OUR stop," George protested.

J.D. had gotten up from his seat and was walking down the empty aisle toward the front door of the bus. "Come on," he called over his shoulder.

The 5:45 M2 Downtown Express had lighter ridership and traffic than its morning rush-hour, Uptown counterpart, which made sense: the dwindling manufacturing base and hospitals were downtown, while most of the homes and apartments were out in the suburbs (Chippewa Falls and other, farther bedroom communities). The Express avoided the Local's traffic lights by using an alternate side-street route, the same one that the Middlestop Heights school system used; although there was less traffic, the Express always seemed to get stuck behind a yellow school bus and thus ended up taking longer than did the Local.

George had been pleasantly surprised and J.D. indifferent when the bus took them past their old elementary school (red brick, tinted windows, animal wire-frame sculptures lining the entryway). George had looked at the baseball field that they used to cross on the way to their wooded clubhouse. Two twisted, rusting poles, sticking out of the dirt, were all that had remained of the backstop fence. The construction crew had cut down more greenery in the past three days and had moved on to tearing apart the infield; the BrewMart Lifestyle Center Billboard that had been previously hidden by the trees and bushes could be seen from the street.

George had asked J.D., "Do you still have the pocket knife?"

J.D. had stoically replied, "I choose to live in the present."

"Aw, come on. Hey, what about the scar?"

J.D. had reluctantly examined his left index finger, with its half-inch scar marking the thirteen year old cut. He had held the finger up to George's face and allowed his friend a moment's smile before curling it up and, in its place, flipping him the bird.

"Come on," J.D. repeated, from the front exit. The bus, which had rejoined the morning route, was pulling into the Middlestop Heights BrewMart store stop.

"Where are we going?" George asked, getting up.

"Some place where we can brainstorm. You'll see."

With a staccato, pneumatic *pshhht*, the door opened. J.D. and George stepped down, and as the bus pulled away, they noticed, along the driver's side, a three-panel, illustrated advertisement that could have been painted by Norman Rockwell: a tradesman, a nurse, and a firefighter, each sipping from his or her steaming BrewMart cup; the tagline, which ran across the bottom, read, "Wake up. Drink a Cup. Get Ready to Face the Day."

"Wow," George said gravely. "And you think *I'm* out of touch."

J.D. did not seem to hear; he looked the other way and took in the store from afar.

Keeping with BrewCorp's mid-century branding, the clear glass, two-story façade was capped with an overhanging, sloped, cantilever roof that met the ground about one hundred feet back. This was not the end of the building, only of the lean-to roof, which served to mask the transition from the transparent entrance foyer to the vast, stucco-walled store proper. The blue-and-green, mug-shaped billboard ("BrewMart Coffee & Living," with googie-style tailfins and chaser lights that might as well have been advertising "Martin and Lewis at The Sahara") stood twice as high as the structure.

J.D. was impressed. The kitsch rejected familiar big-box branding principles so flagrantly that the concept should have died on the drafting table, and yet BrewCorp obviously knew what they were doing: the parking lot remained full, and shoppers could be seen through the façade, packing the escalators and filling the aisles.

George said, "I can't believe one of these is going to be standing on top of our clubhouse."

J.D. gave him another irritated look.

"Give me the stink-eye, why don't you, but tell me why they have to do that to the street?"

J.D. tried to ignore the comment, but he could not shake it off; when it came to ruining the mood, his friend was a pro. "Ok, you know what? When I'm a success, which I will be because I don't waste time and energy on pointless thoughts, I'll build you a new, rusty baseball field, just like the old one, only shittier: George Unger Field. You can go there every day and pretend you're still nine years old, which will prompt real nine-year-olds to stay away for fear of the scary man-child."

George looked at the store. "Why are we here?"

"We're here to make me a vice president with the awesome and uncanny power to hire English majors." J.D. walked toward the store.

George remained behind, arms crossed, for nearly a minute, but in the end he thrust his hands into his pockets and followed the newly paved walkway past the busy parking lot, past the pair of fountains (pedestalled, spinning coffee mugs, angled off-axis and overflowing with water) and through the sliding glass doors.

The aisles of home electronics, décor, furnishing and linens resembled those of a typical retail mega store: flat screen TV's lining the wall, party-size chips and snacks, filling three rows of shelves, off-brand clothing (*Hems of Georgia,* "200 Years of Pants").

What stood out to J.D.—and to George, once he grudgingly sidled up to his friend—was the open floor space that stood between them and the rest of the store: it was made up of coffee tables and creamer and sweetener stands; there must have been seventy or more people concentrated there—a crowd by Middlestop retail shopping standards—yet the noise level was like that of a pub at three o'clock on a Monday afternoon. Conversation was subdued and neutral ("...rain tomorrow; anyway, we need it"), and pallid customers, played-out from their week or month or decade, quietly sipped coffee.

George read the curiosity in J.D.'s face. "The lot's full because it's free." He pointed above the service counter, just to their right.

There was a chalkboard sign, below which a staff of seven, uniformed servers was deftly turning over orders. Four of the workers ran a bank of brewers; the remaining three were at the touch-screen registers, taking orders and swiping discount cards. The sign promised, "Free Coffee Fridays, 5:30 p.m. to 6:30 p.m."

"You know what?" George mumbled to himself. "I could use a-" He got in line.

J.D. followed him to the counter. He pulled out his phone, opened a note-taking app, and began thumbing observations.

The first thing he noticed was the coffee. The customer in front of George, a Chippewa Falls type (power suit, James-Bond-looking watch, designer sunglasses over a clean-shaven, tan face), had just received his; the cup was different from the others, which broadcast the company's happy color palette; this cup, though, was solid white, with the only hue coming from a golden band encircling the top.

Is his the only one? J.D. wondered. *No, wait.* Amidst the rank and file shoppers sat a peppering of suits and sunglasses (and James-Bond-quality watches on tan wrists); the suits were texting, phoning, and taking sips from gold-banded, white cups.

The customer at the counter took his coffee and headed directly to the exit, bypassing the creamer and sugar stations. George moved up, and the server, a sunny undergraduate, raised his eyebrows and smiled. "Welcome to Brewmart." He nodded encouragingly with each word. "What can I get for you?"

"Hello, uh..." George squinted up at a menu on the back wall. "I'll have what he had." He inclined his head in the direction of the exit.

The server took in George's argyle top. "I'll be happy to do that for you. Can I please have your BrewMart Preferred Card?"

J.D. could see the back of his friend's neck reddening; he turned around; there was no one in line behind him; he buttoned the top of his white collar shirt with one hand and with the other fished through his blazer side pockets. Locating his necktie, he pulled it out and listened to the rest of the exchange.

"I don't have a BrewMart Preferred Card," George was saying.

J.D. grinned. As he worked on his knot, he whispered over his shoulder, "Show him your Sigma Tau Delta card."

If the server noticed George elbowing someone in the back, he ignored it. "I'm sorry, but the Gilded Roast is reserved for our BrewMart Preferred cardholders. I'll be happy to get you an application." He reached below the counter and retrieved a five-page form.

"No, no." George held up a hand. He was not interested in putting any more personal assessments above his signature. "I'll just have what the rest of the plebeians are drinking."

J.D. shook his head and laughed silently. "Bro," he whispered.

"I'm sorry?" the server said to George.

"Uh..." George reexamined the menu.

"Medium regular," whispered J.D. as he finished his tie and searched his pockets for another accoutrement.

"Medium regular," George told the server.

The server tapped in the order. "One medium regular!"

A worker at one of the brewers confirmed, "One medium regular, on my screen!"

The server gave his screen several more taps. "If I can just get your name and email, or phone, I can set you up with a regular savings card, good at any BrewMart."

"Not today, thank you," George replied.

"It will keep track of all your points for you. It's paperless."

"What if I like paper?"

George's sarcasm seemed lost on the server, who replied, "You can always print out an e-statement. Just log into your online account at www.Brew-"

"Ok, ok. Give me the plastic. I want the plastic. I love the plastic." George surrendered his name and email to the server, who tapped the dictation into his screen.

The server retrieved, from under the counter, a key ring-sized card, a wallet-sized card, and a brochure (Your NEW BrewMart Savings Card). He scanned the bar codes and placed the cards and brochure, along with George's medium regular coffee, on the counter. "You've got a 500 point enrollment bonus on your card, plus you've earned 100 points with your order; it's good for 10 percent off all in-store merchandise, or you can save up points for bigger deals." A slot in the counter spit out a paper receipt; the server placed it on top of the cards. "Your points are listed on the receipt as well, since you like paper."

George ignored the quip and began arranging the items on the counter for convenient carrying.

J.D., aware that this ritual could go on and on (*so many possible configurations for a coffee, receipt, brochure, and two cards*), elbowed George out of the way as he turned to face the server. He now wore a pair of round, metal-framed, vintage sunglasses. Before the server could welcome him to BrewMart, he said, "I'll have my usual."

"Can I please have your Gilded-"

"My card's at home." J.D. put one hand, the one not texting notes, on the counter and leaned in, so as to stare down the server.

George broke off from his struggle with the coffee and carriables to shoot J.D. a disbelieving look. J.D. stepped on George's foot, causing him to grimace, look back down, and resume arranging his coffee and portables.

"Can I please have your phone or email?" the server asked.

J.D. gave the main number for BrewCorp headquarters.

"Oh," the server remarked before he even tapped the number into his screen. "What's the extension?"

"I don't have one right now. They're shuffling me around while they fix the HVAC."

"I see. It's just that we're really not supposed to…" The sudden smile beneath J.D.'s darkened, round lenses made the server trail off.

"What are you studying?"

"I.T. systems."

"What year?"

"Junior."

"You should think about an internship with us."

Under his breath, George uttered, "Dear criminy." His foot received a second, painful mashing.

The server tapped a code into his screen. "One Gilded, medium!"

"One Gilded, medium…on my screen!" the worker behind him confirmed.

"That's a cool building," the server said.

"Yeah it is," J.D. agreed.

"Sorry I can't give you points for this; it won't let me print you a receipt."

"Mmm-Hmm." J.D. looked at his phone and resumed his note-taking.

"Your order will be up shortly." The server stepped away to collect the order.

George turned to J.D. "Do you sacrifice a goat every night or something?"

"You try too hard, Bro. Just learn to relax."

A series of bells—something one would hear from a slot machine—caught J.D.'s attention, and he looked up. The sound had come from just beyond the coffee plaza, before the shopping aisles, where a line of customers wound its way out of the left side of a community-themed double archway. It was built into a tree mural with blue and green leaves and identically-colored cutout figures (holding hands, forming a ring around the tree). Large marquee letters, done in a whimsical font and self-lit with exposed, white LED globes, formed a sign around the outermost artwork: Citizen Discount Center. A multi-colored ticker display in the crown of the tree announced, "Joe from Inini Village has just earned 1,000,000 points!"

A man, presumably Joe, walked out from under the other side of the archway. He was in his mid-forties. J.D. judged him to be a building tradesman: he had on jeans, a faded red and black checkered, untucked collar shirt (plain white crew-neck underneath), a number-two pencil nestled behind his ear, and a Mosquitoes cap.

Accompanying Joe were his two children: a pre-adolescent girl, texting on her phone, and her glassy-eyed younger sister, who repeatedly flexed a bandaged elbow and shuffled behind in a zig-zag trajectory.

Mrs. Joe brought up the rear and occasionally steered the wandering younger child back on course. Joe led his family toward store shelves with a purposeful stride and a satisfied expression, his lips pursed in a pensive smile and his eyes confidently fixed on the microwave aisle.

The server returned. "One Gilded, medium." He handed J.D. his coffee. J.D. walked over to the condiment station.

George finally settled upon holding everything in one hand and positioning the other hand underneath, as a safety net. He walked into the seating area and looked for a free table. One of the blue ones opened up, but just as George was reaching for one of the seats, a group of college students swooped in and sat down. There were several more such near misses; George, who was familiar with this phenomenon, told himself that he really ought to have known better in the first place and went to the nearest condiment station. No sooner had he begun debating between half and half and skim milk than he noticed five shoppers vacate the green table next to J.D.

J.D., whose back was to the table, and who did not seem to have any way of knowing it was now available, claimed it in one fluid motion. As he sat, he watched George shepherd his coffee across the room: it was a sort of slow-motion Zen ballet that George was inadvertently performing—slowly, methodically sliding one foot forward, pausing, and then sliding the other. He looked like a street mime pretending to be a statue coming to life (one customer, who believed George actually *was* a mime, tossed some coins at him).

As J.D. waited for George to complete the crossing, he took a sip of his coffee. "Mmm." He gazed admiringly at the gold and white cup. It was quite good—a dark roasted, almost metallic flavor, with a hint of chocolate.

George sat down across from him and took a sip of his own coffee; he looked disappointed.

"Let me see that," J.D. said, reaching over to pick up the BrewMart Savings Card brochure. He opened the glossy, folded paper and examined the savings chart that was listed within. One regular coffee was worth 100 points, or 10 percent off of any in-store merchandise; 10 regular coffees were worth 1000 points, or 20 percent off of items designated as weekly specials; at 100 coffees BrewMart obviously considered you a regular customer, and they awarded you 10,000 points, or 30 percent off of weekly specials. At 1000 coffees you were awarded 100,000 points or a 50-percent-off coupon, good for any item in-store; and at 10,000 regular coffees, equal to just one citizen discount certificate, you received 80 percent off any one, in-store purchase (you had to accumulate your points within one year, so you also probably got your stomach pumped).

"Ok," J.D. said, re-folding the brochure, "so what can they do that they aren't already doing?" He took another sip. "What's going to make this chain grow even faster?"

"A raffle," George suggested.

"What would be the point? That's a PR gimmick; everyone obviously already knows this place exists."

"PR can still be useful."

"No it can't."

"Suppose they threw a social event. A ball."

"A ball? Who would come to a ball at a retail store?"

"I would."

"Yeah...you would, wouldn't you."

"Ok, fine. No ball. Bad idea, apparently."

"Because you're trying to get people into the store for the first time, but they're already here."

"So, it's 'How do we get them to come-'?"

"Right. 'How do you get them to come back?'"

"A store-wide sales event."

J.D. picked up George's receipt and thrust it into his face. "Like this? A discount on all merchandise? Already happening."

George reached over and helped himself to a sip of J.D.'s coffee. He closed his eyes. "That is *really* good."

"Hey, hey, hey!" J.D. snatched back his cup. "Get your paws off; drink your plebeian coffee." He took a victory sip and examined George's receipt. George waited just long enough for J.D. to become interested in the piece of paper, and then he tore it out of his hands; George did this knowing what would follow.

J.D. sprung out of his chair, got behind George and put him in a one-armed headlock; with his free hand, he grasped for George's receipt, but George held it out of reach. The head-lock tightened, forcing George to make eye contact with a soccer mom, who shook her head disapprovingly. J.D. stopped reaching for the receipt—he realized that to maintain this strategy would be useless; instead, he positioned his free hand inches above George's scalp and administered a series of small, humiliating forehead slaps.

George remained defiant. "You're…in…the gilded club," he mocked, through crushed vocal cords, "No. Receipt. For. *You*."

J.D. looked around; customers were either ignoring them or else making annoyed faces; that was as far as public concern over the horseplay went. J.D. stuck out his thumb and sharply, repeatedly, poked George in his side ribs, just under his outstretched receipt arm. The jabs achieved the desired result: George retracted his arm to defend the tender spot; J.D. grabbed his wrist and wrenched it around behind his back; George still would not let go of the receipt. J.D. used his thumb to dig into George's inner wrist, causing the receipt fist to open just enough, and then he plucked up the piece of paper.

Grinning triumphantly, J.D. sat down. Unlike George, he had not broken a sweat. He reached for his coffee but realized that it was not in front of him; George had it in his hands.

"Fuck You." George caught his breath and took a long, deep sip. When he put down the cup, he found that he was looking at the checkout registers, which formed the boundary between the glass entrance and the coffee plaza. His eyes opened wide. "I've got it! I've got it! One of those face recognition systems at the checkout to analyze which cashier behaviors make customers want to come back and spend more."

J.D. dismissively rolled his eyes at first, but he stopped reaching for his coffee and put down the receipt.

"Think about it." George held up the brochure. "They can already track a customer's purchase habits; now they can track the way he or she interacts with the cashier. Couldn't they train employees based on that?"

"Totally impractical."

"Why? All they have to do is log on from their plush, executive desks and they can see whatever metrics they want. You make it searchable by expression, so for example you can see all transactions by a particular cashier when he or she is smiling—you see the image stream, but you also see a list of every associated customer, with a graph of his or her purchase history. 'Is that guy's subsequent spending different from previous times? Does he come back sooner or spend more next time if, say, the cashier smiles at him today?'"

J.D. laughed through his nose. "You have no idea what you're talking about. First, there would have to be a Wi-Fi umbrella between the headquarters and all of the stores—or else a Wide Area Network on a set of leased or installed landlines. Do you know what that would cost? I do, because that was my topography project for I.T. seminar. The software didn't even exist...I mean, now there are open source frameworks for real-time retail feeds...ok, so let's assume..."

George recognized the gleam that appeared in J.D.'s eyes as he spoke faster and faster. J.D. droned on, and on, and George's own eyes began to glaze over.

"...searchable database solutions are a dime-a-dozen; I could set it up myself with something off the shelf; it's just a matter of defining a set of expressions in the facial recognition app and plugging it in. It's easy."

"It's easy," George repeated; his inspired tone had given way to a winded irony.

"I could offline it at home. Clean up the bugs and make a demonstration." J.D. sprang to his feet. "Oh, J.D., you are just too awesome!" He strode toward the glass entryway. "Let's go, Bro!"

George stood and patted himself on the back. "Good job," he told himself sarcastically and followed J.D. out of the store.

CHAPTER 6

J.D.'s BEDROOM WAS A scene of barely-controlled chaos, with blueprints and cannibalized circuit boards spread across the bed, assorted plastic connectors from a roller coaster building kit strewn over the floor, and a two week old pile of laundry overflowing from its buckling basket. J.D. rummaged through a large cardboard box filled with rolled and rubber-banded drawings. The design plan he sought was in one of the poster tubes.

Locating the container, he removed the paper and unrolled it; as he hastily spread it across his desk, he knocked over a small, framed photograph. The pane did not shatter as it hit the floor, but it did receive a large, horizontal crack that separated J.D.'s happy mother from his toddler self. Impulsively, he kicked the frame across the room and out of his site; he turned his attention to the desktop blueprint ("Real-Time Fiber Optic Data Feed...Engineer: J.D. Pence").

George appeared at the door.

"You can have the TV tonight," J.D. said, distractedly.

George quietly watched him turn on his PC and arrange the clutter of technical textbooks, journals and drawings into a workable space.

J.D. reached over to his wall-mounted bookshelf. A trio of robotic, stuffed animals stood atop a MIDI sequencing box, which connected to them via an exposed circuit board and four serial cables. J.D. turned on the board; each of the furry heads gave a small twitch. He turned on the sequencer, and a house beat, coming from small, 5.1 surround computer speakers, filled the room.

The heads spoke: "*Win*ner-Takes-*ALL*." Each little figure emitted one word of the crudely-synthesized dialogue. Pronouncements came at irregular intervals, with the tiny heads grooving to the beat one moment and in the next declaring, "No-*Prize*-FOR-*second*-place."

George tried to withstand a few more of the proud utterings; he felt he had to walk away when the heads commanded, "LIM*ITS*-Are-For-lo*sers*."

J.D. reached underneath his blueprint and tore a blank sheet of paper from his desk top blotter; he placed it on top and began to sketch a flowchart; he drew two squares side by side and labeled them "Brewer stream" and "Register stream."

J.D. worked quickly and without stopping. Among his gifts was the ability to follow many cognitive threads simultaneously: he saw what his network needed to do, what the software needed to do, where he would procure the software, what he would tell the sales representative in order to reach the decision-maker, what to tell the decision-maker in order to get the software licenses cheaply, what tweaks he would make in order to get the software to perform as needed, and how to figure the payback for such an enterprise (George could get him this last part, now that he was an accounting intern).

By two o'clock in the morning, J.D. had the basic roadmap in place for his proposal. He was reviewing it, when an angry pounding on the wall interrupted him.

George, who had shut his door, had not been able to get away from J.D.'s music, which had been coming through the wall along with occasional, muffled, electronic outbursts ("make-*IT-hap*pen-BIG-fel*la*."). Doing his best to ignore the noise, he had turned on his computer and begun developing a proposal of his own—or rather, another proposal of his own.

"Sorry bro!" he heard J.D. call out; the blaring, stuffed-animal-spun house music ceased. George stared at the photo project image in front of him: a giant, anthropomorphized coffee mug overlooking a full parking lot, with a fake newspaper headline announcing, "The New Look of BrewCorp." The effect of the silence was like the opposite of a saintly ecstasy: the scales fell from George's eyes, and he saw before him a terrible vision; it was as if a cheerful, Godzilla-sized, brand mascot had decided to settle down and farm a crop of automobiles. George closed the program, opting not to save his work.

CHAPTER 7

GEORGE'S CUBICAL DESK WAS situated among a hive of identical desks in the middle of BrewCorp's happy-colored accounting floor. He sat, frantically thumbing through his five-year-old copy of *Taxes for Morons* and realizing that it was, in fact, too advanced for him.

As an accounting intern, he was expected to be able to conduct cost segregation tax planning. This involved going through hundreds of lines of budget and expense statements for store construction, identifying and separating out any building fixtures that could possibly, or even wishfully, be classified as personal property and applying shorter depreciation periods to them.

There was no one in the department to whom he could turn for help with this totally arcane task: in the weeks since he had begun his internship, he had not made any friends or acquaintances; he had been careful not to after his first day, when he had made the mistake of striking up a conversation with an intern who actually *had* majored in accounting.

"So, make the case for mark-to-market," the overly caffeinated, young man had challenged.

"Uh, wha-well," George had stammered, having no idea what mark-to-market was, "what's your position?"

"It's not about my position, it's what it *is*. BrewCorp doesn't purchase coffee in arrears; they buy ahead; it's a historic cost; why wouldn't you account historically?"

"I agree."

"I'm not asking you to agree," the intern had pushed, "I'm asking you to tell me why it's better to count it the other way."

George had claimed food poisoning and run to the men's room.

After that he had kept to himself and begun looking for a good introductory textbook on accounting. He had checked out a thin paperback volume from the library, hoping that it would be a fast read, but there were no charts or illustrations; only wall-to-wall, 10 point text. George had tried to read it in nightly, two-hour stretches.

He had been struggling through waves of anxiety. It was not just that internal rate of return, spending variance, and Off-Balance-sheet GAAP disclosure requirements were foreign concepts: it was that George felt himself getting sucked into a worldview based entirely upon external value. His passion for covering 19th century gothic novels (using Freudian, Feminist, and Marxist analyses), though highly meaningful to him, had no place in such a world.

Lest he forget that reality, daily performance evaluation emails served as reminders; they were filled with dozens of gloomy, crowd-sourced assessments, compiled from the feed-back of anonymous co-workers.

His anxiety had gotten so bad that three nights into the book he had needed to stop and breathe into a paper bag. He had been reading about depreciation recapture, the process by which, after a piece of property was sold, any previously claimed depreciations were owed back to the government. He had only just gotten used to the idea that he would be

spending time each year figuring out how much less everything was worth in order to claim the depreciation; the idea
of then having to remember to return every such deduction
after a sale, possibly decades later, had sent his mind into a
spiral; a universe of previously unfathomed clerical complex-
ity had unfolded before him, and his bleak, new future had
flashed before his eyes: there would be no more dissertations,
no more lively classroom discussions, and no more Byron or
Coleridge; only year-to-date comparisons, annual accounting
law supplements, and endless emails inquiring about missing
and un-submitted receipts.

Instead of continuing with the immersive reading, George
had decided to purchase a used copy of *Taxes for Morons*, with
the intention of consulting it on an as-needed basis. This
change of tactics, he had hoped, would help avoid another
panic attack. As it turned out, George would have *Taxes for
Morons* to thank for getting him a date with Cerri.

He had not spoken with her since running into her at the
orientation, though he had been thinking about her a good
deal, if fantasies of an 1816-Lake-Geneva-Chateau-style seduc-
tion counted. Her business card, which he took out at least
once a day, had given him hope, and not just sexual hope.
Whenever he recalled the unexpected reunion with his former
classmate, George felt a warm lightness, as though complex-
ity were just a trick of the mind; the universe had once again
settled into familiarity and inclusiveness and was granting him
a long-yearned-for niche. He could not muster the nerve to
call her for fear of breaking the spell.

After three frantic flips through the chapter on business
tax schedules (C, C-EZ and F), George found the paragraphs
on Section 179 depreciation. Minutes earlier, at 4:55 p.m., all
of the accountants had been instructed to reclassify store

equipment purchases from the previous year under Section 179 of the tax code.

George read and re-read the paragraphs, partially out loud. "'You can deduct up to $105,000 of the cost of new or used business equipment...didn't exceed $420,000...has to be used more than 50 percent of the time...provided that all property... didn't exceed $420,000.' $420,000?"

The company had purchased $650,700 in equipment.

George picked up the phone and dialed Cerri's extension, hoping she had not already left for the day.

"Section 179 hotline," she answered.

George blinked, at a loss for words. Cerri had undoubtedly seen his name on her caller ID, but how could she possibly know the reason for his call?

"George?"

"How-? How did you know I'm calling about the-?"

"Everyone in legal got called in at 8:30 this morning. I sort of figured it would take a crisis to get you to pick up the phone."

"Oh, no," George insisted. "I've been meaning to give you a call."

"It's fine; I know how you roll," she said. "You went half the semester without saying a word, then started practically teaching the class."

"I felt like I'd become invisible in there."

"You weren't invisible, you were different."

George nodded. "Yes."

"I like different."

George smiled; his face began to perspire.

"50 percent rule. The additional $250,700 was equipment that we loaned out to a chain of clothing outlets that are incorporated separately from BrewCorp. They had it for more than half the year, so you can claim the $420,000 limit."

"Oh, cheers."

"Cheers."

The call was about to end; George realized that if he let it end, he would regret it; he took a deep breath and then thought, *Bugger it*. "What are you doing tomorrow night?"

There was a pause on Cerri's end. "I'm free."

"Would you like to have dinner?"

There was another, longer pause; George was certain there had just been a terrible misunderstanding, that he had just behaved as desperately and inappropriately as if he had walked up to Cerri at her desk and pulled down his pants.

"Yes George Unger. I *would* like to have dinner with you."

"Fine. Well, uh..." George slid his stapler back and forth across the desk; this helped him to think through the fog of nervous, buzzing joy. "Why don't I cook something—or maybe we should go out?"

"Mmm, either one."

"Well...You know what? I would like to cook you something."

"I would like that."

"Do you have any dietary restrictions?"

"Dolphin."

"No dolphin."

"No, I *have* to have dolphin. It's for my cartilage."

"Seriously?"

"What do *you* think?"

"Oh." George laughed "Well, I'll-"

"Surprise me."

"Ok."

While George and Cerri worked out the logistics for their date (her car; his place), J.D. hurriedly stepped out of the elevator and scanned the cubicles for his friend.

George was just hanging up the phone when J.D found him. J.D. had rarely seen him looking so happy, and he chuckled at the oddness of it. "You look like you've just gotten a bl-" Noticing a woman staring at him from her nearby desk, he caught himself.

"A bluh?"

"Not safe for work," he said quietly. "I got us a ride to happy hour, but they're leaving now." In the weeks since embarking upon his high concept pitch, J.D. had been drinking nightly with his fellow employees and interns, trying to glean as much intelligence as he could about rival proposals. His colleagues' pitches-in-progress had all been variations on the themes of either stepping up BrewCorp's social media presence or else organizing cash mob events at the stores. None of them made J.D. the least bit apprehensive; still he instinctively kept abreast of the latest contest gossip.

"I'm going to be here late," George said, "but guess who I'm having-"

"I gotta go," J.D. interrupted, already on his way back to the elevator. He called over his shoulder, "We're at The Blue Steak! You should come when you're done!"

George shook his head, still smiling, and turned his attention back to taxes.

J.D. REACHED THE PARKING lot just in time to watch his ride peel away from the cul-de-sac. The charcoal colored urban tank kicked up a cloud of dust and loose asphalt as it accelerated around the circle; though the windows were down, the five passengers (blue shirts, white collars, bracers, sunglasses) could not hear J.D.'s shouts over the roar of the engine and the blast of air-conditioning, nor did the driver (black suit, open collar, sunglasses) notice the waving arms in the rearview mirror. J.D. ran after them, but it was useless.

He turned around and waded into the blistering, midsummer heat of the lot, scanning for an alternate prospect.

Twenty yards away, he saw someone with a metal-studded leather purse getting into her economobile (torn-off driver's side mirror, six-inch dent up the center of the hood). He ran over and knocked on Cerri's window; she rolled it down, raising her eyebrows. The car smelled of Nag Champa. "Hey."

"Hey."

"My ride ditched me. I'm trying to get to happy hour ahead of the mob-"

"And the unicycle's in the shop."

"And that."

Cerri nodded politely. "That's a real dilemma." A lengthy silence followed, during which neither one was willing to be the first to break eye-contact.

"I'll throw in a drink," J.D. offered.

"Oh." She let out a theatrical yawn. "Oh, excuse me. Look at-" Another yawn, as she gestured at the dashboard clock. "Look at the time. This has been fun."

J.D. moved around to the passenger's side and climbed in. "Come on."

"You knowww..." she said as though making a very thoughtful suggestion, "I've just come off a seventy-two hour week, I've had no sleep because something happened with my mom and she needed to go to the ER, *and* I'm getting over a sinus infection—so I think your getting into my car, uninvited, right now is verrry, *verrry* hot."

"Is your mom ok?"

"She's fine."

"You need to come with me to happy hour."

"But the thing is, um...?"

"J.D."

"J.D., the thing is, I really *don't*."

"When was the last time you had any fun? Anywhere?"

"This is getting old. Ok, for real now."

"You love it." J.D. smiled his easy smile.

CHAPTER 8

AT A QUARTER PAST nine, George stepped off the bus in front of The Blue Steak.

Tracking down and compiling his allotment of section 179 expenses had taken him until eight o'clock, two hours longer than any of the other interns. Partially, this was due to George's steep learning curve, but mostly it was because receipts for a set of upgraded grocery-aisle freezers had been misfiled; it took him an hour and a half to find out that they had been commingled with the energy efficiency rebate paperwork rather than with the rest of the equipment receipts.

Upon leaving work, he decided that, given the choice between reading himself to sleep at home and shrugging off his day with a pub adventure, he was willing to step outside of his comfort zone and check out The Blue Steak (the phone call with Cerri had put him in a bullish frame of mind).

During his bus ride downtown, George had imagined fin de siècle writers gathering at the one hundred and twenty year old establishment; he had pictured them smoking their pipes and drinking absinthe. As soon as he passed through the restaurant's ebony and etched glass doors, he saw that the social scene was more like something out of late 19th century Wall Street: bankers, businessmen and co-workers were noisily crammed between mahogany-paneled, walls, wrought iron chandeliers with incandescent globes radiated soft, white light, and the smoky haze that floated in the air, between the patrons' heads and the copper-tiled ceiling, came from cigars, not pipes.

George craned his head around, trying to spot J.D., and was not surprised to find that his friend was not there. The sandwich sign outside had advertised happy hour from 5 to 7; J.D. had probably moved on for the night, perhaps convincing some co-workers to join him at Skeeters, a college dive that sold one-dollar watered-down beer near the loft.

Contorting his way between the tightly crammed shoulders and elbows, George tried to secure a spot at the bar, but every time a space opened up in front of him, someone else slipped in to fill it.

After seven or eight frustrating minutes the same momentum that kept him from getting a spot swept him into place atop a leather barstool, and he examined his surroundings.

The focal point of the bar should have been the pair of graying, blue-vested bartenders who were pointing at customers, taking and filling drink orders three at a time, but it was not. Up on the wall behind the bar hung a thick-framed, twelve-foot-wide oil painting: a nude with long, jet-black, wavy hair and a gold leaf headband reclined, across sheets of royal blue velvet and golden satin, upon a Victorian couch; one pale arm rested above her head, and the other dangled lazily off the edge; she smiled out at George expectantly, as if to say, "Hey, Big Spender, are you just going to stand there all day?"

With some effort, George managed to look away; he tried to make eye contact with the nearest bartender, who was vigorously mixing an amber drink in a glass shaker. Taking one hand off of the shaker, the man raised a finger and pointed along the bar for new orders; he pointed at George.

"Hi, could I please get a-,"

A man slid in beside George, reached past, and shoved a $20 bill at the bartender. "Three Guinnesses."

"Three Guinness," the bartender acknowledged as he emptied his shaker into a martini glass; he took the drink to a customer at the far end of the bar, went over to the taps, and began pouring the three beers.

George pulled out his wallet. He had eleven dollars in singles and change. He took out three of the bills, along with two quarters, and as the bartender set the beers down next to him, he held up the money. The bartender did not see; he made change for the Guinness order and then raised his finger, starting at the end of the bar. Two more orders were taken, and then the bartender was again pointing at George.

George held out the money. "Usquebaugh, on the-"

"Cosmo," interrupted a throaty voice on his immediate right.

"Cosmopolitan," the smiling bartender repeated, winking; he turned around to fill the orders.

George turned to see who had just cut him off; she was the woman from orientation, the one with the polka dots and braces. This evening, she wore a strapless, red and black cocktail dress; no one was going to compete with her for the bartender's attention. She saw George's incredulous expression and looked genuinely surprised. "Oh my God, were you in line?"

"Forget it." George felt tired; he realized that he had needed to pee for the last half hour. "Do you know where the rest rooms are located?"

She pointed to a set of double doors. "Through there, down the stairs."

He got up from the bar.

"I'm sooo sorry," the woman insisted. "I didn't mean to cut in front of you."

"Why not? Someone had to do it." Ignoring her puzzled look, George nuzzled his way between the crush of well-dressed patrons, walking where he could and gently nudging backs out of the way; he passed through the double doors and into the welcoming solitude of the hallway beyond.

The only light came from small display fixtures on the wall; a series of illuminated paintings lined the thirty foot passageway. As George walked along, he glanced at some of them. They all seemed to be by the same 17th Century artist, Paulus Potter; he was apparently the Dutch go-to guy for bull-and-cow scenes. Each reproduction was a variation on the bovine theme: bulls and cows grazing, bulls and cows being shepherded to pasture, bulls and other bulls locking horns.

George let out a chuckle as he suddenly thought of *Poe's Fall of the House of Usher*, with its bleak tapestries and rattling trophies. Poe would certainly have appreciated the crowning piece of this gallery, a wall-mounted bull's head that stared amiably, if blankly, from the end of the hall.

The spiral staircase, wrought iron, with a gilt and green patina, was directly beneath the hunting trophy. George had to duck to avoid the animal's massive, furry jaw as he climbed onto the first step. Descending into the darkness, he held onto the rail for support and cautiously felt his way around the first spiral. He rounded the second spiral and began to make out the dimly-lit shape of a circular antechamber. Rounding the third and last spiral, he found himself facing a massive, studded, blue, leather-padded door. Below the small, speak-easy-style window, a brass placard read, "BrewCorp Executive Club. Members Only."

George looked around, trying to locate the bathroom, but there was nothing else there, apart from two more trophy heads: a cow and a bull, side by side on the opposite wall. He turned back to the door, unsure whether to knock, and pressed up against the window, trying to tell whether the pitch black was an unlit room beyond or a cover over the glass.

The cover slid open; a scowling mouth, under a biker moustache, appeared with such abruptness that George stumbled back, tripped over himself, and fell down. He scrambled back to his feet and brushed himself off, staring at the face in the window. The dark sunglasses and turtleneck melted so perfectly into the surrounding darkness that it created the effect of a disembodied mouth and ash white nose and chin, floating in space.

"Private club," the face said, with an irritated, gutteral voice.

Determined not to be intimidated by some bouncer with a chip on his shoulder, George approached the glass. "I know it's a private club, chum. I'm looking for the men's room."

A pale finger appeared next to the floating mouth; an overgrown, bruised fingernail tapped the glass five times, aggressively and rapidly, like some kind of albino woodpecker that preferred windows to trees. George glanced behind him but only saw the stuffed trophy heads; the window cover slammed shut with a loud clunk.

George walked over to the bull head; it was smaller than the one at the top of the stairs. He moved underneath it to examine the wall. Without warning, a nearly seamless door panel opened outward, catching him in the shoulder. The patron, a young man who was snickering at some private joke, bounded past, through the antechamber and up the stairs.

George grabbed hold of the closing wall and walked into the checker-floored bathroom.

There was an odd noise that echoed through the room, a slow, rhythmic creaking. George could not identify the source of the sound, and so he dismissed it as the quirk of an old building. He approached the middle of three, enormous urinals—they were more like bathtubs stood on end—and attended to business. The creaking grew louder and faster; it seemed to be coming from the set of wooden stalls to his right. He tried to ignore the noise but became curious when he heard something smacking the nearest panel, accompanied by a duet of soft wails and grunts. He could not help but look over.

In the gap between the stall's side wall and the floor, a pair of trouser-bound ankles, in 1970's black leather boots, was rocking back and forth. "Naughty girl. Naughty, naughty girl."

George recognized the voice, and his jaw dropped. He shook his head, grinning. Quietly, he finished up and retreated to the bathroom door. A pair of loud and carefree cries made him stop and take a wistful glance back. It is unfortunate that he did, for a pale pair of legs in studded black, ladies' buckle boots, slowly descended into view, followed by a straightjacket purse.

George stopped grinning. "Oh." With his brow furrowing in puzzlement, he hastily opened the door and left.

CHAPTER 9

CERRI WAS QUIET DURING most of the drive to the steakhouse. She listened to a Smashing Pumpkins playlist; J.D. tried to switch to FM radio, and she smacked his hand down. "There's some gum in the arm rest," she eventually offered.

"I'm good."

"You think so?"

"Or not." J.D. rolled his eyes. He found the peppermint gum and handed one stick to Cerri, taking one for himself.

Within ten minutes of arriving at The Blue Steak, J.D. was on a first name basis with nearly every individual seated at the bar.

"Tommy!" He called out; the bartender looked over at him. J.D. pointed down with a circular motion, indicating that he and his new friends were ready for another round. He began to get out his wallet.

"This one's on the house," the bartender said.

"You sure, man?"

Tommy was sure. He liked the kid, whose tales of campus-wide practical jokes were attracting customers.

"So we post it on the school website," J.D. said, resuming his story, "We put up fliers inside all the dorms: 'T.P. Esel

Foundation Competition. Entrants will design and install one proof-of-concept, each, for an exterior building cover frame to hold an ultra-delicate, non-rigid skin. Winning design prize, $5000 cash and an interview with the T.P. Esel Foundation.'" Everyone around him was listening. "We build this whole T.P. Esel page where you can register. It's free, but you have to provide your own materials, and the ultra-delicate skin has to be toilet paper."

"Oh my God," said one, wide-eyed patron.

"Long story short, we say the competition is on homecoming day, and the designated building for the installation is the engineering school.

"Oh man," laughed the bartender, as he distributed Middlestop Pale Ales. Chuckles began to spread along the bar as J.D.'s audience realized where the story was heading.

"So..." J.D. had to stop himself from laughing. "So, that morning, me and my I.T. buddies who built the site, we go for a walk by the engineering building, to see; everyone from the engineering program, *every one*, is putting up, you know, everything from cannibalized tent poles to these really high-tech, geometric, art-in-the-desert-looking, carbon fiber frames, all around the building, and then they just...do it: they toilet paper the entire engineering school."

The bar roared.

"Everyone was so into it, no one ever thought to google 'T.P. Esel Foundation.' 'Esel' is German for 'jackass!'"

A second wave of even louder laughter rolled over the first. The only customer who was not in tears was Cerri, who looked at J.D. with interest as she sipped her club soda. "Your mother must be so proud."

J.D. swung around to face her; he looked confused, as if caught off guard.

Cerri, who had not imagined him capable of such a look, realized that she had accidently landed her throw-away jab on a tender spot. "What?"

The moment passed, and J.D., all smiles again, turned to the bartender. "Hey Tommy, where's the john?"

The bartender pointed to the double doors.

Cerri got up first. "You're never going to find it on your own. Come on." She yanked him up from the bar and led the way through the doors and down the stairs. At the wall under the bull's head, she stopped and turned to face him. "Did I just say something-?"

J.D. pulled her to him and planted a sloppy, drunken kiss.

Cerri kissed him right back. Then she pulled away and slapped him in the face, causing him to gape, wide eyed, at her. She pressed on a panel to her right, and the wall pivoted open. The bathroom was unoccupied.

THREE, NOTABLE MINUTES LATER, Cerri peered over the top of the stall to make sure that the coast was clear. When she climbed back down, she looked impassively at J.D., who was pulling up his trousers and chuckling. He met her eyes. The laughter quickly subsided.

"Enjoy your weekend," Cerri said and unlatched the door.

J.D. grasped her hand. "Just wait a minute." He looked sad again, but then fragments of a sincere smile crept in at the corners of his mouth. Cerri was surprised, and she was even more surprised to find her own gaze softening in return.

THE COBBLESTONE HOUSE WAS a two-story cape-cod, with bars hanging over mended windows—an all too common aesthetic in Middlestop Heights—and faded green graffiti peppering the home's stonework. The economobile pulled into the driveway, and Cerri and J.D. got out.

J.D. looked at the front yard. Instead of grass, there was a wilderness of flowers and herbs, with salvage sculptures scattered throughout. Even by streetlight it was beautiful.

Cerri walked up the driveway, crossing the walkway up to the front door. J.D. followed her, but he stopped short: through the café-curtained living room window, he saw a seated figure, silhouetted in front of a floor lamp; she was hunched over a small table, dealing out oversized cards with a trembling arm. J.D. had the familiar and unpleasant sensation of being watched.

"I should have told you I take care of my mom," Cerri explained, noticing his uncomfortable look.

"That's your mom?"

"Yeah. She won't bother us."

J.D. turned from the window and gave Cerri an excited smile. "You know, I've got this pitch; it's going to be incredible!"

"Mmm-Hmm?"

"Thing is, I really need to work on it this weekend..."

"Mmm-Hmm."

"I want to hang out with you; I just think I need to take a rain check." The enthusiastic smile had deteriorated into a sheepish, pleading look. "Is that okay?"

Cerri glanced at the lawn. "There's more in the back." She returned to the driveway. "Come on, I'll show you my workshop."

J.D. smiled; nevertheless, he replied "Not tonight, okay?"

She saw that he could not quite face her, and so she took him by the chin and gently but firmly brought his eyes up to meet hers. After giving him a searching look, she said, "Okay," and let go.

He turned toward the street but hesitated, looking back.

"You can catch the M2 at the end of the street," Cerri said; then, in a shooing tone, as if telling a child something he should have already known, she added, "Go on."

J.D. did as he was told.

Once Cerri saw that he was out of sight, she allowed herself a look down, at nothing in particular. "Come on." She removed her house key and went back to the front door.

J.D. GOT OFF THE bus six stops early; he wanted to walk in order to clear his head. That girl had done something to his mojo. It was expected that a young man like him would get wild and blow off some steam, so then why was he, all of a sudden, feeling...doubt? He never felt doubt; he did not *do* doubt. He was twenty one, just out of school and working his ass off, and anyone who said differently had no idea what they were talking about. Schmoozing professional colleagues every night of the week *was* work: from drinking a 12-year Islay scotch with a senior project manager, he learned about price-lock contract clauses, for keeping costs down on shipped construction materials; from downing imported, Japanese beer with the network administrator, he found out that I.T. was going to get its budget halved next fiscal year unless there was more work for the department to do; and from previously doing shots of extra añejo, agave tequila with the HR receptionist, he learned that the senior project manager liked 12-year Islay scotches and the network administrator liked imported Japanese beers.

You should be proud, J.D., he told himself, and he reviewed his evening's achievements: he had gotten an older woman to participate in some splendid, once-in-a-lifetime, public restroom hotness (that made him smile); he had also gotten a free round of drinks and, in the process, entertained two loan officers—from competing banks, one civil engineer, an umbrella insurance underwriter, and a bartender, all of whom had given him their contact information (that too made him smile).

By the time J.D. reached his block, he was feeling his old self. He looked up and saw George sitting on their third floor fire escape, preparing a cigar. He waved, but George must not have seen, for he did not wave back.

J.D. let himself into the building and climbed the creaky, wooden steps, two at a time; he was itching to share the men's room story with George who, as was always the case, would get an enormous kick out of it. On the last flight up, J.D. slowed down and paused; it had just occurred to him that perhaps George might be touchy about a story involving a girl he sat next to in class. J.D. could not see why that would be so, but then George was funny that way. Deciding to save it for another time, J.D. climbed the last steps and crossed through the loft, over to the open fire escape door.

George was holding up a flaming piece of paper; it looked like he had lit someone's business card on fire with the Zippo he had just set down, and now he was using the card to light his cigar.

This did not bother J.D. but, rather, filled him with a bubbly affection for his friend, which he expressed in the only way he knew how. "Freak!"

George stared at the burning card. "That's me."

"So tell me about this date," J.D. said, determined to pull George out of his apparent funk.

George blew out the blackened card, continuing to stare. "It's off."

"Aw, that sucks, Bro." For a moment, J.D. felt genuinely outraged for his friend.

Throughout high school and college, George's awkward attempts at dating had never gotten him anything more than a couple of hundred-dollar dinner checks, a few hugs, and a platonic kiss on the cheek. George's rotten luck had been a source of endless amusement to J.D. On one occasion, George, concluding in advance that his date was not going to put out for him, pleaded poverty to her, walked her back to her dorm, and then bought himself dinner for two. The latest rejection, however, did not seem so funny.

J.D. shifted from one foot to the other, growing uneasy at the way his friend would not stop staring at the burnt card. "So, I'm gonna have a pitch ready by the end of the week. The whole network can be up on its feet inside eleven or twelve weeks."

"You must be very proud," George said mechanically.

J.D. figured out what was bothering him about George's face. Whatever frustrations George had to contend with during the course of their friendship, he had always done so with a wide-eyed, comical look of disbelief that said to an unseen audience, *"Can you believe this shit is really happening?"* That look was now gone, and in its place was one of accepted defeat.

"You know," J.D. promised, "as soon as I sell them on it, I'm bringing you onboard, right?" Finally, George looked up, and J.D. saw in his eyes the betrayal, the accusation; then J.D. realized that, somehow, his friend knew. He kept talking.

"You're going to be my right-hand man! I'm going to get you a six-figure salary! We're gonna make a million dollars, right?"

George, to J.D.'s surprise, gave a reassuring smile. "Oh, without a doubt, Bro."

J.D., realizing then that he had obviously been mistaken the moment before, was so comforted that he let out a chuckle of relief. "See! That's what I'm talking about!" He turned, and before his expression could betray any shame, he walked into the kitchen, leaving George to smoke his cigar.

CHAPTER 10

THE FOLLOWING MORNING, GEORGE stuck his disheveled head out from his bedroom doorway and saw that the bathroom was occupied; he had gotten up a half-hour early and still been beaten to the shower. For once, though, he was not annoyed or angry: there was simply nothing to be done.

When the morning bus pulled away without George (J.D. shrugging helplessly from a receding side window), he did not try to chase after it through the rainy street, nor did he shout or get upset: he simply walked up to the bus stop, resumed struggling with a stubborn cowlick and accepted that he would be late for work.

When a box truck barreled through the puddle in front of the bus stop, he did not run back into the apartment to change out of his soaking, muddy clothes: he understood that whether it happened there or at the BrewCorp parking lot, he was going to get splashed that day, and there was nothing he could do.

George got to work twenty minutes late. There was, at least, no crowd of arriving employees in the lobby to witness the loud squish of wet shoes as he walked up to the elevator bank.

While he waited, he glanced at his watch and saw that it was completely fogged. He took it off, held it up to his ear and shook it, trying to determine if the analog timepiece was still running. The elevator doors opened. Staring at the ground, he stepped in and pushed three.

In the pause before the door closed, footsteps approached. George pretended to examine his watch, so as to avoid having to hold the doors. They began to shut, when a black, Italian-style wing tip shoe insinuated itself between them, causing them to retract. The shoe's owner stepped inside and pushed a button.

George, who was starting to get a chill, looked up to distract himself from his discomfort.

The C.E.O. was standing beside him. The leathery-skinned executive removed his horn-rimmed sunglasses and fedora, revealing a peeling, sunburned face.

George stared at him.

The doors shut.

Without thinking, George started talking; the words came easily.

Moments later, the elevator doors opened onto the accounting floor.

"...will provide the company with real-time data," George was insisting, in a hushed but animated voice. "Customer reactions, but also sales volume. I can get this network on its feet inside eleven weeks." He reached out to hold the door open. "This is my floor."

George awaited a response from the C.E.O., who throughout the pitch scrutinized him with an irritated expression. No response came, just a silent frown, playing across the bulldog mouth.

"Sir, my network will give you the flexibility to tailor every store, every piece of inventory, on a minute-by-minute basis." George was not sure that his statement was entirely accurate, but he was determined to make an impression.

The C.E.O. shook his head. He looked disgusted. "Unbelievable. Who gave you this internship?"

"Sh-Sheila Styllavitch," George stammered.

"I don't know who that is," the C.E.O. growled, "but she's done."

"I'm sorry to have bothered you, sir." George stepped back from the elevator and released the door. "Have a good day." He looked down at his soggy shoes, deciding to take the next elevator down and return home, since his internship had clearly just ended.

"What the hell are you doing here?" the C.E.O. demanded, adding, "Why would she put you in accounting?"

George looked up at the C.E.O. "Sir?"

"My office. Tonight. Eight o'clock." The doors started to slide shut between them. "Call me Billy."

CHAPTER 11

SHORTLY BEFORE EIGHT O'CLOCK that evening, George took the
elevator up to the top floor. The night receptionist, a middle
aged woman who wore a scarf, too much makeup, and a vacant
expression, escorted him through an expansive, carpeted floor
that looked like something out of a *Mad Men* episode.

The space was lined with desks, three to a side (alternat-
ing green-blue-green on the left and blue-green-blue on the
right). All of the secretaries, except for two, tired-looking
ladies (more scarfs and caked-on makeup), had gone for the
day, but during normal business hours, each one presumably
serviced the glass paneled office immediately behind her. All
of the vice presidents' blinds were drawn, but the suites, three
to a side, must have been quite spacious.

At the last pair of offices, the floor forked around a cen-
trally-located conference room. The utility core beyond, a
broad, gold column, formed a natural buffer, past which the
floor widened onto a corporate lounging area; angled blue and
green sofas were arranged around an eight-sided coffee table
that was yards across; the seating perfectly paralleled the low,
wooden edges. A tilted coffee cup fountain, like the ones at
the BrewMart store but larger, formed the table's centerpiece.

The receptionist wordlessly took George past this lounging area and up to the set of tall, oak doors at the end of the floor. She swiped her keycard badge into the slot next to them and opened one, standing to the side and staring at George, or rather, *through* him.

"Oh, thank you." George walked into Mr. Hall's reception room.

The woman with the braces was there, the one from orientation, who had so disarmingly cut him off at the bar. She wore an overcoat, underneath which was yet another, 1930's dress (green rayon, with a cream collar flounce). "I'm Maddy Wating, Mr. Hall's executive assistant," she told George, giving no sign of recognition. "This way." She opened the door next to the counter and escorted George through.

The chamber beyond was more of a Great room than an office; the trapezoidal floor plan was arranged into several distinct functions. A fireplace, and plasma wall TV above it, was centrally located along the wall through which Maddy and George had entered, which formed the long base of the trapezoid. Colonial panels, complementing the ceiling coffering, lined the long wall, and near the upper left corner, a bleached shadow box displayed six, white commedia dell'arte theatre masks, with each face portraying a basic emotion: sadness, surprise, and happiness across the top row; disgust, anger, and fear along the bottom. A pair of yellow sofas from the 1920's (wide-ribbed upholstering over the back rest, with carved wooden rails) faced one another, creating a perpendicular channel between the fireplace and an enormous, ornately paneled desk. A narrower and taller, slanted desk stood next to, and angled away from, its larger cousin; it was a standing desk, and judging by the presence of paperwork on it, this seemed to be where the C.E.O. preferred to work.

Maddy walked up to it and brusquely neatened the papers. She then went to the main desk, centered the padded executive chair, and leaned over, resting one hand tentatively on the desktop. "You're to have a seat and wait for him." She stared at something on George's right, the window or the art deco bar cabinet next to it. "He's running late." Offering no further explanation, she buttoned her coat and walked out.

The room was silent, except for a soothing gurgle that seemed to come from the bar cabinet. George walked toward it and caught the faint aroma of a French Roast. He folded back the polished, maple top flaps; inside, he saw a jewel of a coffee urn: it was another antique, with brass facets that cast a sparkling reflection in the frost-striped, mirrored bar top below; crowning it, a glass sphere presented the intermittent splatter of percolating coffee.

George inhaled deeply and closed his eyes. When he opened them, he noticed a framed photo collage on the wall above the bar. Black and white pictures of Mr. Hall's good-looking and youthful relatives filled some of the frames, while nature photography occupied the rest. George glanced from the young couple on bicycles to a seashell, and from small children, huddling joyfully together on a park bench, to a wooded stream.

Something about these pictures struck him as odd; he leaned closer and saw, at the bottom of each photograph, in tiny white print, frame dimensions.

Even though George's clothes had dried, and although one of the open windows let in a hot breeze, he gave off a shiver.

"Hand me that mirror, would you?"

George whirled around, so immersed in the frame he had not heard anyone enter.

Mr. Hall stood behind the large desk, looking at him through the horn-rimmed sunglasses. He was pointing at something, but the last sliver of sun, coming from directly behind him, made it impossible to see what.

George squinted and raised a hand to shade his eyes, but it was no use.

"On the file cabinet, just behind you," Hall said, impatiently.

George turned back and saw the file drawer, just to the right of the bar. He picked up the tabletop mirror that was sitting on top of it and brought it over.

"Close the door please, and have a seat."

George shut the door to reception and took one of the blue-upholstered, French-style armchairs—same period as the sofas.

The C.E.O. sat down as well. He removed some sort of containers from a drawer and placed them on top of the desk.

The sun started to dip below the tree-line, and George was relieved to no longer have to squint. He noticed the C.E.O.'s painful-looking forehead. "Are you alright, sir?"

"Billy."

"Billy. Are you alright?"

"I tee'd off without any goddam sunscreen." Hall took lids off of what George could now see were a pair of round, liquid-filled cases—they resembled oversized contact lens holders. Swiveling his chair around, he placed them on a wall table, under the central picture window.

He arranged the tabletop mirror next to the cases and took off his sunglasses. "You don't come from a technical background. This real-time pipeline of yours...fancy stuff for a humanities graduate."

From one of the containers, he plucked what looked like a small jellyfish: a white, one inch disk with a smaller, solid blue ring in the middle and an even smaller black spot in the center of that. Hall balanced it on his index finger.

Although George could not see the C.E.O.'s face—his back was to him—it looked as though he was inserting the jellyfish into his right eye. "Do you have some hidden asset you're keeping from us?" Hall asked, as he did something with both hands.

"No sir, I'm just a person with an idea." George could see one of Hall's hands in the mirror, and he leaned left to find a more revealing angle.

"That's the greatest resource in the world—people." Hall shifted his head around the mirror, regarding the reflection. Once satisfied, he took out the other disk. "George, being a vice president is...well, it's a new experience." He reached over and shifted the mirror's angle.

George was now able to see his face. There was something in Hall's eye—not the right eye, with the jellyfish thing, which looked perfectly normal in spite of it, but his left eye.

Trying to be as discrete as possible, George craned his head toward the mirror. It took him a moment to register that what he was seeing in the C.E.O.'s reflected eye was not *something* but *nothing*: he was looking at the file cabinet, which was forty feet behind Hall; the reason he was seeing this was because there was nothing between the C.E.O.'s empty eye socket and the back of his head.

The normal, jellyfish eye shifted, looking directly at George. "Things may not make a lot of sense at first, but you'll get used to it if you trust me." Hall brought the remaining disk up to his left socket and worked it in; this created the unnerving, cartoonish effect of a floppy, bizarrely-pigmented eyeball being stretched this way and that. "When you're asked to do something, I expect it done without hesitation." Hall massaged the last wrinkle out of the disk, and a perfectly normal, attractive pair of blue eyes stared at George. "Do we understand one another?"

"Yes." George nodded eagerly, for the gray mask of the world had just slipped a bit, offering him a glimpse of the unreality that he so treasured.

Invisibility as a torturous social stigma was one thing, but being literally invisible? George happily surrendered to his giddiness; he felt like a character in H.G. Wells novel *The Invisible Man*. It briefly occurred to him that 1897, the year Well's tale was published, had been a banner year for characters who cast no reflections; he could not recall what made him think that.

"Good!" Hall bellowed, interrupting George's train of thought. The C.E.O. got up, flashing a warm grin.

George stood as well, and stole a glance at the wall behind him; the toothy smile of the happy theatre mask was identical to the C.E.O.'s.

Hall went to his bar. "I'll expect a final presentation eight weeks from tonight."

"But Billy this project will take eleven weeks to implement," George reminded him."

"No, I've got to meet with my board two months from tonight." Hall reached past the curved, pre-war martini glasses and pulled out a pair of tapered, white coffee mugs.

"I see." George began to feel anxious. "Well, er, I'm sure we could pare it down to ten weeks."

Hall squeezed his eyes shut, shaking his head. "George. George! George!! GEORGE!!!" Opening his eyes, he gave such a piercing stare of irritation that George had to grab onto his chair back for fear of fainting.

"Eight weeks. Not a problem." George bent his knees slightly; blackness receded from the edge of his vision.

The C.E.O. turned a wooden spigot on the coffee urn, filling the two mugs. "And you'll have a demonstration ready for us?"

"Yes."

"With everything: the software, the data, the coffee-"

"Yes, yes-" George froze in mid-nod. "The-I'm sorry, the... coffee?"

Hall set the mugs on the desktop. "We have to be sure our Gilded Roast flavor will still meet our customers' expectations, after we move it through the pipeline."

George, who had been trying for an upbeat expression, could not help but knit his brow. The C.E.O. obviously misunderstood the nature of the project. George chose his next words carefully. "I think I need to clarify something that perhaps I haven't done the best job of communicating."

Hall made a circling motion with his hand. "Speed it up."

"Right, well...look, this pipeline—this network, it doesn't *physically* move coffee around, which-actually what it does is better, Billy-"

"Call me Mr. Hall."

The men looked at each other across the desk, Hall with a look of cold disgust and George with a pleading, gaping surprise, as if he had been slapped.

Hall sat down and pulled out his phone. "I think we're about done here." He began reviewing the latest headlines.

"What do you need, exactly?" George asked.

"I need to shift product from one store to another, at the touch of a button. I don't ever again want to hear that one of our stores wasn't ready when a bus full of senior citizens showed up for coffee. I need to meet all demand."

"I see," George said. He tried to make a mental assessment of what this request would entail but then realized that he had no idea what that could be; he shrugged. "Uh...ok."

Hall looked up from his phone and gestured for George to resume his seat.

As George did, he cast his eyes about the room, nervously hoping to find some definitive clue that would indicate what he was agreeing to. He racked his brain. *1897, 1897...*

Hall slid one of the mugs across the table. "You've got as much money as you need, and Chippewa Falls and the county are going to afford you every courtesy possible." He picked up his mug and nodded at the other one, signaling that George should do the same.

"Oh, uh, thank you sir–"

"Billy."

"Thank you, Billy, but I'd better not; I'll be bouncing off the walls."

"It's decaf. My own personal mud, for special occasions."

George hesitated, staring down at his coffee.

Hall noticed George's apprehension; he reached across the desk and retracted the other mug. "I'm sorry, George, I think this was a mistake on my part."

George shook his head. "No, sir. Please, I-I want this."

Hall shook his head. "We can always revisit it at your annual review."

"I said I WANT IT!" George snatched the mug out of the C.E.O.'s hands.

Hall scrutinized him uncertainly. He raised his mug to make a toast, but George did not wait: he downed his coffee in one, scalding gulp.

CHAPTER 12

J.D. AWOKE TO THE gentle chimes of George's alarm clock. It was usually the other way around: George always shut his alarm off promptly, whereas J.D. always left his to spout abrasive talk radio, all day.

It was already eight. J.D. jumped out of bed; the t-shirt and shorts he had slept in were the same ones he had been wearing since the weekend. He had crammed together his proposal on Saturday and Sunday and then, so as to polish it, he called in sick on Monday.

He walked to George's door. "Bro!" He knocked, but there was no answer. He tried the knob, but the door was locked. "You're gonna be late! Today's the day!"

Still no answer.

Anxious not to be late himself, J.D. walked into the bathroom and started the shower.

WHEN HE EVENTUALLY STRODE across the BrewCorp campus, J.D. exuded the momentum of a human juggernaut; he was a man on a mission.

On Saturday night, he had gone drinking with the last few holdouts, co-workers whose confidence in their pitches J.D. had not been able to shake.

He had cleared most of the field by using technical and logistical arguments, delivered with an easy smile and a supportive attitude ("That's brilliant, man; how'd you manage to track income earned from each dollar spent on social media? *No* one's been able to lick that! You *haven't?* Oh, well, you'll figure it out"); the result was that the targeted colleagues had experienced intense self-doubt, along with gratitude for the concerned peer who had instilled it.

The few rivals who were immune had nonetheless recognized that they lacked J.D.'s *sine qua non* pitchmanship; J.D. had brokered a "most favored nations" arrangement with them: he would present each of the proposals, acting as their representative; in turn, each of the pitches would be modified to credit any competing peers as contributors; it would be a win-win for all, particularly for J.D., who had effectively monopolized the contest.

He planned to approach the C.E.O. mid-morning, when Mr. Hall regularly could be seen sipping Gilded Roast coffee as he toured the headquarters. J.D. visualized this scenario as he crossed the parking lot.

There was a new urban tank next to the main entrance; it was black like the other vice presidents' rides, but it was parked in the normally empty handicapped space.

J.D. walked up to the vehicle and peered into the tinted driver's side window. On the dashboard, just below the hanging handicapped tag, lay a pair of cigars.

He walked around and looked at the license plate; it read, "GEORGE-1".

Alarmed, J.D. power-walked into the front lobby. Unconsciously, he had been counting on his aggressive gait to carry him past whatever obstacle lay waiting there, but no amount of striding could sweep aside the event banner hanging over the reception counter: "Congratulations George Unger on Your Promotion to Vice President in Charge of BrewCorp Data and Coffee Pipeline Development."

"There's still some left," said the receptionist. She was excitedly pointing at the bakery box on top of her counter, next to a stack of plates and a cup of plastic forks.

J.D. approached the counter and looked down. Two thirds of the three foot by five foot cake had been eaten, but the iced lettering in the middle was intact: "Congratulations George!" Taking a moment to improve his expression and unclench his fists, J.D. looked up at the receptionist. "Morning Shel."

"Good morning, J.D.," she replied, smiling encouragingly.

"I gotta congratulate him personally. Can I get a badge?"

Her smile took on a chastising quality. "Now, you know I can't do that without calling upstairs."

"Come on." J.D. flashed a mischievous smile, "I happen to know you can do a lot of things."

Shel blushed.

J.D. GLANCED AROUND AS he walked onto the executive floor. He noticed Hall's assistant standing in his path, exchanging hushed laughter with another executive secretary. She saw him, but he pretended to ignore her and walked past; even with the guest badge clipped to his lapel, he knew that he had to keep moving purposefully in order to look as though he belonged there.

Passing by long stretches of closed shutters, J.D. stopped when he reached the last pair of offices. The morning sun backlit the set of blinds on his right, projecting shadows from the two figures within; the standing one was using hand gestures to demonstrate something to the seated one. The door placard confirmed: "George Unger, Vice President." The seated figure appeared to have the shakes.

J.D. did not like ideas such as synchronicity or kismet—irrational ideas. He preferred to subscribe to the laws of probability: it allowed for randomly encountering more than one silhouetted, trembling, seated figure within a 96 hour period, allowed for both encounters to relate to George, and even allowed for J.D. to feel, both times, somehow ambushed.

He approached the secretary and could smell her caked on, powder makeup. She looked up; her thick, red-silver eye shadow only accentuated the burnt-out hollowness of her expression.

"I'm here to see Mr. Unger," he told her.

"And you are?" she asked in a distant, disinterested voice.

"Oh, I'm J.D."

"You'll need an appointment. If you'd care to-"

He did not wait to hear the rest but instead took out his phone and speed-dialed. From behind the blinds came the muffled notes of Bach's Toccata and Fugue in D minor. The seated shadow answered his phone.

"Let me in, Bro," J.D. instructed. There was no response. "George. Let. Me. In."

"-st...inut...eeting," said George's fragmentary voice. The call was dropped.

J.D. saw that his phone had no reception bars. He walked up to the office partition and knocked loudly on the glass.

"Excuse me!" the secretary protested, suddenly fully present. She picked up the landline headset from her desk console. "Security."

A hand wearing a fancy watch parted the office blinds, and J.D. felt nauseous with despair: suddenly he knew—even though he could not explain how—that all of his mojo had been permanently taken away. The face that appeared wore perfectly circular, heavily-tinted sunglasses and a wavy, Jay Gatsby haircut supported with a generous amount of product. The only features by which J.D. could identify his friend were the nose and mouth. The newly-minted executive held up a manicured finger and waved at the secretary, who hung up her phone.

For an instant, the face retreated behind the blinds; then they parted to reveal a silent, comical scene of Richard Sytry gravely instructing George in the use of a desktop coffee brewer.

One of the coveted, gold-rimmed, white mugs had been issued to George, and he placed it under the unit's spray-head. Following Sytry's muffled directions, he opened a large cartridge holder at the top of the unit, and inserted a Gilded Roast flavor cartridge that looked like an oversized coffee cream packet; George locked the holder shut. He held a finger over the lit button at the bottom of the unit and looked to his instructor. Sytry gave George a nod, and George pushed the button. He looked quite pleased as his mug began to fill.

Sytry pivoted toward the door and walked out, past J.D., leaving an eddy of air-conditioned cologne in his wake.

"Hey, man," George called to J.D. as he returned to his chair, "Thanks for stopping by."

J.D. strode into the office and shut the glass door.

"It's been insane. In! Sane!" George raised his arms and held them apart to emphasize just how physically big the insanity was. "It's all moving, Bro; everything is moving so quickly."

From across the desk, J.D. stared down at his friend, who was bouncing a leg and fidgeting with a glass paperweight. George's twitchy behavior reminded J.D. of a stereotypical auto dealership owner, pushing unbeatable deals. "Are you on something?"

"Too much coffee." George reached for his mug and took a hearty swig. "This stuff is just too fucking good!" If he had expected his reply to cut the tension between them, he was mistaken: J.D. had rarely heard his friend curse, and never casually.

George noticed the dismayed expression. "Sit down."

J.D. did not budge.

"Or don't." George turned his head to stare through a tinted partition, which looked onto a smaller, unused space; then, as if remembering there was someone else in the room with him, he looked back. "So listen, we're going to build your pipeline."

J.D. inclined his head and stared into the sunglasses. "What is this?"

"I ran into Hall in the elevator." George again looked away and then wrestled his gaze back. "I mean, you've always said 'George, you gotta act, you gotta act,' so I acted." He took J.D.'s emerging look of gaping astonishment as a positive sign. "The schedule's going to be a little tight—Oh, yeah: and you're going to need to adapt the design so we can move coffee through it." George took another gulp and set his mug down.

J.D. made no indication of intending to respond to this directive.

George prompted, "What do you think is the best way to do that?"

J.D. leaned far across the desk and, supporting himself on two outstretched fists, he invaded George's personal space. Arching his eyebrows, and bobbing his head with each word, he incredulously clarified, "What do I think is the best way to send coffee through a fiber optic network that you stole from me?"

"Whoa, whoa, whoa!" George protested, throwing up his well-manicured hand defensively. "No one is stealing anything. We're all on the same-"

J.D. cut him off with a raised, silencing palm. Looking into the air with an expression of deep concentration, he dropped the palm down next to George's half-filled mug. Having apparently found a solution to the engineering problem before him, he nodded sagely and said, "Maybe there *is* a way to send coffee through an impermeable material. Let's run a test."

Before George could react, J.D. picked up the mug and tossed the coffee at his new suit, soaking the collar-shirt, bracers, jacket and tie and causing George to flinch in surprise. "Did *that* get through to you?"

J.D. stormed out of the office.

At the elevator, he jabbed the down button seventeen times. He was about to take the fire stairs when the doors in front of him parted.

Cerri came out, brushing past; she turned around, brightening. "Oh, hey."

"Hey," J.D. replied half-heartedly. He stepped into the elevator.

"Do you have a minute?"

"Not really," J.D. sighed. "Could you please just leave me a voicemail?"

The doors began to close; Cerri reached in and held them open. "Thing is, we're closing right now. It's the anchor store for the Inini Town shopping center."

"I-I-" He looked this way and that, trying to find a polite way to excuse himself, becoming increasingly agitated.

Cerri did not notice, or if she did, she pushed on anyway. "My boss is working with a new appraiser; he'd like another pair of eyes. Could you just come down for two minutes?"

There was an annoyed edge to her voice, and picking up on it, J.D. snapped, "I'm not the answer to your problems!"

They stood there: J.D. glaring at Cerri, regretting his words but carried by his belligerent momentum, and Cerri staring guardedly back. She dropped her hand and let the doors close between them.

J.D. SOLDIERED THROUGH THE day, bumbling through a mental fog of confusion and anger.

By the time he got off work, he had entertained several ideas for blowing off steam: he could get drunk at Skeeters and pick up a coed; he could look up his former Differential Equations professor (she and he kept up via email, and she had just gotten out of a relationship); or he could go up to Montreal, play blackjack at the casino and get a lap dance on Saint Catherine Street. Montreal won out as getting J.D. the farthest away from the unsexy complications of reality.

As his M2 pulled out from the BrewCorp stop, he prepared a mental list of what would be needed: passport, change of underwear, and condoms. From the apartment, he could either call his buddy from I.T. seminar, Mike P., who had a car, or he could put a bus ticket on his credit card.

Thirty minutes later, stepping off the M2, J.D. had reached the conclusion that Mike P. would only slow things down; the car owner had a habit of allowing his tank to get precipitously low while he window shopped for the cheapest gas station;

the car would likely stall, as it had on several previous trips, besides J.D. wanted to be on his own.

He looked up from his walking and was irritated to discover that he had not gotten off at the stop in front of his apartment; he was standing behind the orange plastic fencing, looking out at the grove. The torn earth and construction equipment, parked for the day, had advanced to within yards of his and George's old poker spot. J.D. smacked the nearby Property of BrewCorp signpost, resentfully acknowledging that a trip out of town was not in the cards.

He stood there for a long time, preoccupied with thoughts more complicated than any mechanical engineering equation or lossless transmission formula: questions about the line between self-advocacy and betrayal of others. The mental loop that had ensnared him came down to three ideas, chasing one after the other: *I'm not responsible for his feelings; I take care of my friend;* and *He had no cause to do what he did.*

Again J.D. felt nauseating despair.

Turning around, he allowed his eyes to adjust to the twilight and eventually discerned the idling, black tank. Through the open driver's side window, George regarded him while sipping coffee. There was someone with George, a woman's outline in the passenger seat, but it was too dark for J.D. to make out a face.

"Stay," George told her. He removed his sunglasses and placed them on the dashboard (*He's doing coke,* J.D. thought. *When did that start?*). He swiped up a pair of cigars from the dashboard and climbed out.

J.D. turned back to the grove. George went up to him, holding out one of the cigars; J.D. made no move to accept. George wedged it into the breast pocket of his suit jacket and bit off the end of the other. He took out his Zippo and lit it, working the flame evenly around the edge.

"I didn't steal," George said. "I grabbed an opportunity so you and I could bring your idea to fruition." He took a series of increasingly smoky puffs.

J.D. shook his head at the torn-up field. "I would never do anything like that to you."

George cackled, causing smoke to shoot out of his nose and mouth. "Middlestop High, 2003. My mom and Bob were in Charleston for the weekend, and I told you I was planning a Georgian-themed masquerade ball."

J.D. grinned at the memory, in spite of himself. "That was never gonna get you laid."

"You went and told the football team I was having a heavy metal costume party," George said.

"Yeah," J.D. sheepishly acknowledged.

"*Yeah*," George repeated, bitterly.

"No one was ever going to come to your Lord Byron party, except other virgins."

"At least some of them might have been female. Instead, Chuck Rand, The Tootch, and the rest of the all-star, all-male headbangers gave me a trashed house, a citation from the Middlestop Heights police and a grounding that is technically still in effect."

"That's not the same thing at all! It was just a party-"

"It wasn't what I *wanted*!" George, who was getting more and more animated, took a deep puff from the cigar and chased it with a gulp of coffee. "Summer, 2001: I told you I wanted to be a filmmaker."

"I got you my dad's videocamera on loan," J.D. reminded him.

"What you did," George corrected, "was pour lighter fluid on my favorite action figures so you could get video of them exploding; you set my folks' living room on fire."

Forced to concede the point, J.D. nodded, looking at the grove in search of a counter argument. "In fourth grade you said 'Let's do a lemonade stand.' You didn't know how; you just had a dream, and I made that happen for you, remember?" J.D. pointed into the grove. "The whole street showed up."

"You told them it was a subscription service!" George cried out. "You watered down the lemonade, which I got stuck serving all summer and never got paid for; you pocketed the money and took Cathy Chatwick to see *The Matrix*! She'd sat next to me that whole year; we did homework together after school; she was interested in me; you *knew* she was interested in me!"

J.D.'s face crinkled in disbelief. "You were *ten*! We were *ten*! Do you stay up at night thinking about this stuff?"

"No." Instantly, George's anger was gone, shrugged off with self-effacing laughter. "Look, let's move on. So I made V.P. So what? You're the engineer, not me: if you don't want to build it, it doesn't get built. So what are we going to do?"

"You're talking about pumping coffee back and forth over a fifty square mile geographic region," J.D. ran a hand through his hair. "What you're talking about is setting up a private utility. Do you have any idea how to do that? Because I sure don't."

George said nothing but stared at his friend while taking another gulp. He looked like a hyperactive child on his best behavior—as if one wrong move would get him sent to his room without supper; then J.D. realized: *he's worried I'll say no; not just worried, but terrified.*

If someone had later asked J.D. what swayed him, he would have said it was the opportunity for career advancement, and he would have meant it. He would not have said that it was because his best and oldest friend was in some sort of trouble; for him to do so would have been to acknowledge a wrinkle of imperfection in the otherwise unblemished world view that he had, as a college freshman, passionately adopted upon reading *The Fountainhead*.

In any case, J.D. let out a grumpy sigh and told George, "We're gonna build the thing."

George tried to conceal his obvious relief by looking down at his jacket; he dug out the spare cigar. "This is the right decision—you'll see! Your mom would be proud!"

"Would you please shut up." J.D. grudgingly accepted the cigar and pulled out his own Zippo. The two smoked in silence. After several minutes, J.D. looked at George's ride. "Who you got in there?"

"She's a friend," George said, cagily.

"Yeah?" J.D. awaited more details, but none were forthcoming; George puffed calmly, staring up at the darkening sky. J.D. asked, "Where are you taking her?"

"Out for a drink."

CHAPTER 13

DURING THE NEXT SIX weeks, J.D. threw himself into building the coffee and data pipeline with a single-minded intensity that would in one way or another affect all of his personal and professional relationships. The stress did not come from the data-gathering components—the facial recognition checkout cameras, the software, and the private wireless umbrella; it came from the physical distribution of the coffee.

J.D.'s struggle to produce a timely design for the pipeline had been fruitless; in order to break through the creative block and meet his deadlines, he resorted to cannibalizing an artificial heart valve prototype. He had learned about the specialized implant during one of two, obligatory dinners that he and the designer, who had not yet secured a patent, ate together each year. J.D.'s questions about the device, in concert with the designer's three doubles of scotch (Usquebaugh, 18-year), resulted in J.D.'s being given a spontaneous, ten minute demonstration of the working model by the designer—his dad. They would not speak to one another again for over a year.

That relationship was the most egregious casualty of J.D.'s obsessive work, but it was by no means the last: as Project Management and Engineering Consultant, J.D. required regular input from an assortment of puzzled, unenthusiastic, and sometimes irate stakeholders.

The problem with shouldering this responsibility was that he had to do it clandestinely: George, who had managed to get him hired full-time, had grossly overestimated his clout with Human Resources; the best he could do was to get J.D. a salaried position designing flush sensors for the stores' men's-room urinals. In order to minimize conflicts with his official duties, J.D. conducted pipeline business during off-hours, breaks, and stolen moments, when his regular supervisor was nowhere in sight.

Project time grew so scarce that J.D. adopted unorthodox and aggressive tactics to get in touch with any unresponsive vendors, contractors, store managers, or county officials: he looked up home phone numbers, procured a second cell phone, so as not to be immediately identifiable on caller ID's, and several times he waited outside of houses and apartments, greeting avoidant associates as they arrived home from work. J.D.'s tone was always disarming and friendly, but his underlying message was clear: *the sooner you deal with me, the less I will fuck with you.*

The resentful blowback to his leadership style was limited to a single, isolated incident: during a Saturday afternoon, while sunning on his apartment roof, as he did every week at that time, J.D. heard a loud slap on the blacktop—the sound of liquid-filled plastic hitting hardened tar. Jumping up from his towel, he looked over at the noise: a contractor bag, filled with watery feces, had come out of nowhere and landed ten feet away, partially exploding. J.D. never learned the identity of the literal shit slinger, but by the third week of the project, when his emails were receiving prompt replies, and his phone calls were no longer getting bounced into voicemails, the incident had been all but forgotten.

There remained, among J.D.'s newly-cooperative colleagues, one critical holdout: the man who had given him the job. George had pledged any resources that J.D. would require, without question and without corporate interference, but the tension between the two quickly grew. George pulled promised personnel and cashflow away from the project, submitted last-minute verbal change requests, and dragged J.D. into the types of situations from which George was supposed to be shielding him.

GEORGE'S HANDLING OF THE project's legal complications became a case in point.

The city of Middlestop was filing court injunctions to prevent the snaking of miles of flexible coffee tubing; the lines were to be piggybacked on top of water mains that ran between the headquarters and the thirteen stores. BrewCorp had paid permit fees for the work taking place in Middlestop but had refused to pay for additional work in Inini Village, Middlestop Heights, and Chippewa Falls—townships that were serviced by Middlestop's water lines but were not part of the city. The lawsuits were merely the latest act in a bitter, decades-long, drama that had been playing out between those suburbs and the city proper; at stake were not only permit fees but also tax revenues and service contracts for the miles of proposed coffee lines. Chippewa County, whose appellate court would be hearing the suits, was an enthusiastic facilitator of regional commercial development, and the court's prompt dismissal of the injunctions was a foregone conclusion.

Still, George had decided that, for the sake of procedural correctness, J.D. ought to give a deposition to the company's legal counsel. "Tell them it's my idea," George instructed him, reasoning, "that way you'll be protected if there's a wrinkle."

J.D. was so inundated that he did not initially refuse to cooperate; he hoped to just get it over with and move on; then he learned that the lawyer who would be interviewing him was Peter Mendes, Cerri's boss, and that she would be accompanying him.

J.D. rescheduled six times; Mendes finally took the hint and cc'd him an email to George concluding that testimony would not be needed. That was the end of the deposition, almost. The following morning, J.D. found a brochure in his in-box: *Patent Your Genius* (As Seen on TV). Below the bright yellow 800 number was a cheaply compiled montage of thick-outlined photographs: an overweight couple pedaling atop their four-wheeled, tandem couch-cycle, a wrist-worn writing pad, and a transparent P-trap sink drain, shaped like a crazy straw. An attached red sticky note read, "Whichever of you two cooked this up, pls call these guys. The world needs to know." It smelled of Nag Champa.

THROUGHOUT THE LONG WEEKS of construction, George was apologetic for, and at times surprised by, any inconveniences his directives caused J.D. ("Wait, what do you mean you haven't been home since Tuesday?").

At the end of week seven, a phone call between the vice president and his project consultant took an unexpected turn.

It was the day of the initial hook up. That morning, the coffee tubes had been joined to a massive industrial pump in the headquarters' basement; they had already been connected, at the other end, to each of the individual BrewMart stores via smaller branching tubes (housing J.D.'s cannibalized regulator valves). Another set of lines ran from the top of the pump vertically, through the building's utility core and onto the roof, where a converted water tower, once installed, would receive them and buffer any excess coffee in the system.

J.D. and the engineering crew had expected the rooftop expansion tank's construction to be straightforward, but it proved a tedious process that seemed to lull everyone involved into an ineffectual stupor.

As the afternoon wore on, pneumatic, overhead pounding was replaced by the clanking of metal on metal, as hoisted sections of the tank collided with the previously installed sections.

For half an hour, the crew tried to hammer the tank's cover into place, until they realized that it was out of alignment and needed to be repositioned; then, dozens of thunderous crashes, spaced moments apart, reverberated throughout the building as the metal cover was hoisted, repositioned, dumped onto the cylindrical rim, then raised and repositioned again, in trial-and-error fashion.

J.D. had been on a call with a supply chain company and was trying to find out why an order of carbon steel had not yet arrived from Brazil ("An equatorial blizzard? No shit!"), when his other line lit up.

"Ok, thanks," J.D. told the supply chain representative, ending the call. He picked up the second line. "This is Pence."

"How much longer is your crew going to be dicking around up there?" George demanded.

He must have been in a meeting upstairs; J.D. could make out some of the vice presidents' murmuring voices in the background; one was reporting that the cold brewing taste tests scored well. The chatter was intermittently drowned out by heavy roof top thuds.

Before J.D. could reply, his regular supervisor walked up to the cubical. "Why haven't I gotten your schematics for the low-flow urinals?" He had a habit of accosting subordinates while they were preoccupied on the phone.

"Please hold," J.D. told George, and he turned to face the supervisor. "I'll have them on your desk by five."

The supervisor looked at the pile of papers on the desk. Though J.D. had the foresight to keep a urinal blueprint on top of the other papers, his boss could clearly see the coffee pipeline schematics protruding from underneath.

"Have you seen how your performance evaluations are trending this week?" he asked J.D.

J.D. had seen. Those co-workers who had agreed to let him pitch for them were, not surprisingly, upset to learn that he was unable to convince George to share credit with them; their discontent correlated closely with a six-week dip in J.D.'s previously-glowing, peer-sourced reviews.

"You should take a look," the supervisor concluded ominously and walked off.

J.D. resumed the call, trying to ignore the fact that his career was now in George's hands. "They're gonna stay up there until it's all finished. Look, you tell me 'speed it up; do it cheaper.' This is the only way to do that."

"I'm sorry," George said, "are you telling me you can't?"

"No, I'm not saying that."

There was no immediate reply.

The C.E.O. was telling someone, "Board members don't get...I need to see....up and running early...prime them-"

The buzz of a running coffee brewer cut in, making the rest inaudible.

"Look, Bro-" J.D. began.

"No, *you* look: speed it up *more*. If you can't do that, I have to get someone who can."

"Oh, is that right? I'd like to see you find-"

"Hold on-"

The brewer in the background was suddenly making a gurgling noise. Then silence. There was a bang of skin on plastic, and the C.E.O. was complaining, "What's wrong with this thing?"

"I gotta go," George told J.D. "Just get it finished."

There was a click.

J.D. was about to put down the receiver when he heard the company's hold music. It seemed George had immediately dialed another extension, and in doing so he had unintentionally set up a conference call.

J.D. could have ignored the misdial and worked on his urinal plans, but curiosity got the better of him; he decided to try and use his company-issued pin code to listen in.

He dialed in the four-digit code.

The elevator music stopped, and the line was silent. A chime sounded, and a recorded voice announced, "*J.D. Pence* has joined the call."

Well, that's that, J.D. thought. All of the executives would have heard the announcement, and George, figuring out his mistake, would hang up.

Only, they did not hear the announcement because they were too busy shouting at each other.

"...just told me his team is moving as fast as they can!" George was insisting.

"Your engineer isn't responsible for this project," the C.E.O. replied, "*You* are!"

"Dispensary," answered a new voice on the line; this was George's intended call.

"This is Unger in C.R.1," said George, tensely, "We need coffee."

"Yes sir, we're working on it." The dispensary worker must have had his phone on speaker, for there was another layer of sound, an echoing of indecipherable shouted orders accompanied by the scuffling of boots on concrete. "They cut something up on the roof. That's what's causing the disruption."

J.D. then understood why George had been pulling project resources and making late change requests: the executives must have wanted to tie this dispensary, which apparently fed their in-suite brewers, directly into the pipeline.

"I don't care what's causing it!" George barked at the dispensary worker. "Fix it!"

The C.E.O. added, "Mal, do whatever you have to do."

"Yes sir," replied the dispensary worker.

What happened next was unclear. The dispensary worker stopped talking, but his line stayed open; J.D. made out the muddy echo of stepped-up activity, of heavy shoes or boots on concrete. A distant, raised voice cried out in protest; a vicious punch sounded, much clearer and closer—like knuckle on bone—followed by something heavy crashing into a hard surface—J.D. could not tell if it was the construction work or something happening with the executives. It sounded like a three way wrestling match had started, and then—J.D. was sure he heard it—an animal let out a deep, warning growl, as if one of the vice presidents had a protective Doberman with him. An echoing, distant, high-pitched scream, overlapped with the end of the dog snarl; complete silence followed.

J.D. thought he had been disconnected, but then he heard the coffee brewer sputter back to life. It buzzed for ten seconds and came to a normal stop, and judging by the sound of casters rolling across floor and the squeak of a spring, it seemed that someone had returned to his seat. There was a leathery creak and the sound of more casters rolling.

"Sit down," the C.E.O. said, in a disgusted tone. Another roll and squeak. "Thank you, Mal."

"Yes sir," replied the dispensary worker.

J.D. heard the C.E.O. say, "I move to suspend Vice President Unger's coffee privileges until his project meets-," but then the call cut out.

J.D. turned to the urinal blueprints. He was not surprised when, a few minutes later, a call came from George's office extension.

"I need to be up and running in one week," George said, sounding shaken.

J.D., unsure of what he had just overheard, kept his outrage in check. "You understand it'll take a full week to test this system; we discussed this."

"We'll test at night. Get it done."

WITH A TREMBLING HAND, George hung up the receiver. He stared at his fingers. They were beginning to prune. He was shaking all over.

He fumbled for the empty mug on his desk and placed it underneath his brewer. He pushed the single, red-lit button at the base of the unit; nothing happened. He urgently tilted the unit forward, causing the mug to tumble to the floor; the handle broke off. He did not care; he examined the tubing that ran from the bottom of the brewer into a hole in the countertop. It was clear and empty.

George picked up his desk phone again and dialed a two-digit extension and closed the blinds. "I need you in my office, ASAP."

CHAPTER 14

J.D. SCRAMBLED THROUGH THE week in a haphazard frenzy, racing to meet George's new deadline. Any construction not directly related to the pipeline was postponed; the facial recognition system would have to wait, as would the upgrades to the fire control system (new sprinklers and automatic, 2-hour-rated fire doors). He had been working around the clock for three days straight, propped up on energy drinks.

Employees often stayed past one in the morning, but by two thirty, when J.D. was still going strong, all of his co-workers had gone; after that the headquarters building assumed a phantasmagoric quality: the reduced HVAC running mode made the air clammy and oppressive; J.D.'s skin would occasionally tingle with an unseasonable static that refused to discharge a spark, even when he reached for a metal doorknob; the air would become intermittently still, and the temperature would swing from hot to cold.

The strangeness of the atmosphere reminded J.D. of a time when he was boy, playing in the front yard: he saw a funnel cloud overhead; the passing tornado never touched down, but its greenish vacuum had tugged menacingly at him, causing his ears to pop.

J.D.'s custom-built server and remote control workstation for the pipeline had been installed on the executive floor, in the formerly empty space next to George's office. The glass-partitioned room had been selected midway through the project, when George had issued another of his bizarre change orders and demanded that all data, backups included, be kept within sight of his office. J.D. hated the location: he could not look at his friend without feeling somehow diminished; it was a terrible, nauseating sensation.

That was not the only thing that gave offense: while J.D. was there, configuring the software, he would occasionally smell a rotten staleness; the stench would only last for a second, and as soon as J.D. took another sniff, the stink would be gone; he knew he had not imagined it, and his frequent sniffing started to become an unattractive habit.

He visited the pump room for the first time at the end of the week. As he pushed the elevator's *B1* button, hairs stood up on the back of his neck. He could have performed the diagnostics from the workstation upstairs, but this was J.D.'s first opportunity to see the system in operation, and he was determined to witness his handiwork springing to life. Stepping out of the elevator, he traversed the long, darkened basement hallway.

Taking out his single-issue key, J.D. placed it into a solitary, cylinder lock and turned it one-quarter, counter-clockwise. He pushed open the heavy security door and walked through; it hissed slowly shut behind him. He passed a pair of empty wall guides, which would eventually house the descending, fire-rated door; then he entered the pump room.

Even in his wired state, J.D. had to stop and gape. He had pulled off many stunts in his young life, but nothing compared with the baroque mechanism standing before him; it was like a steampunk set piece from a Terry Gilliam film, with its converging, angular pipework, analogue pressure and temperature gauges, and patchwork of round and square panels. J.D. looked up; he had not been aware of it while slapping together the design, but the filtration unit on top resembled a giant, mechanical mosquito, with a segmented recirculation line that looked like a large proboscis.

J.D. shook his head. "Dude."

Until that moment, all of his motivation came from an ambition to succeed; now, as he realized that any snags associated with the pipeline's quirky design would fall squarely on his shoulders, he became motivated by the fear of failure.

Logging into the private server from his company tablet, he loaded the control software and opened the *Diagnostics* app. An analogue pressure gauge appeared on the screen, under the alert, *Initializing...*

For several seconds, nothing happened; J.D. felt himself tense; he wondered if there was a bad control link somewhere, but then the pump issued a mechanical click, followed by a rising whine; hidden gears and pump wheels whirred up to speed.

J.D. selected *Variable Demand Test Battery*, which would randomly simulate coffee demand signals from each of the stores, creating an approximation of day-to-day operating conditions.

During normal operation, the signals would be generated by what were being dubbed Smart Coffee Dispensers: in-store brewers that had been retrofitted to do nothing more than heat and pour cold-brewed Gilded Roast drawn from the system.

The tests began to run. Water converged on the pump through eight clear tubes (the dispensary would load the actual product once all of the diagnostics passed). Bands of air moved through the water, as though each main was an enormous drinking straw with a giant, unseen thumb opening and closing over the end. The last traveling bands emptied into the pump. The needle on the test gauge crept from the red left side over to the green right. The flow reversed course, sending intermittent bands outward; it reversed course several more times. Air and water sloshed back and forth through the mains in a seemingly random pattern, while the needle crept further into the green.

The tests ran for five minutes, during which J.D. urged his creation, "Come on, bitch!"

Finally, all of the water entered the pump; J.D. heard it rush up the vertical pipes to the rooftop tank and settle; through a round, two foot diameter inspection window in the mechanism, he verified that a translucent siphoning bulb was pulsating, draining water out of the machine's large metal cavity.

He looked at his tablet screen; the gauge was replaced with a test report, listing *Passed* all the way down.

"That's right," J.D. proclaimed as he generated a PDF copy of the report. "Who's the boss? I'm the boss."

He swaggered back down the hallway, relieved at having cleared this last major technical hurtle. The moment he stepped into the elevator, however, the nervous energy that had been keeping him going left, and by the time the doors opened onto the top floor, J.D. could hardly stand; he staggered, bleary eyed toward George's office.

Even though most of the vice presidents had left for the day, the parade of black, angular shapes, silhouetted by exterior building lights against drawn blinds, gave each office an eerie feeling of life; it was like walking past a series of shadow theatres at some surreal, midnight carnival.

J.D. passed the office belonging to the head of marketing, John Fourneus, and stopped; he backed up. Not a moment earlier, out of the corner of his eye, he had seen what looked like a shadow of a large dog; the animal had appeared to be sitting on top of the desk, but now J.D. only saw the outline of a seated, late-working vice president. Shaking himself awake, he pushed on, virtually dizzy with fatigue.

He approached George's office and discerned a woman's profile looming over a seated shadow. Unsure whether or not he was interrupting something, he pulled out his phone and quick-dialed. The muffled organ chords sounded, and the seated shadow picked up his phone.

"I'm coming over," J.D. announced.

"...eeh v...ts."

"Say again?"

"imme...ive..."

The call was dropped.

J.D. looked at his phone; he had one bar. On a hunch, he continued to stare at it as he drew nearer to George's office. The last bar disappeared. He backtracked a dozen steps, and the bar returned. He walked forward into the dead spot again, and the bar disappeared. A *No Service* message appeared on the display. J.D. looked up; he was just outside of George's office.

"We're done here," George said, from the other side of the glass; the seated shadow stood and faced the woman's profile.

"Can I at least-?"

"I said we're done here."

The profile exhaled loudly, sounding frustrated. "You know, I don't have to-"

"Don't argue with me, just do what I say."

She stood motionless, then picked something up off the desk and secured it around her neck. "Fine."

The door opened, and Maddy Wating stormed out.

J.D. recognized the braces and polka dots, but the scarf and dark-ringed, watery eyes were unfamiliar. He had only ever come across the C.E.O.'s assistant when she was laughing with colleagues or breaking up her boss with a whispered piece of juicy gossip, as only she was allowed to do.

She gave J.D. a polite smile as she passed him. She stopped and turned, looking back at the office.

George appeared at the doorway; his tie needed straightening, but otherwise he looked refreshed and rested. "Maddy..." He stared her down until she turned and resumed her march to the elevator.

As soon as she was out of earshot, J.D. asked, "What was that about?"

George ignored the question. "What's happening?"

J.D. tried to hand his friend the tablet with the test log, but George would not take it. "Just tell me if we're up or not."

"We're up."

"For real?" George brightened.

"For real," J.D. confirmed unenthusiastically.

The vice president raised a palm for a high five, but J.D. kept his hands at his sides; George instead slapped him on the back. "I couldn't have done this without you."

"Tell your boss."

"I will, next quarter, when everyone sees our overhead has shrunk and store efficiency has shot-"

"'Next quarter, next quarter.'" J.D. turned and walked away.

"Come on, let's have a drink."

"Goodnight," J.D. said, without looking back.

CHAPTER 15

GEORGE'S TEXT MESSAGE ARRIVED just as J.D. was climbing into bed. He tried to ignore it but got a follow-up call. First, George reminded him that it was an employee's contractual responsibility to be available, by phone and email, twenty four hours a day, then he notified J.D. of the change: originally, the demonstration had been scheduled for the following week, but after receiving the perfect test results, George had wasted no time in pushing the date up—to 9:30 a.m. the coming morning. He had, at least, saved J.D. the trouble of overseeing replacing the test water with actual product ("No, no. You get some sleep. I *insist.*").

Five hours later, J.D. did not shower, shave or brush his teeth; he merely rolled out of bed, watered down his hair, and wriggled into a blazer and chinos. He was still groggy, but that was not the reason for his scruffy appearance: he had a plan, and it would require him to play against type.

By nine twenty five, J.D. was sitting at his workstation, with the C.E.O., George, and the other executives looking over his shoulders. After taking a moment to rub his hands together and warm them, J.D. began tweaking the keyboard settings.

George addressed the C.E.O. and vice presidents. "Before we get started, for those of you who don't know him, this is J.D. Pence."

J.D. sat up straighter and twisted around to face his audience; he made eye contact with the C.E.O. He did not nod or smile but gave each executive a brief, unimpressed glance as if to say, "So, you're the leadership, huh?"

"J.D. managed day-to-day construction," George continued, "and made sure that my creative vision was protected."

Oh really? J.D. thought as he held his neutral expression.

"Hold it, Unger" interrupted Mark Amon, knitting his bleached eyebrows as he pointed at J.D. "Isn't this our urinal sensor new-hire?"

"You gave this to the urinal guy?" asked a wiry, red-haired executive who had been thumbing through stock index reports on his company-issued phone. J.D. recognized him as the C.F.O., Mike Ballum (*his* cellular data service seemed to working fine, J.D. noted).

Duke Bunet, Vice President in Charge of Human Resources (bald, stout, golden dragon cufflinks) chimed in. "Does he have any credentials at all?"

George began, "J.D. graduated at the top of his class-"

"Great, an *academic* urinal guy," Amon concluded.

John Fourneus, who was standing next to the C.E.O., turned to him. "Billy, every time someone flushes, the coffee's going to taste like piss."

"Who can tell me what I-three-E twelve-twenty-two dash two-thousand-eleven is?" J.D. cut in. It was time, he decided, to make his move. The room fell silent as all eyes turned to him. "Anyone? No? The set of standards for all the overhead fiber optic cables I've been installing for you? It's pretty important." He turned to Ballum. "What about thirteen-seventy-nine dash two thousand, Mike? May I call you Mike?"

Ballum said nothing but gave J.D. a puzzled, narrow-eyed look.

"'Recommended Practice for Data Communications Between Remote Terminal Units and Intelligent Electronic Devices in a Substation,'" J.D. recited. "Ever heard of it? Because the flow sensors and valves that make this whole thing work are all 'Intelligent Electronic Devices in a Substation.'" He turned to face George. "What about P-fifteen-eighty-eight, vision guy? 'Standard for Clock Synchronization Protocol for Networked Measurement and control systems?' Or maybe you have some other way of keeping this entire system working correctly—after all, it's *your* big idea."

Eyes turned to George, who responded with a forced smile.

"Here's an easy one, John," J.D. said to Fourneus. "What do all those standards have in common?"

Fourneus shook his head. "No idea."

J.D. looked around at the other executives. "No one? Come on. Anyone who knows anything about load smoothing knows this one: they all belong-"

"They're smart grid standards," Mr. Hall interrupted, staring at him.

J.D. stared back; he had not figured upon the C.E.O.'s being familiar with anything more technical than how to change a coffee filter. "That's correct."

Hall nodded. "Alright, kid, enough. Let's see it."

J.D. turned to his workstation; he caught George's resentful expression and, with a small rush of smugness, thought *message delivered*. "It will take a few seconds to load," he explained. He used a series of keyboard shortcuts to instruct the system to cycle up to normal operation.

A red progress bar appeared on the display and crawled to the right. J.D. no longer doubted that the demonstration would be a success and that Billy Hall personally liked the way he thought; his moment had come.

J.D. had not been aware of it before but realized he had been holding his breath; he started to relax, letting the air out slowly.

Then he stopped.

Something was wrong, not with the demonstration or the pipeline but with the room: something was *off*. It was much, much too quiet.

He stole a glance at the executives behind him.

No one's chest was moving with the normal, subtle rhythm of idle respiration. None seemed to be deliberately holding his breath, and yet none was breathing.

J.D. looked over his other shoulder, at George—George, who virtually hyperventilated whenever he was in a room with people. George was as silent and still as the rest.

The computer chimed, and J.D. returned his attention to the workstation. The completed progress bar disappeared.

Even from four floors away, the shudder of a vast underground machine starting up could be felt.

Next to the keyboard, a new executive Smart Dispenser emitted a brief, angry hiss from the cartridge holder. Although the Gilded Roast flavor cartridges would no longer be used, George had refused to let J.D. do away with that legacy design element ("Whoa, let's not get too far ahead of ourselves, Bro"). The unit settled into silence.

J.D. positioned an empty mug under the spout and pushed the button. The cup filled with steaming, aromatic coffee.

He removed the mug and turned to face the C.E.O. "This Gilded Roast came from BrewMart stores several miles away. It was cold-brewed and loaded this morning; it's been circulating since then, and when I pushed the button, some of it was shunted here and heated; right now, our rooftop buffer tank is adding the balance back into the system." He handed the mug to Hall.

The C.E.O. took a sip as George and the other executives anxiously watched. Hall closed his eyes, as if receiving a telepathic message from the cosmos. Then he opened them and nodded.

He passed the cup to Richard Sytry. The vice president took a sip; his eyes grew wide, and he wordlessly passed the cup on to Mark Amon. As the leadership passed the coffee around, the room grew colder than before—colder, J.D. concluded, than could reasonably be attributed to an over-driven HVAC system.

"What are you doing about security?" The C.E.O. asked.

J.D. realized that Hall was talking to him. "Uh, well, all the usual protocols, once they're installed, plus fire: 2-hour-rated, automatic doors on the basement levels, and a building-wide deluge system: if one sprinkler goes, they all go."

"Get them installed by the end of next week," Hall ordered.

"I need to put in the facial recognition hardware as well," J.D. pointed out, hoping to break the C.E.O.'s gathering momentum. "That's two weeks, minimum."

"Put in everything. Just finish it and send George the bill."

J.D. was starting to get a bad feeling. "I can't do it that fast."

"Why not?" Hall demanded.

"You guys haven't given me the resources," J.D. protested, injecting a note of defensiveness; he had decided that going all in on his performance as a negative employee was the surest way out of whatever George had gotten him into. "You've got George telling me, 'Get it done in seven weeks,' and then pulling funds. You need someone who can work with unpredictable cashflow; I'm not your guy."

"You're our guy," the C.E.O. said, dismissively, and J.D.'s affected neurosis turned into genuine, quiet panic as he watched Hall turn to George. "J.D. gets carte blanche to finish up. You understand?"

"But-But, Billy," George stammered, "I have a whole portfolio of development projects moving forward."

"This one is top priority." Seeing George's irritated look, Hall barked, "I'm not asking, Mr. Unger. You understand?"

"Yes sir." George shot J.D. a bitter glance.

"And I want this whole system isolated: *he*"—Hall indicated J.D. with a tilt of his head—"should be the only person with access."

"I'm not sure I-" J.D. began to protest.

"It'll be done ASAP," George reassured the Hall.

Hall turned back to J.D. "I don't want any product moving through while maintenance is being done. Is that clear?"

J.D. shook his head. "That's not going to be possible. You have to have periodic, real-world-"

George cut in. "We'll move water through for maintenance."

Before J.D. could say or do anything more to extricate himself from the project, the C.E.O. announced to the group, "Mr. Unger's coffee privileges are reinstated," and with that Hall strolled out of the office, followed by George and the rest of the vice presidents.

CHAPTER 16

J.D.'S PROFESSIONAL EXPERIENCE OVER the next week felt like a textbook case study of efficient project management: George had finally paid out over several hundred thousand dollars in construction arrears, and he put the general contractor on a regular bank roll for the remainder of the work; J.D. was freed from having to monitor daily cashflows and was no longer receiving either project change orders or urinal sensor directives. He was left with the virtually ceremonial task of visiting stores, inspecting worksites, and confirming that fire and I.T. crews were hitting their daily marks, which they were.

He should have been encouraged by the unimpeded progress; instead he grew more bothered with each passing day. George had signaled forgiveness of J.D.'s political maneuvering by giving him a ride to work each morning, and yet during the commute hardly a word was exchanged between them.

J.D., hoping to get a simple explanation for what he had heard during the demonstration—or rather, what he had not heard—would turn the car radio volume down to a conversational level, but George would suddenly place a call to China and begin arguing in fluent Mandarin (from the peppering of English, J.D. surmised that the fight concerned the price of repair parts for the new coffee dispensers).

"When did you learn Mandarin?" J.D. asked George, one morning.

"Night classes," George replied as he quick-dialed another sales manager, launching into flawless Pashtun.

When not on the phone, George went out of his way to cultivate other, more flamboyant evasions. One time, spotting a pair of MU coeds at a Chippewa bus stop, he pulled over and gave them a lift to their school; somehow, between the bus stop and the university, he had convinced them to toplessly serenade him with show tunes. J.D. could only sit and watch the risqué spectacle, flummoxed at finding his own former mojo inexplicably dancing for a new master.

Only one substantive conversation took place during this time; it happened the day J.D. found, in the back seat of George's ride, a large, groaning, spotted Hyena. It went something like this:

"That's a fucking Hyena."

"Oh, yeah. He's tame."

"Get rid of it."

"Ok."

That was it. J.D then warily backed out of George's front passenger seat and walked over to the bus stop.

Work on the project ramped down with little fanfare; J.D. signed a Certificate of Substantial Completion on a Friday and issued a light punch list to the weekend skeleton crew.

On Monday, BrewCorp rolled out its Coffee and Data Pipeline. There was neither a social media blitz nor any local television or radio advertising—just a small sticker affixed to each store's front entrance, announcing, "BrewCorp Guarantees Gilded Roast Availability at This Establishment 24/7." By the end of the day, according to J.D.'s real-time data sampling, sales volume was up 30% from the baseline for the year, and customer foot traffic had risen over 50%.

"GREAT MOTHERFUCKING DAY, HUH?" George stood at the bathroom mirror, tweaking his tie's knot.

J.D., who had just walked into the apartment, made no immediate reply but instead studied his friend's reflection.

George picked up his sunglasses from the sink top and put them on. "The Board's meeting at the club. Hall and I are going to talk to them about you."

J.D. glanced around suspiciously. "Where's that damn animal?"

"I got rid of it." George walked to his bedroom door and tried the knob.

"It's not in there?"

"No, it's not in there." Satisfied that his room was locked, George strode across the open kitchen, ignoring the spaghetti and grease stains that it was his turn to clean.

"How do you get rid of an exotic pet? How did you even get it?"

"I know a guy who knows a guy." George opened the front door. "You can have the TV, Bro. I won't be back until late." He walked out, leaving the door open behind him.

J.D. went up to the door and locked it shut. He peered out of the window next to it and saw a black, tinted company limousine, bearing the license plate BRCRP-2, idling across the street. Whether such transportation was standard for board meetings, or whether George had already grown bored with his smaller car-tank, J.D. did not care. He waited for his friend to disappear into the vehicle; as soon as the obsidian-veneered stretch pulled away, J.D. started up his desktop computer.

The first search engine result for "doorknob lock picking" turned out to be spot on, but since there were no hairpins in the apartment—and since J.D. could not find a paper clip—a pair of drafters calipers became the tool of choice. George's lock, like all of the other fixtures in the apartment, was cheaply made, and the eighth-of-an-inch-wide keyhole easily accommodated the implement's hooked end. It took J.D. less than thirty seconds to tease all four pins into retraction. He tried the knob, and it turned cleanly.

"That's right." J.D. straightened up from his crouching position and gave the door a triumphant shove. He looked into the room.

The calipers fell from his limp hand, clattering against a pair of uneven floor planks.

The coffin was made of plain pine and looked to be about as cheap a model as one could get: there was no polish and no ornamentation, save for the pair of silk boxers draped carelessly over the edge of the open, one-piece lid.

J.D. walked around to the other side to get a look inside. He was relieved to find that it was unoccupied, apart from a light coating of dirt. Actually, it looked quite comfortable. Silk sheets covered what felt, to J.D.'s prodding hands, like a contoured foam mattress; atop a feather pillow lay a folded late edition of a financial paper, along with a gentleman's magazine and a hastily-opened pack of tissue.

J.D. examined the rest of the room, which had undergone a transformation since the last time he had seen it: there was no longer a bed, and opposite the coffin stood a combination vanity table and mirror; a small wine refrigerator sat below the fluttering, parted curtains of an open window. J.D. moved closer to the cooler and leaned down to examine it; he could just make out, through darkened glass, half a dozen clear plastic bags filled with dark fluid; he reached for the door but stopped short of opening it.

"Aw man," J.D. uttered grimly, as the situation became clear: his lovelorn and socially awkward friend, in a desperate bid to get laid, had obviously gained entry into some vamp-goth fringe of Middlestop's club culture, and judging by the plastic bags, George had gotten into some hardcore stuff—biting, drinking, and hard drugs.

J.D. searched the room but did not find any controlled substances. The only noteworthy object, aside from the coffin and miniature blood bank, was a set of cosmetic hair and skin products arranged on top of the vanity. He examined the white labels, squinting to make out very fine print (HAIR #6, SPF-10K; SKIN TONE #13, SPF-15K).

These items posed, in his mind, a different, more alarming danger than the physical risks of cocaine abuse and even blood ingestion: going to the length of applying fake SPF-ten-thousand sunscreen suggested that George was either role playing during the work day or, even worse, had cracked under the strain of years of partner-less masturbation (*What must that be like?* J.D. could not imagine) and convinced himself that his skin, to the delight of teenage girls everywhere, sparkled in sunlight.

Before he could run an intervention, J.D. would need to find out the specific nature of George's downward spiral. He went to the kitchen, reached under the free-standing, crumbling corkboard counter, and opened the wobbly top drawer of his plastic tool cabinet. He retrieved his tape measure, his cordless drill, his lithium ion battery pack and a bit case. Taking the items to his room, J.D. compared the assorted drill bits to the lens of his USB webcam. The closest match was the 3/8" bit. Hopefully George would not notice the hole.

J.D. brought the tape and a pencil into George's room. He examined the wall bordering his own room and located—amidst peeled cream paint, old nails, and unpatched screw holes—a suitable dimple. He made a small pencil mark and measured its distance up from the floor, and then in from the door.

Returning to his own room, J.D. brushed aside the slacks and shirts hanging on his side of the common wall. Replicating the measurements from next door he drilled through. He went back to George's side and checked the hole; it was on its mark, though hardly noticeable. He swept up the wood shavings and re-locked the door.

J.D. went back to the tool cabinet; in the middle drawer he found a roll of heavy-duty duct tape. Using ten strips, he secured the webcam over his side of the peephole.

On the off chance that George might wander into J.D.'s room during the sting, J.D. made his camera's USB cable scarce by tacking it along the bottom of the baseboard and along the doorway molding.

He pushed his hanging clothes back into place in front of the webcam and sat down at his desk to examine the video feed on his monitor. George's room received no direct light in late afternoon; the only discernible object was a large billboard that faced the window from across the street—a BrewMart advertisement ("Wake up. Drink a Cup. Get Ready to Face the Day."). J.D. turned on the camera's low light setting; the image became black and white, and the details of the room appeared, bathed in the billboard's reflected sunlight.

Opening a lengthy playlist, J.D. brought out his old box of brightly-colored building connectors, and ordered pork dumplings and house fried rice from the hole-in-the-wall takeout downstairs.

J.D. sat on his floor, free-assembling abstract plastic shapes. He had not spent a quiet night at home since grade school, and the music (Charles Mingus—at once cheerful and yet angry; quirky and yet familiar; uncontrollable and yet civilized), combined with the comfort of greasy food and with J.D.'s play-building, cast a mercurial spell over the evening. At certain points a suffocating feeling would force J.D. to take a walk up the street, but at others, a nostalgic contentment would inspire him to look up old music videos.

Each time he checked his video feed, J.D. merely saw an empty room with a vanity, an open window, and a coffin; by three in the morning, after eight vigilant hours, he decided to go to bed. He put away the hundreds of toy connectors and disassembled what had evolved into a red, yellow and blue, plastic replica of his childhood house.

As he closed the building kit, he chanced to look up at his computer screen.

The billboard was bathed in bright, nighttime illumination provided by its bank of sodium vapor foot lights; a shadow blotted out part of the sign. The black spot grew, and J.D. realized that it was not a shadow but a hovering *thing*.

The shape filled the window as it drew nearer, occluding more of the billboard's light and rendering the already grainy image too dark to make out. The detail returned, however, as the floating silhouette cleared the window and passed into the room.

It pivoted upright over the coffin and descended until it stood inside, at the foot; then, with a slowness that defied gravity, it tilted backwards, sinking behind the open lid and pulling it shut.

CHAPTER 17

GEORGE'S ALARM CLOCK SOUNDED at five that morning, just as the sky was beginning to lighten. The understated chimes were easy to sleep through, but the interred slumberer awoke immediately.

A reverse death rattle came from within the coffin; the lid burst open, and a bruised corpse rose into the air and floated down to the refrigerator; it took out one of the bags and held it up to its sagging face. The dead man opened his jaw wide. As if on cue, a two-inch long fang, thin and curved—like a rattlesnake's but longer—shot out from behind the front teeth; he used it to rip open the top of the bag. The fang retracted into his mouth and, in its place, out wagged an obscenely long tongue, or not so much a tongue as a fleshy, pink tube, tipped with a large sucker. The seemingly intelligent organ threaded its way into the bag, dipped into the dark liquid and began to drink. The tube swelled as fluid coursed through it. The bag emptied so quickly and so completely that it collapsed around the proboscis, making it look like some vacuum-sealed piece of deli meat and forcing the corpse to wrestle itself free. The bruising disappeared, and the drooping skin became firm.

The dead man went over to the vanity and sat. He faced the mirror, but neither his dull red eyes, nor his ashen skin appeared in it; only his tank top shirt and boxers cast a reflection, and they seemed to float in space.

He gathered his cosmetics. He removed a tinted, large contact lens from a container and put it in; a floating, hazel eye appeared in the mirror; it became the left of a pair as the second lens was worked in. A gray hand grasped a hairspray bottle and applied the product generously; the thick, pigmented mousse revitalized the stringy hair, which the dead man slicked back. He took the most time applying a pigmented moisturizer; deathly pale flesh resolved itself into a simulacrum of living skin. The remaining beauty products made the missing eyebrows, lips and teeth presentable.

Bit by bit, George Unger appeared in the mirror.

J.D. watched all of this from his bedroom floor, where he sat propped up against the foot of his bed, wearing the previous day's clothes and Middlestop Mosquitoes cap. He had not gone to sleep; he had not put his building kit back on his shelf; he had not moved in hours.

"GET DRESSED. I GOTTA go." George paced back and forth through the kitchen, holding his phone to his ear with one hand and holding his mug of coffee with the other.

J.D. quietly regarded his friend from the small, makeshift kitchen table (a plywood wheel, balanced atop three piles of cinder blocks). His bowl of cereal sat untouched, drowning in its milk. "I'll be in later."

George looked from J.D. to the cereal. "What's wrong, Bro?"

"I got a stomach thing. I'm hoping it's just a 24-hour bug." J.D.'s burnt out expression and lethargic tone backed up the claim.

"Feel better," George said absently; he turned and left.

For the next hour and a half, J.D. researched vampire lore. If he had not been distraught for his friend, he would have given up the search after five minutes: he could find no indisputable online resource documenting supernatural events; what he did find felt like it was cobbled together by film and goth divas, each looking to claim his or her corner of the internet.

Most of the purported facts were already familiar to J.D., as they would be to anyone who had ever watched an episode of *Buffy* or read an Anne Rice novel; he found inconsistent, sometimes contradictory, assertions: vampires had to be invited in, vampires could go where they pleased; sunlight destroyed them, sunlight weakened them; crosses repelled them, crosses insulted them, crosses made them cackle defiantly. Several sites mentioned sunflower seeds, which were supposed to detain an undead ghoul by forcing him to pause and inventory each kernel. There seemed to be more of a consensus that garlic was an effective repellant, and it was universally suggested that staking the heart was a reliable method of dispatch.

J.D. stood up, determined to collect some solid data. Pressing half a dozen garlic cloves into a solution of water and dish soap, he converted a travel-size sprayer into a weaponized cosmetic remover.

FROM BEHIND HIS WORKSTATION, J.D. waited for George to join the other fellow executives for their afternoon coffee break.

Once George was out of his office, J.D. walked through the open door, took out the spray bottle, and spritzed the keyboard. He waved his hand back and forth to dissipate the odor and went back to his own office.

Five minutes later, George returned from his break, barking Spanish into his cell phone. "Ellos nos dan un buen precio, pero nosotros podemos hacer mejor si il tambien nos suministra los navios!"

He frowned, sniffing the air; nevertheless, he hunched over his desk and, cradling the phone between his head and shoulder, began to type on his keyboard. "Diga me su informacion...S-O-L-D-"

George's eyes grew wide as his fingertips released plumes of smoke. Stifling a scream, he ran to his door, leaving trails of red, dried powder on the floor and white smoke in the air. He kicked his door shut, all the while nodding at the cradled phone.

Sitting on the other side of the partially open blinds, J.D. watched his friend huddle over a corner water cooler, nudge open the cold tap with his elbow and hold his melting finger tips beneath the stream.

J.D. turned back to his work. A freak interaction between some household chemicals, an herb, and a hand crème was, he felt, the most plausible explanation for what he had just seen. Still, he wanted more data.

FOR FIVE NIGHTS, J.D. patiently observed the video feed of his friend's room; he became satisfied that there was a routine to George's nocturnal movements and that the hours between eleven p.m. and four a.m. offered a safe window in which to operate. To keep up appearances, J.D. made it his business to be out of the apartment for several evenings before conducting his next experiment. He took special care to leave half-emptied beer bottles scattered throughout the living room and to make regular, flirtatious, after-work calls—always within ear-shot of George—to his single, female co-workers.

On the night of what was to be his next experiment, J.D. was late getting home. He had intended to arrive by 11:30, but there was an unannounced service suspension along his bus route (a box truck, driving at high speed, had leapt into a massive, notoriously neglected pothole on the westbound lane of the Inini bridge and actually tumbled *through* the split concrete and missing rebar, into the river below); four hours and eight transfers later, J.D. walked into the apartment; it was 4:45 in the morning.

He went directly to George's room, not bothering to review the surveillance feed. The coffin was shut, and there was a terrible smell that made him almost throw up; he went to the bathroom and stuffed wads of tissue into his nostrils.

J.D. returned and stood uncertainly in the doorway. Gathering his nerve, he tiptoed to the vanity. Every rustle he made, every creak, seemed amplified as he quietly, frantically rifled through the cosmetics. In his jumpiness, he kept looking over his shoulder for any sign of movement behind him; during one such distracted glance, he knocked one of the containers off of the table; it hit the floor with a loud clatter.

He scurried out to the hallway, where he stood for five minutes, peering at the casket, but nothing happened. He took a tentative step forward, followed by another, and then another, until he was standing over the fallen plastic case. He picked it up and saw that it was the one he had been looking for: SKIN TONE #13, SPF-15K.

J.D. carried the bottle to the kitchen sink. He emptied half of the contents into the drain and replaced the missing product with a mixture of tanning butter and dish soap. He shook the container and dispensed a sample; it looked unchanged. Returning the cosmetic to the vanity, J.D. put everything back in its place.

He turned to go but stopped and stared at the casket.

J.D. did not understand why he did what he did next; he only knew that his friend had no right to put him in the situation he was in; spurred on by that feeling of betrayal, he reached out and gave the lid a shove. Underneath it, he saw, up close, red, unseeing eyes and blackened, wasting flesh, and as he stood looking down at the barely-recognizable corpse of his best friend, all of the fear drained out of him. "Fuck You."

J.D. went to go get a screwdriver.

GEORGE PUSHED AGAINST THE inside of the lid for the fortieth time, but still it would not open. He had spent the past five minutes trying to get out of his box. He was doing it the same way he had done it every morning, but this morning the box would not let him leave. He tried using both hands; the lid refused to budge. He could hear the alarm outside and realized he was going to be late. Irritable and hungry, he snarled his frustration and beat randomly at the padded panel above him.

After one of his punches, a sliver of pre-dawn light came through; he pushed on the same spot, far to the left of where he normally put his palm; the lid moved cleanly, but it opened the wrong way. George sat up and examined the sides of the box: the hinges had been moved to the opposite side.

Confused, George fumbled his way to the vanity to put on his face. He needed to have a cup of coffee; he could not even begin to work out what had happened until he had done that. And why did he keep smelling dish soap?

He put on his suit and sunglasses, poured himself a double cup from the kitchen carafe—J.D. would just have to make his own—and tucked the market report section of the paper under his arm. He knocked on J.D.'s door but saw the note taped there ("Went in EARLY, Bro"). He went down to the street.

The morning was hot and sunny, baking the peeling, old building and crumbling sidewalk in hard, yellow light. George swaggered out into the day. He made it ten steps before getting the comical look of a cartoon character who had just looked down after running several yards off of a cliff.

"What's burning?" he actually asked out loud before noticing that his hands had begun to literally fry.

George ran back toward the building and desperately groped his pants pocket for the key. No sooner had he fished it out than his sunlit, sizzling right hand burst into flame. He dropped the coffee and periodical and swatted at the burning skin, but the hand he was swatting with, along with its sleeve, caught fire. George let out a shriek. Other exposed parts of him spontaneously combusted, a neck here, an ear there, burning any adjacent fabric in the process. By the time he had gotten the door open and retreated through it, he looked like an action stunt double who had been set aflame.

Across the street, sitting at the downtown M2 bus stop, J.D. folded up his copy of *The Middlestop People's Chronicle*, got up, and jaywalked over to catch his uptown bus.

CHAPTER 18

"YOU WANTED TO SEE me?" J.D. asked, poking his head into the office.

"Shut the door," George said quietly. His lobster-red face and hands were badly peeling; a pile of ash lay on the desk in front of him.

J.D. shut the door and stood unassumingly in front of the desk. He had just gotten into work and found the sticky note summons on his door.

Looking down at the foot of George's desk, he saw that a beach towel from the apartment had been carelessly tossed into the trash can; its singed edges spilled over the sides of the titanium mesh cylinder.

"Have a seat," George said.

J.D. sat down, balancing his briefcase on his lap.

"Ok," George began. "So you're obviously aware that there's a new...situation." His tone was so measured that he might as well have been explaining that casual Fridays had just been suspended. "It will be an adjustment, but I'm confident we'll get through it, as long as we're both on the same page." George sat patiently, awaiting a response.

"You're a vampire," J.D. said, matter-of-factly; he might as well have been stating that his employment contract expressly guaranteed casual Fridays. "We're not on the same page; we're not even in the same model of the universe."

George raised his hands in cautioning. "There's a lot of misinformation out there about what this means, ok? And we should clear up any misconceptions you've gotten."

J.D. considered this. "You're a *vampire*."

"Shhh." George looked past.

J.D. followed his gaze. Richard Sytry was peering in through the blinds, looking concerned.

George gave the vice president a reassuring wave. Sytry slowly turned and walked away. George turned back to J.D. "Let's tone down the labeling, okay? I'm just like everybody else, only better suited for a 24-hour, free-market, global economy."

"If you're just like everybody else, why don't you have a reflection? Why do you spontaneously combust in sunlight? Why does being around you make me want to curl up and die? I've never felt like this in my life!" J.D. held up his cell phone, showing George the *No Service* message. "Why do you interfere with my reception?"

George chuckled. "I know, isn't that whacked? It's something about my presence violating the laws of science and nature!" He held up his own phone; it looked just like J.D.'s but without the scuff marks. "You'll need a special model. I'll work on getting you one."

"How did this happen?" J.D. demanded.

George shook his head. "Sorry, Bro, that's above your pay grade."

J.D. reached into his briefcase and then flung his arm toward George. A handful of sunflower seeds spilled onto the desktop.

George's reaction was immediate and seemed to surprise even him: he huddled protectively over his paper blotter, holding his nose within inches of the desktop surface, and began to point to each newly-broadcast kernel, silently mouthing a count.

"Did you know vampires are obsessive seed counters?" J.D. asked.

"Uh, no," George distractedly managed to answer. "I thought that was just children's public television."

"Well, I'm here to clear up any misconceptions you've gotten."

"Would you please put these away?"

J.D. insisted, "I want to know how this happened."

"I couldn't, even if you locked me in a granary-DAMMIT!" George banged his fist on the desk, causing the seeds to jump. He was forced to start over. "I'll tell you the rest though. Please, Bro."

J.D. swept the pips back into his case.

George sat back. He tried to gently wipe the newly-formed beads of sweat from his burnt forehead, but finding his skin painful to the touch, he put down his hand. "It's not like they go around making others whenever they feel like it."

"Who?"

"The only time a position opens up is if they lose one."

"Wait a minute." J.D. silently followed a disturbing line of thought. "Of *course* no one was breathing! You, Sytry, Bunet, Hall, the whole top floor."

"We breathe," George said, a little too defensively. "We totally breathe." His chest heaved with a series of deep breaths. "Look, let's just focus on our own-"

"And they were talking about some exec or board member!" J.D. recalled. "At our orientation! G.L.! They were talking about a replacement!"

George fidgeted with his padded arm rests as he watched understanding dawn on his friend's face. "Actually, now there's a good story: technically, G.L.'s a missing person, but the talk is someone staked him." George leaned in, conspiratorially, and confided, "From what I understand, the stuff with crosses is all bullshit, but a stake through the heart? G.L. turns into a pile of ashes. It's the perfect crime: no corpus, no habeus." The words seemed to be spilling out of him. "But is it a crime to kill someone who's already dead? But I digress-"

"I don't get you." J.D. stood up, unable to hear any more. "I-I don't get you!"

"Shhh."

"How could you choose something this twisted?"

George's face changed. His eyebrows shot up, as if he needed to make certain that he had heard correctly. "Twisted?" Gone were the sheepish grin and placating tone.

George came around the desk, his expression becoming one of open bitterness. He stood in front of J.D., inches from his face. "You want to know what's twisted? When the crazy wino with the shopping bags and broken TV set always—*always*—sits right next you on the bus and informs you that *you* bear the mark of Cain, that's twisted." He ticked off finger after finger. "When you drink from one of eight open soda cans, the one filled with your bunkmates' tobacco spit that they deliberately offered to you? Twisted! When you unknowingly track dog shit through the immaculate halls of the Dean of Freshman's house at an Ivy League school, right before your admission interview. Twisted!" His low voice took on an unearthly, guttural character. It was not loud, but it was big—too big for his body; it seemed to fill the room. "When you dream you're a superhero who flies only 3 feet off the ground, and slower than everyone who's walking, Twisted!"

The room grew colder, as if George's tirade was sucking up all warmth.

"And when you finally manage to find *someone*," George cursed in an impossibly deep, hurt-filled growl, which was at once sad and terrible to behold, "and your best friend takes her to the Blue Steak men's room and there *shags* her, while *you* happen to be taking a leak? Twisted!"

J.D. drew back, unable and unwilling to make sense of what he was hearing. "Is that what this is about?"

George shook his head, looking at his friend with a mixture of disgust and pity. "You can't possibly imagine what it's like to lose, every day, for your entire life. How could you? Well, you know what would be really twisted? Taking more of the same from God when you have the chance to shove it back in his face."

No rebuttal came to aid J.D. against the naked words. They hung in the air like the acrid smoke of an electrical fire.

Throughout their years of friendship, J.D. and George had never held a serious discussion about spirituality or religion. J.D. had, on one occasion, shared with George his theory that everyone, including George, was merely a projection of his own psyche, but that was during their one flirtation with mush-rooms—and it had been a bad trip (George had rocked back and forth, convinced that he was a figment of J.D.'s imagination, and J.D., who had reassured George of his reality, had been secretly convinced all along that he was, in actuality, providing moral support to an imaginary friend). J.D. had always felt comfortable in his atheism, and George...well, it had been difficult to say just what George really believed. J.D. had regularly enjoyed watching his friend look up at the heavens in response to some random mishap—receiving a dolloping of bird droppings on the head, or accidently spilling meat sauce on a high school varsity wrestling captain—and dryly intone to the almighty, "Thanks for that." J.D. never realized that it ran deeper than a comical bit of Yiddish theatre.

"Look, you should be happy for me," George said, shrugging off his unearthly rage with a smug chuckle. "I finally get what you've always known: it's eat or be eaten." He sat back down and took a sip of his morning coffee.

J.D. stared at the cup. "Vampires don't eat. They drink."

George frowned up at him, confused until he realized J.D.'s meaning. "Oh, no. No, Bro," he insisted. "Never during business hours."

"Never during business hours?"

George smiled. "Well, a man's gotta live, doesn't he?"

"I want you out of the apartment."

George laughed again, but as he saw that J.D. was serious, he frowned and then smirked, seeming amused. "Oh, what? You're suddenly afraid to get a little blood on your hands?"

"Get out, moutherfucker," J.D. said softly.

Hearing a knuckle crack, George looked from J.D.'s impassive face down to the clenched fist; he stopped smiling. "You're in *my* office. *You* get out, motherfucker."

J.D. trembled; he struggled to think through his anger; he chewed on his lower lip and told himself to just leave. Quickly, he turned away and began walking.

He had made it halfway to the door when George called after: "Oh, I'm sorry. That was out of line. You don't have a mother."

To throw a full round house against a seated opponent from J.D.'s standing position would have been difficult and unrewarding; instead, J.D. pushed off the floor with his left foot, and with his right fist he launched a superhero-style punch into George's face. When it connected, J.D. expected to feel the crunch of imploding cartilage; instead he felt the sharp pain of unyielding mortar; he let out a yelp. George's sunburned face remained otherwise unblemished.

George shot out an arm, grabbing J.D. by the throat. He launched out of his chair, flinging the two of them through the air, until the mortal man's back was pinned against the glass partition with his head sticking halfway through a foam ceiling panel.

George drew back his lips, making a deep, resonant, animal growl. One of his fingernails, which had all elongated into small talons in the space of a few seconds, had made a cut in J.D.'s neck; a trickle of blood ran down George's thumb. Without thinking, he stuck out his tongue and sucked up the bright red drops.

The growl stuck in his throat. His eyes grew wide, crazed. He opened his mouth, and the long fang appeared.

There was knock at the door.

The fang went away, and George came back to his senses.

Sytry stuck his head in. "What's the problem?" he asked the two men up on the wall.

"No problem." George dropped himself and J.D. onto the plush carpeting; he released his friend's neck. J.D. doubled over in a coughing fit.

"People are working," Sytry reminded them. "Keep it down."

"Ok," George acknowledged. He straightened his sleeves and checked his tie knot.

Sytry turned to go but paused. He eyed George's peeling skin. "Have you seen tomorrow's weather?"

"Yeah, I saw." George nodded. "Sunny."

Sytry walked out, mumbling to himself, "This goddam weather."

George returned to his seat and pretended to read emails.

J.D., still recovering from his brief strangulation, stood for a few moments to take stock of the situation. He could not bring himself to face George, and George was ignoring him.

Realizing that there was nothing more to say, J.D. grabbed his briefcase, opened the door, and tottered out.

As he crossed the hallway, staring down at his feet, he became aware of hushed conversation in front of him.

"A special purpose entity?"

"That's what Duke said."

More dazed from his confrontation than he realized, he stumbled into a pair of pale legs in studded, leather boots. Grimacing, he took a step back and made himself look up.

"Sorry," he said, staring into Cerri's resentful eyes.

"Uh-huh." She did not sound convinced.

Nancy, Duke Bunet's red headed administrative assistant, was standing next to her. "I'm still waiting for that ballgame," she told J.D.

He had been seeing Nancy, on and off, since orientation. Neither he nor she really had much to say to one another during their hours together, but they implicitly agreed to put up with the awkward silences and small talk for what seemed to J.D. like a common, recreational purpose.

"I know, I need to get those tick-," he began but noticed Cerri looking from one to the other. In that awkward moment, he was able to fathom how a series of unpleasant coincidences could send George's personal cosmology into a tailspin. "You know, I've actually been incredibly busy."

Nancy stared at him, blankly.

A loud yawn made J.D. turn back to Cerri, who was snoring loudly and staring him down with bored eyes.

"I'm sorry," he said to both of them and brushed past, aiming for the sanctuary of his office.

As soon as he got there, he felt the exposure of his uncovered glass partitions (his hallway blinds had been removed on George's orders). He hunched behind his computer display but could see Cerri and Nancy still staring at him from across the floor; they spoke amongst themselves, shaking their heads, and even sharing a giggle, as though studying an amusing animal at the zoo.

CHAPTER 19

"YOU CAN PRETTY MUCH do what you want with the common area," J.D. told the young man he led from the living room into the kitchen. "I'm basically only here nights and weekends."

In the pursuit of roommate referrals, J.D. had telephoned or emailed dozens of his former classmates; none had responded, except for an ex-girlfriend who had hung up on him. Reluctantly, he had then posted on Craigslist and was not surprised to have gotten a flood of emails from undergraduates looking to live off campus.

To add a sub lessee, J.D. would need to get his landlord's permission, and *that* relationship was also strained: J.D. owed one month's back rent; catching up on it was proving difficult, since student loans ate up half of his BrewCorp salary. J.D. needed a responsible roommate—someone whom his landlord would readily approve.

The young man to whom he was showing the apartment that Saturday afternoon was just such a prospect: the kid had graduated high school cum laude (all AP courses), would be starting his freshman year in the Finance and Business Administration program, working part-time at Chippewa Medical

Clinic, and most importantly, would be co-signing with his parents, who ran a successful 30-year auto dealership.

There had already been ten showings, and each time, J.D. had persuaded the applicant to pay a five-dollar, non-refundable processing fee without actually seeing George's room (instead, they saw J.D.'s, which was comparably-sized).

The current showing was more complicated: George's movers had arrived thirty minutes ahead of the star prospect, and the packing crew had already started carrying shrink-wrapped furniture out of his bedroom.

"I don't want to get in their way," J.D. explained to the student. "My bedroom's the same dimensions; I'll show you." He started toward his room.

The young man did not follow. "What's the public transportation like?" He drifted down the hall, toward George's room.

J.D. walked up behind him. "I think you dropped something."

The young man turned around and frowned; a five dollar bill had just drifted to the floor. "I don't think that's mine."

"I saw it fall out of your pocket." J.D. picked up the money and handed it over. When it came time to fill out an application, the young man would, J.D. hoped, conclude that his fee had been waived. "You're at M.U.?"

The young man nodded, and J.D. was relieved to have temporarily regained his attention.

"It's great. Lots of options for getting there. There's the M2 bus, there's-" J.D. noticed, behind the young man's back, six movers carrying the coffin out of the bedroom. J.D. backed toward his room, gesturing for the prospect to accompany him. "Well, there's mainly the M2, but you can sleep during the ride."

The prospect began to follow J.D.

"I know I was always glad to get that extra hour," J.D. continued. He backed into his bedroom.

The young man followed him to his door and looked approvingly at the layout and roominess of the space. A loud floorboard creak prompted the student to turn around. "What's that?"

"What's what?"

"That." The young man pointed at the Dadaist funeral procession—six, uniformed pallbearers, each one bearing the insignia *Bill's VIP Moving and Storage*—passing through the kitchen. "Is that a...? Is that a...?"

"Yep. That's a coffin alright. Good eye."

They watched the movers carry the box out of the apartment; creaks sounded from the stairway below.

"I'll let you know," the young man said, hastily retreating through the common area, toward the open apartment door.

J.D. called after him, "So I can go ahead and pull the ad, right?" and walked out into the kitchen. He had no reason to go there, but keeping his legs moving helped him to think through his situation.

One option would be to sublet the apartment in secret, for which purpose any of the other nine applicants would be suitable. Over time, though, the risk of his getting caught in an illegal sublet would only grow.

It also occurred to J.D. that he did not want a roommate; given the way he was feeling, he would prefer to have as little human contact as possible. In order to carry the entire lease as a single tenant, he saw only one possibility: Hall seemed to consider him indispensable to the operation and upkeep of the pipeline; he could demand an advance on the raise he was going to ask for in the fall: a pay bump, into the high five figures, stock options, one-to-one employer-matching on his

401k, and a bus card (he was initially going to demand his own company ride, but the thought of driving a mobile fortress to the grocery had bothered him).

"I've got him right here." George emerged from his emptied bedroom, squinting at J.D. from behind his sunglasses. He was on the phone, and as he approached J.D., he held it out. "We need to double product through the pipeline. What's the best way, without a second pump?"

"Oh, that's easy," J.D. said loudly to the phone, hoping his sarcasm would carry. "Just redline the compressors and replace every moving part in six months."

George put the phone back to his ear. "Did you get that?" He turned away and gave a series of quiet nods.

J.D. surmised that his angry, throw-away response was being taken seriously. "That's right," he warned. "Replace a one-of-a-kind, municipal capacity pump, *every six months*."

George ended the call. "Have it done by Monday." He glanced around the apartment. "We're done here," he said and strode out the door.

CHAPTER 20

"Every six months," J.D. muttered, shaking his head as he consulted a thick hardcopy of the pump schematics. Whatever the company's short-term cashflow needs, he could not imagine any accounting scenario in which an unbudgeted, semi-annual expenditure of over a million dollars looked good.

Standing in front of the pump, he thumbed through his printout, trying to locate a set of codes. Finding them deep within the two-hundred page document, he searched the machine's panelling for the keypad; he found it next to a sampling dipstick. He entered the codes, and a small LED display above the keypad confirmed, *Motor Safeties: Unlocked.*

Taking out his tablet, J.D. went into the pipeline's advanced settings and applied the overclock. A warning message appeared: *Are you sure you want to do this?* He clicked through it and started the diagnostic cycle.

Stepping back from the unit, J.D. closed his eyes to listen to the deepening thumping that filled the room, as a bank of air-driven pistons revved up to twice their previous speeds. He decided that the pump sounded alright, or at least not about to explode, and opened his eyes. He watched the test water flow back and forth through the network of tubes. There were no signs of systemic distress, apart from the higher frequency at which the bands of roiling water and air were flowing into, and out of, the main lines.

J.D. went back to the elevator. On his way there, he tested the self-locking security door. He knew that his eyes and ears were blunt instruments compared to the maintenance software, but relying entirely on automated safety diagnostics made him uneasy. The door closed itself three times out of three. Passing beneath the newly installed automatic fire door, he stopped to inspect its accompanying control console.

J.D. monitored the remaining stress tests from his workstation. The pipeline passed the entire battery. With some lingering trepidation, he ordered the dispensary to reload the Gilded Roast.

Throughout the day, he followed the pipeline's activity from his workstation. He began to notice an unusual pattern: on the hour, all of the green arrow icons, indicating the direction of flow, would align toward the headquarters building, meaning that all store product was directed back into the pump and buffer tank. This was to be expected during testing cycles, but in normal, demand-driven, operation, such a random convergence would be rare to see in a week, much less in an hour.

At four O'clock, after witnessing the phenomenon for the fifth consecutive time, J.D. pulled up video feed from the Middlestop Heights store. Eight pairs of live thumbnails appeared, displaying cashiers and customers at each of the store's eight checkout lanes.

He enlarged the first register's feed and studied the close-ups of the cashier and his customer. Overlaying each face was a geometric network of line graphics, which interfaced with a statistics sidebar.

J.D. closed the sidebar and turned off the facial overlays. He was not sure what he expected to find, but he did not see anything out of the ordinary, just a gum-chewing teenager, distractedly purchasing a gamer's flight stick while watching a movie on his smart phone.

He enlarged the next lane's feed, and the one after that; there was nothing unusual.

He enlarged the fourth set. A staggering customer was hoisting a karaoke machine onto the counter; it seemed to expend all of the man's strength to do it. The box did not look big or heavy, and the theatricality of the customer's effort reminded J.D. of a Charlie Chaplin or Buster Keaton comedy.

The man looked familiar, and J.D. realized that he was Joe, the Inini Village tradesman who had enjoyed a few seconds of fame as the high-scoring citizen discount participant. Joe wore his same Mosquitos cap and open, checkered shirt, but he looked terrible: pale, with sunken, unfocused eyes and dark circles.

J.D. zoomed out; Joe's wife and two girls were there next to him. The whole family looked exhausted. Their collective stupor was briefly interrupted when Joe, swaying unsteadily, fell. His wife, jolted into alarm, let out a brief, terrified yelp as she caught him; then she settled back into her malaise. The youngest girl tottered as well; her older sister reached out to steady her. The smaller girl took the offered hand; as she did so, J.D. saw that she had been rubbing a bandage on her inner elbow. The wife and older daughter also wore bandages, each one located in the same place. Joe wore long sleeves, but J.D. noticed that one of them was unbuttoned.

J.D. pulled up the transaction and saw that Joe's family had, just minutes earlier, received another citizen discount.

CHAPTER 21

USING A HOLE PUNCH, J.D. made a small opening in his shirt pocket. He worked alone, sitting on the salvaged couch, in the middle of the living room.

George's absence, although relieving J.D. from spells of irrational despair, had augmented the loft's sense of urban decay into an atmosphere of desolation. The quirky antiques that George had accumulated—his mahogany hat and coat stand, his miniature grandfather clock, his coromandel chest—had covered exposed lath strips and missing floor boards and filled the space. With those items gone, the living room felt oppressively open and impersonal.

The only furniture left was the couch and a second-hand entertainment center, which they had found at a thrift store up the street (initially, George had, under protest, split the cost with J.D., condemning the cardboard and plywood cabinet as a "gauche monstrosity" that lacked history. When George moved out, J.D. offered to reimburse his half, but George snorted derisively and told J.D., "Consider it a gift.").

The small, CRT television was on, with the volume turned up. J.D. did not care about the home renovation show that was on; he just wanted to have some sound in the apartment—and to take advantage of his last few days of subscription service before calling the cable provider to cancel.

He placed his phone in the shirt pocket and positioned the lens behind the hole. Satisfied that it lined up cleanly, he taped the phone into place and went to the bathroom mirror to inspect his handy work.

The lens was only a shade darker than the gunmetal oxford; the installation looked not like a camera but like a perfectly round ink stain. J.D. used a pen to make the hole appear less circular. The resulting camouflage looked perfect.

It occurred to J.D. that he was getting quite good at surveillance.

Entering the Middlestop Heights store, he joined the line at the tree-themed citizen discount archway. There were six customers already there.

"What about you honey, what have you done?" an elderly lady in front of him asked a six or seven year old boy (J.D. guessed that this was her grandson or perhaps great grandson).

"I don't know," the shy boy replied.

"What about the candy?" his pre-adolescent sister prompted him.

"I sold chocolate bars for..." The boy stopped to consider how best to summarize his volunteer work. "So children with diabetes could get help."

"Oooh, Raymond"–The old lady gave the boy a big, wrinkly smile—"what a good boy!" She pulled him into a one-handed hug, shifting her other hand's grip on her cane, so as not to lose balance. "What about you, cute stuff?" she asked the young girl. "What you done for the community?"

"We planted trees at school last spring. Does that count?"

"Sure it count." The old lady hugged the girl. She turned to the third child, a sullen-faced teenage girl. "What about you?"

The older girl crossed her arms. "I don't gotta do nothing for the community."

"Say what now?"

J.D. found himself admiring how quickly and easily the old lady shifted from nurturer to matron.

"What the community done for me?" the teenager said coolly, staring at the floor.

"That ain't right," the old lady told her.

"What the community—"—she began moving her head from side to side for emphasis.

"No, that ain't right, girl. *You* ain't right." The old lady stared at the defiant teenager, who refused to face her.

A sales manager appeared under the archway. "Please step all the way in!" His peppy voice and plastered-on smile reminded J.D. of a theme park employee.

The customers followed him into the tree. They passed through a short hallway and emerged into what looked like a grownup-scaled version of a children's section in a well-funded library. Cartoonish reliefs of bulging bicycles, mid-century store fronts and colorful awnings crowded the sky-blue walls; green and blue clad mannequins, peppered throughout, waved at one another, picked up after their leashed, plastic dogs, played chess, and cheerfully greeted foot patrolmen; from the ceiling, recessed speakers embedded in fluffy clouds filled the panorama with an upbeat murmur of bicycle bells, barks and banter.

The sales manager led the group to a street side café installation (real fencing and tables, jutting out from a fake front). "That's right, all the way in. And please take a seat."

J.D. sat at one of the tables, taking in the eatery's façade. The painted window displayed a hanging, chalked-in list of Eastern European specials: potato dumplings, schnitzel, pierogies, blintzes, and beef goulash.

The sales manager consulted his clipboard as the rest of the customers found seats. "Welcome to the BrewMart Citizen Discount program," he recited exuberantly. "I'm Mike; I'll be your program counselor." He beamed at the group.

J.D. could not fault him for throwing himself into his work, still the intensity of the presentation made him uncomfortable.

"We want to thank you for all you do for the community. Now, each of you is sitting in front of a discount application and a pencil."

J.D. looked at the hardbound menu, sitting on top of his table. He opened it and found the pencil and form nestled within.

"Oh," the old lady interrupted, squinting at her copy of the paperwork. "What documentation was I supposed to bring?"

"None at all," the sales manager replied.

The old lady frowned. "I never heard of application that don't require-"

"Nana," hushed the teenage girl.

The sales manager reassured the old lady, "Please don't worry about a thing. No one has failed an assessment yet."

The old lady looked from him to the teenager and shook her head doubtfully.

The sales manager said to the group, "In just under ten minutes, you'll each receive a coupon, good today only, for 50 percent off *any* in-store merchandise. Just bring your completed applications and pencils up to the front when you're ready."

Customers took up their writing implements and jotted down responses; the added scribbling of pencil on paper gave the neighborhood soundtrack a dissonant feeling; J.D. had the unpleasant sensation of being stuck in a classroom on a gorgeous day.

He examined his form. Under the BrewCorp header was a single sentence: "1. Please briefly describe what makes you a good citizen?" J.D. considered whether or not to compose a genuine response; the erroneous question mark eventually swayed him to strike a line through the text.

He got up, handed his questionnaire to the sales manager, and started back to his seat.

"Excuse me, sir?"

J.D. turned around.

"You'll need to sign." The sales manager pointed at the faded, boilerplate paragraph and signature line at the bottom of the page.

J.D. took the form and examined the statement, which read:

Applicant understands that any and all reproductions of the BrewCorp Citizen Discount evaluation process, including, but not limited to, still photography, video and audio recording, and blogging, are strictly prohibited. Applicant further affirms that he/she is entering into the BrewCorp Citizen Discount program of his/her own free will and fully consents to the evaluation process.

J.D. signed the affirmation and handed the form back. The small boy walked past him and handed in his table's applications. The last remaining submissions were brought up by a middle-aged man wearing business casual attire (either a tenured professor or an early retiree) and a young couple (medical workers, judging by their blue scrub tops).

"Great!" The sales manager placed the papers in his leather bound folder, went over to the fake restaurant front and opened a real door. "Now if you'll please follow me, I'll show you to the assessment room."

The group followed him inside.

"A little bit of history," he called over his shoulder as he led the customers down a long flight of steps. "The BrewMart Citizen Discount program was created by BrewCorp's C.E.O. and founding father, Billy Hall."

At the bottom of the steps, the wall mural (traditionally-uniformed chefs tossing pizzas, slicing tomatoes, and waving to the passers bye) transitioned to sterile white, as the group entered a long corridor.

"Billy believed that people are the world's greatest resource, and he wanted to reward individuals who work to improve the community."

The lighting became dimmer and intermittent. J.D. glanced around; the fluorescent bulbs were buzzing, flickering, and, in some places, missing; water stains and drywall cut outs increasingly marred the walls; and the floor's previously smooth concrete had become a crumbling, irregular patchwork of bad repairs.

J.D. reached into his shirt pocket and tapped his phone. With a muffled beep, it started recording.

"What kinda discount program take people down some creepy basement?" the old lady protested. She pulled the young boy close to her and instructed her two girls, "We going back."

"I'm sorry ma'am," the sales manager apologized, as he approached a dead bolted door. "I should have explained our appearance; we're undergoing renovation."

He twisted the lock's knob until it clicked open, and he turned to face the group. "Hundreds of ordinary folks come down here every day. You see, here at BrewCorp, we understand that you're working to build a better life, and we think you deserve some recognition." He stood to one side and pulled open the door.

CHAPTER 22

THE FIRST THING J.D. became aware of was a herd of gray-faced people lumbering aimlessly through a mall. Deafening, goofy elevator music shook the space. J.D. then realized he was watching television.

His jaw ached; he realized he had been smiling for hours. He straightened his mouth and rubbed his lower face. His neck hurt from staring straight ahead.

He turned his head and saw that he was in his living room. He had no idea how he had gotten there.

The staggering bodies appeared on a 60-inch screen. The HDTV sat in a new, cherry and glass entertainment center, as did a Blu-ray player, an amplifier, and a pair of six-hundred watt speakers.

J.D. searched his couch for a stereo remote. On his left, he saw a certificate of completion for the citizens discount program. Next to it lay a cardboard-framed 4x6 photograph, in which the sales manager was presenting him with the certificate: his face wore an uncharacteristic, open-mouthed grin; the caption below read, "Keep Making Us Proud!" Seeing this made him smile again, in spite of his jaw: at that moment, he inexplicably felt the same gratitude for the sales manager as he might for an inspiring high school teacher or nurturing sports coach. Locating the remote, on his right, he lowered the volume. His morning radio alarm was blaring, down the hall.

Standing too quickly, J.D. steadied himself against the couch back. He waited for the blackness to recede from his vision and for balance to return to his limbs. Once he could be certain of not collapsing, he navigated a maze of newly opened cardboard boxes and plodded to the shower.

While reaching for the bath faucet, he caught himself in the mirror. The dark circles under his eyes and the unseasonable pallor of his skin did not make an impression on him, but the unfamiliar bulge in his shirt pocket did. With some effort, he yanked the phone free. The duct tape puzzled him, but he pulled off the strips and threw them into the trash.

BY THE TIME J.D. shuffled into work, his grin had faded, giving way to a spiritless expression that alternated between confusion and vapidity. For three hours, he slouched at his workstation, monitoring nothing, gaping into the display, as though waiting for something. A second morning coffee did not improve his motivation. He browsed media and entertainment websites—this went against company policy, but he could not stop himself: he simply had no internal direction.

What broke through his mind fog was a call from George, who had been out of the office all morning. "Have you fixed the flow rate, like I asked?"

"Yes," J.D. replied, straightening up. "I got you 97 percent more volume; that's the upper limit."

DRIP

"OK, good," George said with audible relief. "I need you
to stay late tonight: I need all the stats and analysis to date.
Give me everything, nice and formatted. We've gotta show it
to the board tomorrow."

J.D. grinned, feeling a renewed sense of purpose. "Ok," he
said, nodding emphatically. The line went dead (George's new,
efficient etiquette for ending a phone conversation).

J.D. opened a drop-down menu and began formatting the
required reports. A soft musical sting caught his attention; he
glanced at his phone; there was a reminder notification: "You
have one new unplayed video. Press to view."

He tapped the text.

A dingy hallway appeared; people were moving toward a
large door. There was something familiar about the location,
but J.D. could not recall when or where he had seen it. The
sales manager stood next to the door, with backs of heads
intermittently filling and vacating the image, as people shuffled forward.

The sales manager pulled open the door; the room beyond
was too dark for the camera to pick up. Heads and shoulders
filed in, and loud, anxious chatter filled the recording.

J.D. turned down the sound.

The camera followed the last person across the thresh-
old, and for a moment there was just blackness and nervous
breathing. There was a metallic clank, followed by the click
of a deadbolt slipping into place.

J.D. did not like this experience. He extended a thumb over
the video, intending to stop it, when a pair of red, glowing
orbs pierced the blackness.

J.D. jerked back in his seat. The recording's screams filled
his head. He suddenly saw, with perfect clarity, what was too
dark for his camera to discern:

Webbed, pointy ears and white, buttoned, high-collared lab coats, like something out of 1930's Hollywood.

The corpse-white faces were partially obscured by black gas masks with elongated, hose-fed snouts; the corrugated, elephantine trunks that trailed from the snouts terminated in tanks that each of the seven things wore on its back.

One of them glided among the panicking customers, staring at each person until his or her cry became a stifled whine.

J.D. had tried to avoid the thing's gaze, but his body would not listen. Bright red embers glowed behind the ghoul technician's large, round goggles, and J.D.'s scream died in his throat.

Another of the things crept up alongside and clutched his arm in its groping, withered fingers. J.D.'s legs betrayed him, and he mechanically followed his escort. He lay down on a stone slab; he knew what he was doing but could not stop himself.

Across from him, four of the things eased the old lady and children down onto more of the blocks; the disconnection between terrified faces and subservient limbs was horrible to witness. The lab-coated figures hunched close over the family. The old lady's quivering lips settled, and her eyes dulled. The struggling children became stupefied as well.

J.D.'s captor moved to the center of the room, where it was joined by the other technicians. Moments later, when they drifted back to the supine customers, each of the things was carrying a long needle and a line of clear surgical tubing.

J.D. was unable to move anything below his neck; he twisted his head left and right. There were a dozen slabs, arranged in a circle. The young couple and the old man lay on either side of him; under the things' red gazes, they rolled up their sleeves.

The things began jabbing customers; blood filled the far tubes.

J.D. watched his technician approach. "My name is James Pence," he whispered to himself, trying to unfreeze his mind. "My father is Robert Pence, my mother was Kate Pence."

Red flowed out of the customers, through long lengths of tubing; J.D.'s eyes followed the blood.

"When I was four I stole seven coins out of Mister Farver's antique oven. I felt bad and gave them back, and then he forgave me."

Each of the undulating lines snaked its way along the floor and toward the center of the room; from there they all climbed to a dangling, arterial convergence and disappeared up into the darkness, like the ganglia of some giant, red jellyfish.

"My kindergarten teacher was Mrs. Williams. In the fall we put leaves in wax paper."

J.D. watched the ghoul attending to the old man yank the needle out of his arm; the thing was apparently dissatisfied with its own food supply and tore the hose loose from its mask, causing red to dribble onto the floor; it hunched over the old man's inner elbow.

"When I was six I caught a firefly and noticed some were green and some were yellow."

A pale sucker darted out of the thing's torn snout and fastened itself to the man's arm; the only sign that the man, who was completely paralyzed, knew what was happening was a line of tears that streamed from each of his wide eyes.

"When I was eight I ate a Daddy Longlegs on a dare and got to see Jill Mars's..."

The red eyes drew near to J.D., and his voice faded into the distance; his left hand automatically rolled up a sleeve.

That was all he could remember.

The video filled in the rest. Following the sound of a lock opening, the camera swung around and showed the sales manager standing in the doorway. "Congratulations! Keep up the good work!" He handed certificates to stumbling, bewildered customers.

As the old lady and her children received theirs, a flash illuminated their uncomprehending faces; something had been taken from them—something dearer than blood. They staggered purposelessly down the hall.

J.D.'s bandaged arm reached into frame; the sales manager placed a certificate into the limp fingers and pointed off screen. The camera swung in that direction; a technician with a disposable camera snapped a picture. There was a flash; for an instant everything was lit—the circle of slabs, the tentacles of tubing, the bat-eared ghouls—and then the background returned to darkness. The image swung around to the sales manager ("Thank you, and keep up the good work!") and then followed the unsteady customers into the hallway.

The video ended.

Whatever the spell J.D. had been under, it was now lifted. He unbuttoned his right cuff, praying to discover that his experience had been a psychotic hallucination. He rolled up his sleeve; the bandage on his inner elbow was no delusion. He tore it off, revealing an angry, raised puncture wound underneath; it looked like a bruised insect bite from hell. Once satisfied that it was not going to bleed through, J.D. hastily re-buttoned his sleeve.

He looked around the workstation room, trying to find some distraction from his distress. Absently, he glanced from his arm to the workstation to the desktop coffee dispenser. He repeated this circuit several times before wondering why his gaze gravitated to the same three items.

Then it hit him.

"Oh, Christ."

He stood. Since the glass office had no blinds, he used his body to obscure his work from general view.

He opened the brewer's top lid and removed the redundant Gilded Roast cartridge. He examined the blackened, wet plastic. "Made in Vietnam," stated the small engraving on its side. He set it down on a napkin and wiped off his fingers. He shut the lid, placed his mug underneath the spout and pushed the button: nothing happened.

Reopening the lid, he noticed a small, recessed switch that matched a nub on the cartridge. He straightened a paper clip and lodged it into the compartment until he felt the mechanism click. He closed the lid again.

He looked behind him.

Just outside the partition, George's secretary was immersed in composing a correspondence; there was no one else nearby.

He pushed the button.

The brewer emitted a noisy gurgle—without the cartridge, it was louder than usual—followed by an ordinary stream of coffee.

J.D. was so relieved to see this that he almost laughed out loud. Whatever these bloodsuckers were doing to people, it had nothing to do with him: he was, if not innocent, at least not guilty.

The machine's buzz lowered in pitch, and the pouring coffee thickened and began to lighten.

With growing dread, J.D. realized that the unit had been merely purging cartridge-colored water. The backup was probably left over from his overclock. The actual Gilded Roast came up behind the water, and the stream changed.

J.D. saw, spurting into his mug, red, arterial blood.

"You know too much, Pence," said a cold voice.

J.D. whirled around and found himself gaping into Richard Sytry's sunglasses. There was nothing he could say or do.

"How *did* you get us double the capacity?"

It took J.D. a moment to register what the vice president was asking. He then flashed Sytry his most confident grin. "It's what you pay me for."

"You've just licked distribution, you know that?" One corner of Sytry's mouth turned up, and J.D. realized that he was smiling. The executive must have been in an even better mood than his expression indicated; he must have been ecstatic to the point of carelessness, otherwise, he would have glimpsed the exposed cartridge behind J.D.'s back, or at least smelled the aroma of warm, freshly poured blood. "You're going to be famous," Sytry said; then he turned and left.

J.D. THREW UP IN the men's room on the legal floor. He chose that location because he did not want to risk being seen by an executive—and also because he was headed in that direction.

He arrived at Cerri's desk a few minutes later, just in time to see her marching into Pete Mendes office with what looked like a commercial mortgage application.

"What is this?" J.D. heard Cerri protest; he saw her thrust the packet at her boss's tired face. "We have over seven million dollars in liabilities! Why aren't they listed?"

"Jesus, keep your voice down," Mendes warned her. "Shut the door."

The door closed; if Cerri had seen J.D. across the hallway, she did not acknowledge him.

He walked up to the office and waited.

The glass door and walls, and the fabric blinds, did little to mask the conversation within. Cerri's voice was lowered but her tone remained irate. "Nancy in accounting says Duke Bunet just ordered the entire pipeline project onto an S.P.E. *Poof*, it's off our balance sheet."

"That's what I hear," J.D. heard Mendes confirm. "There's nothing anyone can do." He sounded certain in his hopelessness, like the world's leading brain surgeon telling a patient that a tumor was inoperable.

J.D. did not know Pete Mendes personally, but he knew of the old-school lawyer's reputation. Mendes had worked for decades in the loan department of Middlestop First Savings, a local bank that had provided conventional mortgages to many of greater Middlestop's homeowners. Mendes moved the first black families into the east side in the seventies and helped to demonstrate that integrated neighborhoods maintained and increased their property values.

Unlike their competitors, Middlestop First Savings refused to package subprime loans, and in 2005, unable to generate enough new business, the bank closed, and Mendes came to work for BrewCorp. The rumored friction between the upper management and Pete Mendes was not surprising: he was being asked to put together deals to build BrewMart stores on undeveloped land in Inini Village and Chippewa Falls; in every case, a perfectly suitable, aging shopping strip existed within shouting distance of the green land, but since the older, developed space was located inside of Middlestop, or Middlestop Heights—or some other township that could not offer a ten-year, 100 percent tax abatement—Mendes was ordered not to look at it. Consequently, whenever the attorney landed a real estate deal, he had to reluctantly defend BrewMart against the losing township's inevitable anti-poaching lawsuit.

Cerri's voice urged, "We can call the SEC! We can call IRS! We can call our loan underwriters!"

"The minute we get off the phone with them, someone will call Richard Sytry and tell him he has a coupla whistleblowers. Nancy'd be out on her ears, even though she had nothing to do with it, along with a dozen others." Mendes's voice grew shaky. "Think of your mother's medical bills. Think of my kid. Cerri, for God's sake."

The office fell into silence; J.D. recalled hearing that Mendes had a semi-dependent, adult son with severe autism.

"This place is so wrong," Cerri said in a clipped, tight voice.

"I know it is, but a lot of decent people, with families, work here. Please, don't make things any worse."

The door handle turned. J.D. backed up several yards so as to appear to be approaching.

Cerri strode out of the office so quickly that she bumped into him. Before he could stifle himself, J.D. blurted out, "We have to stop meeting like this." Cerri just stared. Her mascara was starting to run.

"Look, I-I need to talk to you," J.D. quietly began again. "There's something going on upstairs, and I don't know who else to-"

The smack landed hard across his jaw. She smacked him a second time and strode past.

Mendes, who had seen this from his desk, stood up to reprimand her, but J.D. held up a hand. "It's ok."

The attorney nodded, sat back down and stared despondently at the mortgage application Cerri had left. Sighing, he picked up a pen and, added his signature.

CHAPTER 23

A LATE-SUMMER BREEZE SWEPT through downtown. To George, who had been wandering the streets since dusk, the wind felt like freedom: freedom from embarrassment, freedom from disappointment, freedom from inhibition, freedom from intimidation; freedom from *George*.

What shall I do now? He thought. *Shall I fly alongside an airplane and terrify the passengers? Shall I walk into an ER, complaining of chest pains, and drive the medical residents crazy? Shall I pay Sheila a visit and show her my tiny, little fang?*

George passed through the public square. An evening home game was letting out, and due to the unseasonably warm September weather, there were more spectators than usual; he brushed against the passing bodies and gazed, through dark spectacles, at the multitude of faces, smelling the tantalizing blend of warm-blooded scents. He wondered how his colleagues contented themselves with just a few, rationed cups a day.

But, of course, they don't, he acknowledged with a smirk. *Not really.*

Two blocks ahead, he spotted the familiar awning of The Blue Steak; he decided to walk in that direction. A young lady was standing near the entrance to the restaurant, holding a dozen individually-wrapped, red roses. George recognized her.

She's the one from the bus: the one who hummed Beethoven with such a sweet voice; the one who smiled for him but not for me.

"How about a rose for your lady?" the girl called to a t-shirted pedestrian; she held out one of the flowers; he ignored her. She added, "Just two dollars for a rose."

A well-dressed middle-aged couple, holding a pair of play-bills, approached from the opposite direction.

"How about a rose for the lady?"

The man did not smile, but he and his companion slowed down as they strolled up to her.

"I'm starting music school in the fall," she explained. "I'm on a scholarship, but someone stole my violin."

The man and his companion looked at each other uncertainly. The lady asked, "What about your folks?"

"My mom's in foreclosure," the flower girl replied. She could see that the couple was skeptical and stated, matter-of-factly, "We're not looking for handouts. We all work."

"Ok," the man said and took out his wallet. "We'll take two." He exchanged four singles for a pair of roses.

"Thank you so much," the girl said, placing the money in her coffee tin.

"Study hard," the man said, as the couple resumed their walk. "I will."

The girl noticed George crossing the street toward her. "Hello, sir, can I interest you in a rose?"

Holding his first two fingers apart, in a "V," George reached under his sunglasses and awkwardly clawed at his contact lenses.

"I'm starting at the music institute in two weeks, on a scholarship, but someone stole my..." She fell silent as George peered over the tops of his spectacles and gazed into her face.

His red eyes cast no reflection in hers. He flicked the white and hazel lenses off of his finger tips and moved closer. She retreated slowly, matching each of his advancing footsteps with a step back.

There was a long, narrow alleyway next to the steakhouse. George guided her deep into its recesses—away from the sounds and lights of the street; away from the passing foot traffic. He cornered her between the steakhouse's darkened brick wall and an open, peeling dumpster.

He drew his lips into an open-mouthed rictus. It was a theatrical expression, but he wanted to give her a dramatic view of his sucker-tongued maw.

You never saw me before, he thought, *but you do now, don't you? Now, you couldn't ignore me if you tried.*

The girl gaped vacantly into his jaw; a tear rolled down one of her cheeks. To the old George, this silent cry for help would have aroused compassion and moral horror, but to the new one, it was a turn-on. Keeping his eyes on her vaguely despondent face, he moved down to the girl's neck and pressed his mouth against it. He pushed his fang against the soft skin.

"Hey Bro, do you have a second?"

The suddenly shy fang retracted, leaving the skin intact. George knew the voice behind him. He felt as if he had just been caught jerking off. "Hey," he replied into the girl's forehead. "Uh, how did you find me?

"It's The Blue Steak, man; it's where all the big boys come to drink."

"Ok, I need a minute J.D.," George said irritably.

"I know what's in the pipeline. I've seen it."

George's face contorted; for the next few seconds he bit down on the "F" of a silent "Ffffffffffffffffffffffffffffffffffff ffffffffffffffffffffffffffuck!" He closed his mouth and pushed up his sunglasses.

The girl's face sprang to life; she frowned at George in confusion. "I'm sorry, I..." She turned around and noticed J.D., and as she looked from one man to the other, her face flushed with embarrassment.

"You lost, sunshine?" J.D. asked, neutrally. When she did not reply, he pointed a thumb behind him. "This way is out."

She scurried uncertainly past him.

He watched the disoriented girl make her way to the safety of the street; then he turned back to George. "So, I need you to get me into your club."

"Wait, what?" George said. He shook himself, trying to throw off the aroused hunger to which satisfaction had been denied. "Say that again."

"I think I'm executive material. I want to know more. So, let's get me in."

George bared his fang at J.D., and before he could stop himself, he wheeled around and dove further into the alleyway. He returned clutching a gray, matted rat that he had heard scratching along the ground. He had no patience for a drink; he took a deep bite into the rodent's side. "You want me to get you into the club?" he mumbled through his mouthful of rat.

"Correct." If the crunching sounds bothered J.D., he did not let it show.

George spat out a pair of ribs. "So, we're friends now?"

"Yeah, we're frien-" J.D. looked away. "Look, I get it: you needed to catch a break, and you took your shot. I want to see what I'm missing out on."

George searched J.D.'s face; for an uncomfortable moment, the two of them looked at each other. George tried to read J.D., and J.D. submitted to the silent scrutiny, flashing his familiar grin. George took another bite from the now limp carcass; J.D.'s smile briefly faltered.

"I don't think that's a good idea," George decided, tossing aside the remains and wiping his hands against one another. "How are you going to swim with sharks if you can't stand the sight of blood?"

"Come on," J.D. said, unconcerned. "Let's go."

"Do you know what they would do if they caught us?"

J.D. chuckled. "You know, you haven't changed at all. Still whining about 'Don't get us into trouble, don't get us into trouble.' I thought you were going out for yourself, to be your own man, but you're just Hall's little bitch."

"I'm not‑!" George began to protest, but he lowered his voice. "You know what? I don't have to take this. I can fly." He rose off the ground until his knees hovered just above J.D.'s face. "That's right," he boasted, gloating down at his friend. "I have the power of flight! What do you have?"

J.D. squinted up at him, amused. "Is that as high as you get? For real? That's like three feet."

George's leer turned to a look of indignation. "It increases over time. In a hundred years, when you're mouldering in the ground, I'll be twice as high. And it's not three feet, it's *four*."

"Oh my God!" J.D. began to giggle uncontrollably. "It's your superhero dream!"

"Shut up."

"You're"—J.D. struggled to get the words out—"You're The Little Vampire That Could." He doubled over and wiped his eyes. "'Can I turn into a giant bat?'" he asked, in a small child's voice; in a grownup voice, he answered, "'Maybe next year, little buddy; for now you get to transform into a chipmunk.'"

"Would you please cut that out." George waited for the laughter to subside and then floated down to the pavement.

This caused J.D. to burst into a renewed fit.

George, to his own surprise, snorted; the dead man could no longer experience true, punch-drunk hilarity, but his body laughed nonetheless.

Once the shared chortling subsided, J.D. told George, "You're getting me into that club."

"No, I'm not," George replied, shaking his head.

"Yes, you are."

"No, I'm not."

"Yes, you are."

So began the familiar contest, which had been fought dozens of times over as many years. The topic changed with each debate, but the format never varied, with J.D. insisting, "Yes-you-are-Yes-you-are-Yes-you-are," and George asserting, "No-I'm-not, No-I'm-not, No-I'm-not." The outcome would be the same as always.

"WE WALK IN, YOU look around, we walk out," George instructed from the side of a large pedestal sink. "That's it. You got me?"

"I got you," J.D. replied mockingly as he dispensed a final dollop of Skin Tone #13 from George's bottle. He blended the lotion into his face and examined his smooth complexion and newly moussed hair in the mirror. Satisfied with his makeover (passing as undead-passing-for-alive) he turned and walked toward the door.

George grabbed him by his collar and lapel, nearly choking him.

"What?" J.D. asked impatiently.

George's hazel eyes stared into his (sunglasses, George had disclosed, were rarely worn in the club, except by the bouncers). "If anyone recognizes you, they will *kill us*." George maintained his stifling grip until he had extracted a nod of understanding from J.D.

Leaving the men's room, they crossed through The Blue Steak's basement lobby. George stepped in front of J.D. and tapped the glass on the red-cushioned door. The cover abruptly slid back, and the scowling, biker moustache appeared. The sunglasses darted suspiciously back and forth between the two men but lingered on J.D.

"Midstream," George said. The glasses shifted back to him, and the cover slid shut.

The door opened; no one was on the other side.

"Stay close," George whispered to J.D., and he led him inside.

They walked through a short hallway lined with vintage red and gold wallpaper. The undulating, abstract patterns seemed to point the way to the velvet curtain up ahead. Muffled sounds of a clarinet section drifted through the heavy fabric, and J.D. recognized the introduction to Duke Ellington's *The Mooche*.

As George approached the curtain, it pulled to one side, as if tugged by an invisible hand.

J.D. found himself staring into an immense, art deco speak-easy. The reflection of gas-lit chandeliers against golden walls bathed the space in an amber glow. Round dinner tables and private booths filled the room; most of the dozens of members who occupied them wore 1920's formal ware, but J.D. was able to pick out Elizabethan collars, 17th century waistcoats, 18th century, silk suits, and 19th century capes as well.

During the musical bridge, a deep thumping, coming from J.D.'s right, shook the floor on every fourth beat. J.D. turned and saw why: on the thrust stage at the near end of the long room, a bandleader rose into the air, raised aloft by enormous flapping wings, protruding from the back of his tailcoat; with perfect timing, the webbed appendages rested, and their owner landed with a thud, in rhythmic accompaniment to his eight, fellow musicians.

"Ok, now you've seen it," George said tensely. "Let's go."

Before George could grab hold of his arm, J.D. moved into the room, strolling down a raised walkway that bounded the club's perimeter.

He saw a waiter, carrying a tray of red martinis, briskly approaching from the opposite direction. J.D. veered left, toward the closest, curtained alcove. He ducked through the wine-colored fabric, hoping to find an empty booth.

Instead, he encountered a pair of wrinkled men, one wearing a fedora and pinstripes, the other wearing an Ottoman turban and robes and sporting a waxed, tapered moustache; they shared a blood-filled hookah, and, fortunately for J.D., their attention was riveted to a wall display screen opposite him; it featured a series of graphs, with securities index names that he had never heard of: *NOSFER, BLOODAQ STOKEX.*

"Our blood banks have been recession-proof for the past three quarters," the pinstriped man was boasting; his speech filled the air with red, perfumed smoke.

J.D. silently backed out of the curtains and steered to the right of the oncoming waiter; he ran his hand along the walkway's brass railing in order to affect a leisurely stroll.

"Drink, sir?" the stiff-backed waiter asked, stopping next to him.

A bluff, J.D. had always believed, sank or swam based on the cadence of delivery, not on the soundness of logic or the plausibility of story, and so, without pausing to consider his words, he shot back, "Not tonight, Jeeves. Doctor says I'm getting too much iron."

The waiter frowned, looking alarmed.

J.D. added a mischievous wink.

"Very good, sir. 'Too much iron.' I'll have to remember that."

"You do that," J.D. encouraged.

The waiter continued down the walkway, passing George, who was trying to catch up with J.D. George stopped to sniff the bloody cocktails. He snatched one of the rounded martini glasses and gulped down the drink.

J.D. put more distance between himself and George, and he resumed his reconnaissance of the room. Looking up, he saw that each of the six surrounding walls vaulted into a flat, copper-plated ceiling. Covering the quarter round transitions was a series of 72, framed portraits.

The chiaroscuro oil paintings looked like something Rembrandt would have produced, had he ever painted monsters: all but a few of the subjects had animal heads, mostly lions and birds; some of the figures had wings and feathers, others had clawed appendages, and still others had human limbs. The crowned figure, directly above J.D., had a human head, but the faces of a cat and a frog grew out of his neck; the multi-species monarch rested upon eight enormous spider legs. The disquieting effect of the portraiture above was complemented by the alcoves below, where grinning, plaster grotesques punctuated the trim work that ran along the top of each niche.

Something about the paintings and sculptures made J.D. uneasy, something apart from their subject matter: their placement around the room was somehow unsettling. He took in all of the architectural lines—the trim work, the frames, the wall corners—and, with a sudden feeling of claustrophobia, he realized that the room was shaped like a giant coffin.

Hoping to find less disturbing design elements, J.D. cast his eyes down; he saw that he was running out of platform:

the brass bars and etched glass paneling that constituted the hand rail terminated in a bar, which occupied the remainder of his side of the narrowing room.

The bar and stools rose a good six feet higher than usual, as did the floor behind the bar countertop; this allowed the bartender, a wild-eyed man in a white serving jacket and black necktie, to serve drinks without need of a ladder or stilts. To climb up into one of the front barstools, though, would be impossible. The questionable ergonomics of this arrangement became justified when one of two patrons levitated himself off of his stool and floated down to the floor.

The remaining bar customer tapped his empty glass onto the countertop. The bartender, ignoring the red bottles behind him came forward. He tugged back one of his white sleeves; a miniature tap protruded from a thick band of medical dressing that encircled his wrist. He held his hand over the customer's empty glass and pulled back the tiny knob. The glass began to fill.

J.D., who was powerless to help the mesmerized bartender, turned away, picking up his pace and feeling that he should complete his survey as quickly as possible.

Seeing that the platform resumed on the other side of the room, he climbed down and waded through dinner tables, making his way across. His zigzag path took him past a large, bibbed diner who was aggressively carving a piece from the red mess on his plate.

J.D. recognized the signature superior vena cava and ascending aorta of a partially-devoured human heart.

The sound of shattering glass sounded behind him; he looked back at the bar.

The staggering bartender had knocked several bottles off of the shelving and was struggling to support himself against the display; the lone patron, ignoring him, sipped from a full glass.

Everywhere J.D. looked there was some new horror quietly unfolding: to his left, a server used a chain leash to drag a bewildered debutant to a waiting guest; to his right, shark-toothed diners blithely applauded the band, while their lady companion sat hunched over, face down in her bowl, with a trickle of blood pooling onto the table; ahead of him, a pair of gentlemen, smoking thick cigars, admired the limp figure seated across from them—a young lady, whose head lolled to one side, revealing oozing holes in her neck.

J.D. searched for an exit. Upon reaching the opposite wall, he eagerly climbed out of the tabled section and regained the platform.

His relief from the gruesome spectacles below was short-lived. The walkway took him past an occupied booth with an open curtain; the mink-festooned, grande dame who was installed there was simultaneously holding court over the phone while entrancing a young man seated next to her. J.D. recognized the dazed victim: he was Brett—J.D. and George's former classmate.

"Those drivers are for amateurs, honey," the lady proclaimed, waving a bejeweled hand in Brett's face; he closed his eyes and offered her his neck. "I neh-er thlithe with whine," she continued, lisping heavily around the long, white needle that had descended from her upper palate. "Neh-er. Excuthe eeh one owent, dear."

The woman clutched Brett's neck and pulled him into her, biting down hard. When she lifted her head, her pulsating sucker was clamped over his jugular.

Resuming the conversation, she offered, "I'll loan you why thare thet," and then, gazing down at Brett, she added, "I'll hath why woy ring it toworrow."

George caught up with J.D. and calmly whispered, "Are you out of your mind?"

J.D. turned to face him. In spite of the fear in George's eyes, he was all smiles.

"Do you see who this is behind me?" J.D. whispered back, inclining his head toward Brett.

George, who was watching something else over J.D.'s shoulder, ignored the question. "The waiter is pointing you out to the bouncer. We need to go."

"Ok."

George led J.D. toward the entrance. They traversed the platform and approached the last alcove before the stage; the entranceway stood on the other side.

The alcove curtain in front of them opened and Richard Sytry stepped out. Fortunately for J.D., the vice president was glaring at the server across the room. "Gremory!" Sytry bellowed.

J.D. whirled around to avoid recognition and found himself face to face with the bouncer. If the security guard had been intimidating in the dark, then the ample lighting of the club made him doubly so: he stood a foot taller than J.D., had a bald head and webbed ears, and when he removed his sunglasses, oversized, feral red eyes appraised the trespasser.

J.D. turned away, hoping that if he ignored him, the bouncer would go away. He tried to stay directly behind George so as not to draw Sytry's attention. From this position, he could see a disoriented woman, perhaps in her forties, seated at the vice president's booth; she wore a black collar around her throat.

"Yes Mr. Sytry?" the waiter said as he appeared in front of the surly vice president.

"This is the second time this week the kitchen's screwed up my order!"

The impassive waiter looked from the empty bowl on the table to the seated woman, and back up to Sytry. "I'm sorry sir, I'll take care of it." He reached behind the woman's back and retrieved a length of chain, which tugged at the woman's collar; forcing her to stand, he led her away.

"If I wanted aged meat," Sytry hollered after them, "I would have asked for it!"

A cold, powerful grip on J.D.'s shoulder spun him around, and the bouncer took a series of short, doglike sniffs. The red eyes opened wide with alarm, and a long-nailed finger pointed at J.D.'s chest. The bouncer let out a high-pitched, ear-splitting squeal.

The music abruptly stopped. There was a blur and a rush of air, and suddenly J.D. and George were surrounded by the club guests; one after another, they bared their fangs.

J.D. searched for an opening in the tight circle, but none was to be found; the air grew cold as the inflamed faces closed in. J.D. turned to George, hoping to receive some guidance, but George was no less a target of the silent mob; the panicked junior executive made a series of jerky, evasive movements—he looked like a street cat confronted with a homeowner's water hose; then, instinctively, he grabbed J.D and wrenched him around to use as a human shield. J.D. did not know exactly what awaited him, but he felt fairly certain that he was about to die badly. He hoped that when the first attacker grabbed him he would just wake up screaming in his bed.

The reassuring recognition that he was dreaming never came. Instead, what hit him was the cold certainty that he had reached the end of his life and the limit of all he would ever do or think or experience. All of his gifts would not change this, nor would his youth or passion, nor even his dream of one day designing a faster-than-light spaceship. The ever-sustaining conviction that he would live a full and meaningful life had abandoned him.

Since he could do nothing else, he struggled free of George and put up his fists; he knew that this would amount to little more than a symbolic gesture, but he was determined not to permit his last thought to be, *I am helpless.*

A voice from within the crowd entreated, "No, no!" Billy Hall pushed his way through. "It's alright," the C.E.O. reassured the mob. He laid a hand on J.D.'s back. "This is who we have to thank for all of our recent good fortune! This is the architect of our pipeline!"

Fangs disappeared, and expressions around the circle changed from threatening to welcoming.

"Say hi to J.D. Pence," Hall said, patting J.D. on the back.

In unison, the room cheered, "Hi J.D.!"

The adulation in the vampires' faces made J.D. uncomfortable, nevertheless he smiled and waved. "Hi guys."

"Now, on with the party!" Hall ordered.

The bandleader returned to the stage, took up his clarinet, and tapped out, on one of his wing tipped shoes, the first, syncopated beats of Benny Goodman's *Sing Sing Sing.* His band took up the introduction, and the circle dispersed, giving way to conversation and up-tempo Lindy hops.

Hall turned to J.D. "Come with me." J.D. and George began to follow him, but he gave George a stern look. "Just J.D."

George stood for a moment, looking as if he had been slapped, then he stormed across the stage and through the entrance curtain, exiting the club in a huff.

Hall moved toward another curtain, which stood across the stage from the entrance. J.D. followed him. On the other side of the fabric stood a hallway lined with seven padded doors. Hall walked down to the last one and retrieved a magnetic card from the vest of his dinner jacket. He slid the plastic into a slot in the wall; the door opened.

Entering the room beyond, Hall turned and looked expectantly at J.D. "This way."

"Is this where you tell me to enter freely and of my own will?" J.D. quipped. In seventh grade, George had foisted his copy of *Dracula* onto J.D., insisting that it was required reading. He never got past the first three chapters; nevertheless the Count's famous invitation to Jonathan Harker, issued from the doorway of his grim castle, had made an impression.

The C.E.O. rubbed his nose and thought about the question. "Kid," he replied, "you already did that when you decided to work for us. Anyway, that's a technicality. Come on." He turned and receded from the doorway.

J.D. studied the placard next to the keycard slot. It stated, simply: Suite No. 7.

He stepped into the private lounge, prepared to see coffins, rats and skeletal human remains; instead, he saw his own version of paradise. On the opposite wall, across plush carpeting, stood a fully-stocked circuit bending workshop, complete with legacy PCI sound cards, LCD learning computers ("Children Ages 9 and Up!"), robotics kits, and animatronic dolls, as well as vintage items from the 70's and 80's. On a pegboard wall, just above the table, hung soldering tools and tinkering implements of every kind. To the left of the circuit bending area stood a one-lane bowling alley.

"Would you care for an Armagnac?" offered a smoky voice.

Turning toward it, J.D. saw shelf upon shelf of prized scotches and brandies, including half-a-dozen pre-Prohibition whiskeys, a 20-year-old Lowland Malt, and two bottles of Usquebaugh 43-year Islay—the distillery's oldest and rarest release.

Cerri stood behind the bar, wearing a low-cut, sleeveless, black dress, which she highlighted with a sommelier's tastevin necklace; she gazed at J.D., with one eyebrow raised invitingly.

J.D. walked up to her and then saw that she was not actually Cerri but, rather, a dead ringer, whose eerily similar height, posture and complexion had been supplemented by red hair streaks and an eyebrow stud.

"Two glasses of Usquebaugh 43, please, one rock each," said Hall, from the other side of the room. The C.E.O. had taken a seat in one of two traditional smoking chairs and was trimming the ends off of a pair of cigars.

"Nothing for me." J.D. stared at Cerri's doppleganger.

The sommelier brought the C.E.O. his amber drink, setting it down on the small table between the two chairs.

"Show him the sensory room," Hall instructed her.

She smiled and grasped J.D.'s hand, leading him halfway down the bowling alley. There was a recessed door on the right; she opened it and guided him into what could best be described as a recreational master bedroom. The leather water-bed that dominated the space was much larger than a standard, or even a California, king ("It's a *Caesar*," the sommelier said; her explanation, though intoned seductively, meant nothing to J.D.); the mirrored ceiling housed an array of black pipes, which J.D. surmised were for mounting the harnesses and swings that were on display in the open, walk-in closet.

The sommelier took out her smart phone and made a series of taps and slides. The Japanese-style paper walls lit up; J.D. found himself standing in the midst of a rain forest.

"There are over six-hundred environments to choose from," said the woman. She cycled through a sample of wall videos: storm clouds, a log-cabin living room and fireplace—complete with roaring fire—a mountain campsite, a roiling nebula.

"Mmm, here's one of my favorites." The bedroom transformed into the inside of a bathroom stall, which J.D. recognized as belonging to the Blue Steak men's room.

J.D. stared her. "What is this?"

"What's what?"

"Who are you?"

"I'm whoever you want me to be."

"What's your name?"

The sommelier paused, as though trying to remember something. "What name would you like?"

"No," J.D. pressed. "What's *your* name? Your *real* name."

"Um..." She furrowed her brow.

"Thank you, that's all!" called Hall from the other room.

The sommelier turned and walked out. J.D. followed her back through the suite. She passed by the seated C.E.O. and, wordlessly, opened the padded door and left.

"As of Monday," Hall told J.D., matter-of-factly, "I'm making you a junior executive."

J.D. normally would have welcomed such an offer. As it was, he stood in place, looking horrified.

"It's not a vice presidency, but you'll receive a substantial raise, and that way the big boys will get to know you better, get comfortable with you." Hall gestured, with his lit cigar, at the empty chair next to him.

J.D. did not move.

The C.E.O. lightly chewed the cigar in one corner of his jowly mouth, sucked once and unleashed a cloud of sweet smoke. "We need you to stay."

"Oh." J.D. looked down.

Hall frowned. "What exactly do you think is going on with the company?"

"I know what's going on," J.D. said to his shoes.

Under the bushy, gray eyebrows, a twinkle lit up the blue, lensed eyes. "Let me guess." Hall held out his right palm, as if inviting J.D. to dance. "You built something that you think could be hurting friends and neighbors. You risked coming here because you want to know how many of us there are, how much harm you've caused."

J.D. would have liked to maintain his sullen silence, but it was pointless: Hall was in charge of the situation, and both of them knew it. "How many of you are there?"

"Too many to count."

"How much harm have I caused?"

The C.E.O. let out another smoky cloud and sized up his guest, trying to decide whether or not J.D. could handle what he was about to tell him. At last, he leaned forward in his seat. "None, and I need you to keep it that way." He removed the cigar from his mouth and rested it on a porcelain and chrome ashtray on top of the table. Looking down at the Persian rug beneath him, he shook his head. "Listen, I haven't handled the same bullshit decade after decade because I've enjoyed it; I do it because it *has* to be done. Most people will never understand that—understand what it's like for us." He waved a finger between himself and J.D.

"Which 'us' would that be?"

"The strong ones!" Hall snapped, as if annoyed at having to explain the obvious. "The ones who not only survive in this world but thrive! You and I are the ones who have to hold back the jungle; it's on us."

The complement aroused a sudden flash of indignation in J.D. "You don't hold back the jungle! You *are* the jungle!"

"No I am *not*, son," the C.E.O. said calmly. "The jungle is what you and I are protecting people from."

J.D. stepped in closer to the C.E.O. and leaned over him. He wanted to make it abundantly clear that he was nobody's chump. "I just watched one of your crew eating a heart, another biting an old schoolmate's neck, and a third making the bartender bleed out!"

Hall held up a hand. "The heart belonged to a cadaver. We have a source. As for Ernie, the barkeep, he'll be fine in a couple of days; he's been serving us for years."

"How do you sit there with a straight face and tell me you look out for the public?"

The C.E.O. stood and pointed toward the padded door, shaking his finger at it for emphasis. "Because we regulate all of that feeding!"

J.D. frowned back at him in stunned silence.

"We set limits!" Hall continued, "And the patrons respect those limits because they know if they don't, they stop getting fed!" He paused to allow his words to sink in. "I think you'll agree that latte-drinking yuppies and mildly anemic soccer moms in the mall are preferable to a cabal of bloody fiends filling the streets with desiccated corpses!"

"But those people out there getting bit–"

"Will *live!*" Hall leveled his stern gaze at J.D. "Are people tired? Yes. Are they under the weather? Yes. Is it unpleasant? Yes. Now put yourself in my shoes for a minute: do you cancel a program that keeps tens of thousands from being killed?"

J.D. had no reply; Hall's revelation was making his head swim, and when the C.E.O. returned to his seat, J.D. sat down as well. "You're saying my pipeline–?"

"Was doing tremendous good...for about a week. Police blotter shows that assaults and homicides—I'm talking about our kind of homicides—dropped seventy percent."

"For a week?"

"Yep. Demand caught up."

"I overclocked the pump."

"Sure, that's helping," Hall replied, adding, "for the time being. Demand is catching up."

J.D. suddenly understood why the C.E.O. seemed concerned. "Because I built it." He had learned about the phenomenon during a poorly-attended guest lecture on neighborhood-oriented development. The speaker had maintained that building highways to alleviate automobile congestion often had precisely the opposite effect.

The C.E.O. sniffed at his scotch and allowed himself a sip. "What do you think would happen if it failed?"

J.D. thought about it. "Shit."

The two of them sat in silence, each man mulling over his own predicament.

"I can set it up so it won't," J.D. promised. "You really won't need me after that. I can come in on a consulting basis. It'll pretty much run itself."

"'It will run itself,'" Hall repeated. "That's just what a commodities broker told me when I leveraged most of the assets from a five and dime chain into steel. That was in the second quarter of 1929. My boss and I lost our shirts." He had a faraway look in his eyes. "Well, you can come back from losing your shirt. I lost mine a couple of times before that. One year, I put everything I had into San Francisco real estate and lost it in an earthquake."

"1906? You were there for The Great Earthquake?"

"I was there for that one and the one before, but I didn't lose anything in 1868 because I didn't *have* anything. Anyway, this would be different." The eyes refocused on J.D. "If things fall apart, no one will make it out. I'm not going to let that happen—and neither are you."

A series of urgent knocks sounded, and the door swung open. Sytry was on the other side, gesturing for the two of them to accompany him. "We've got a problem."

J.D. and the C.E.O. followed the vice president back down the hallway, into the main room and over to his booth.

There, in front of the closed curtains, stood George, who had returned from outside and was inspecting a wound on his lower arm. The long gash was closing up before the group's eyes, even as dried, red granules of powder poured out of it. George chuckled at the oddity.

Sytry reported, "Stupid bastard dragged a girl in from outside. He was in such a hurry, he didn't put her all the way under; while he was drinking, she grabbed a knife off the table and sliced him."

Hall's expression darkened. "Where is she?" he asked George, but George was so fascinated by his arm that he did not hear. "George!"

George stopped giggling and straightened up. "Sorry, sir." He turned to the curtain behind him and drew it aside.

It took J.D. a moment to recognize her because of the angle: she was draped diagonally across the table, on her back, with her head dangling over the edge, but as J.D. stared at the upside-down, pale face and glazed eyes, his general moral disgust at seeing a murdered body rolled back, and in its place, a wave of heartbreak smashed into him, for he realized she was the girl he had just saved. Her mouth, which had previously blessed J.D. with its warm smile, was now drawn open in despondent resignation.

"I'm sorry," George stammered. "I-I just...I got a bit carried away, that's all."

J.D. looked up at his old friend and started to grasp that he was looking at a killer. He took a disgusted step back.

"Is that your blood on her mouth?" Hall asked.

The three executives turned to stare at the ring of red powder lining the girl's parted lips.

"I must have caught her there when I back handed her," George admitted. Seeing the disapproving looks his colleagues were giving him, he protested, "She cut me!"

"That's not the issue," Sytry pointed out impatiently. "She may have-" the vice president leaned in close to George and whispered the rest.

"Alright," Hall decided. "Rich, get in touch with Haagenti; tell him we need a suicide: the usual stuff in case there's an open casket."

Sytry gave a curt nod, pivoted and strode away, toward the private lounges.

"Why would anyone want an open casket for a suicide?" George asked.

"Because people are crazy," Hall replied distractedly.

J.D. stared down at the punctured neck. He could feel the C.E.O.'s eyes on him. For a few moments no one said anything.

George, uncomfortable with the silence deadpanned, "Guess we're going to have a woman on the board."

"George," Hall said, "I want you to take J.D. straight home."

"Yes sir." George turned to go but saw that J.D. had not moved. George reached out to tug at his sleeve, but J.D. took another step back.

"And George," Hall added.

"Yes?"

"See me in my office, first thing Monday."

"Yes, sir," George cheerlessly acknowledged.

"J.D.?" Hall said gravely, and J.D. forced himself to look up from the body on the table. "Remember what we discussed."

"SEE WHAT YOU MADE me do?" George accused J.D., as he accelerated past a bus, cutting it off. "The old prick's going to lockout my brewer for weeks!"

George's ride had been parked ten minutes away from The Blue Steak, in a municipal lot. Throughout the walk there, he had frequently looked over his shoulder, past J.D. J.D. had wanted to get himself home, but George would not allow it; he was convinced that Sytry, or another of the vice presidents, was following him; he was sure that if he did not personally see J.D. back to the apartment, Hall would know.

The black car roared through intersection after intersection, narrowly beating each light.

J.D. clutched the edge of his seat, as George vented at him. "I've got, maybe, five days' worth of stuff in my fridge, then I'm stuck chasing squirrels and stray cats."

J.D. could not muster the energy to respond. He kept picturing the wretched, open mouth and sad, lifeless eyes and thinking about what his friend had done to the poor girl. For the first, inescapable time in his life, J.D. saw that he was sullied; the dead girl on the table, whose fate had, arguably, nothing to do with him, made him feel like filth.

"Doesn't the library hold a blood drive every few weeks?" George asked. "I'll bet I could sneak a bag with water and food coloring in there. I could get seated next to an older donor or someone whose snoozing—pose like I'm there to give; then, when no one's looking, I could just take out my bag and-"

"Let me help you get clean," J.D. earnestly cut in.

"Get clean? I'm sorry, do you mean resign from BrewCorp? Because making V.P. is the best thing that ever happened to me."

J.D. could not think of anything to say that would sway George.

"What did you two talk about? In the lounge? You and Hall. Am I getting fired?"

J.D. sighed. "No. He just wants to make sure the...product keeps moving."

"Oh yeah." George smiled in relief. "The product," he chuckled. "We have everything we need, don't we?"

"We do."

"Yes we do!" George nodded enthusiastically. "Everything we need!" He let out a manic yell and floored the gas petal.

CHAPTER 24

OVER THE WEEKEND, J.D. had tried to list possible exit strategies for himself, but by Sunday night, all he had managed to jot down was, "1) They'll never let me leave," and "2) I'll never let myself leave."

On Monday, J.D. and his new gray suit were paraded through each of BrewCorp headquarters' five floors. Billy Hall, flanked by his vice presidents, gripped the newly-minted junior executive's shoulder with a paternal arm, steering him toward senior accountants and internal auditors and making jovial introductions.

The entourage arrived on the legal floor. J.D. saw Cerri looking at him from behind the gathering crowd of curious employees. He wanted to scream to her for help; instead, he flashed his winning grin and shook hands with the chief counsel.

The tour concluded on the top floor. J.D. was marched past the rows of desks, waving at the sallow, scarved secretaries as though he were stumping for political office. The slack faces stared blankly ahead; the only one who seemed to be aware of what was going on was Maddy Wating; the C.E.O.'s secretary walked up to Hall, holding out a sheet of correspondence and a pen; as her boss signed the document, she stole a glance at J.D.; it was an ostensibly neutral look, yet it happened so quickly—a flick of the head toward him, then a flick back—as to seem the slightest bit hostile.

A champagne fountain had been set up in front of the C.E.O.'s office. The server, who J.D. recognized as the bartender from the club, hobbled into the executives' midst, laboring to hold up a shaking tray of overflowing, rattling flutes. Hall raised his glass; the vice presidents lifted theirs as well. J.D. had no choice but to do the same.

J.D. SLAMMED HIS FOURTH shot glass down onto the bar counter, where it joined the other three. The junior executive had been drinking consistently, following the morning's promotional toast.

As soon as the other executives had returned to their work, J.D. had left and taken the bus down to Skeeters. Since it had only been eleven in the morning, the bar was closed; J.D. had gone up to his apartment and thrown back shots of cheap vodka. He ignored the scotch.

Since he had been too agitated to sleep, he had gathered his putty knife, roll of drywall tape, and bucket of joint compound from the kitchen and made repairs to the walls. He had patched and drunk until five and then gone back to Skeeters. Finding the bar open, J.D. had knocked back stale beers through the end of happy hour.

Monday nights, like most week nights, were slow: students and regulars trickled in during the evening, but never enough of them to bring life to the establishment. J.D. wondered how it managed to remain open—he had been dragging George there since high school, when he used fake ID's to get in. *It's probably run by space aliens*, he thought, only half-joking. *Bet the pinball machine in back is actually a rectal probe.*

He regarded the proprietor, who had come around to his side and was now perched on a stool, sipping beer. The man did not particularly look like a space alien: he wore a Mosquitoes cap that seemed to push his gangly neck down into his sunken shoulders; his face was leathery, with raccoon eyes and a thick, graying moustache.

"Hey, man," J.D. said, trying not to slur his words, "what's your name?"

"Jimmy," he rasped.

"I'm J.D."

The man nodded.

"Jimmy, how long have you been here?"

"I come here two years ago," the man replied.

"Oh, you're not the owner?"

"This' my brother inlaw's place. He took it over from his dad in '08; then I come from the Bends plant in '13."

"You were a welder?" J.D. asked; the Bends plant had been a keystone of Middlestop's fading steel industry.

"I am."

"You're retired?"

"Forced to, when they downsized in '10. You?"

"I work for a bunch of bloodsuckers."

Jimmy grunted an acknowledgement.

J.D. had been around people like Jimmy all of his young life: reticent townies, whom he stood next to at the checkout line or sat behind at the ball game or waited with at the bus stop. Until now, he had never started a conversation with any of them. He had always assumed that the unsmiling faces and standoffish demeanors signaled some kind of collective attitude problem on their parts; it had never before occurred to him that life might have taught someone like Jimmy not to say or show too much.

"You a lifer?" J.D. asked.

Jimmy nodded. "My folks had a farm on the east side."

"Changed a lot, right?"

Jimmy nodded and got up as three more patrons walked in. "Another Tequila?"

"Yeah." J.D. watched Jimmy go back behind the bar and pour his shot.

"Congratulations, J.D.," said a woman's voice.

He swiveled around to find Maddy Wating sitting next to him.

"Hey Maddy," he glumly acknowledged. "I've never seen you down here; do you live in the neighborhood?"

"I live five minutes from here," Maddy replied, with what sounded to him like a note of innuendo. She watched as another shot was placed in front of him. "You look like you could use someone to celebrate with."

J.D. eyed the polka dot blouse, which was, this evening, buttoned all the way to the pointed collar. No, he concluded: an invitation for anything hotter than fresh-baked scones and a game of Bridge had to be the product of his imagination. "I'm not really in a celebrating mood."

Maddy inclined her head toward him; he was surprised to see a pair of attractive, large, thick-browed eyes staring into his. "Why don't you let me worry about that?" She leaned closer. "*Give* it to me. Tonight."

That, J.D. decided, was that. He had been desperate for distraction, and a kinky invitation from the C.E.O.'s seemingly-untouchable secretary was the stuff of 1970's porn. Downing his shot, he stood and waited for the floor to become level. When it did, he called to Jimmy and, carefully enunciating each syllable, asked him to close the tab.

MADDY'S BUILDING WAS FARTHER away than she had suggested. Following a ten minute cab ride (the only detail of which J.D. could recall was the patter of rain on the car's roof), J.D. found himself leaning against a cream-colored, laminate counter and slicing a softened lemon. The one-bedroom apartment was tidy, if outdated. The wood trims of forty-year-old kitchenette cabinetry clashed with everything else—except for a series of permanent coffee rings, staining the porous countertop.

J.D. added the lemon peel to a glass of straight gin; he looked through the amply-stocked bar, just right of the discolored porcelain sink. He found the bitters and added a few dashes. Once satisfied with the unnamed drink's color, J.D. took up his glass and lurched out into the living room, sloshing the liquid onto gray carpeting.

Reaching the couch, he shoved aside an assortment of yarns and needles and dropped down, spilling gin onto a darkening, plush leather cushion. Taking a swig, he balanced his glass on one of the armrests and glanced around.

The furnishings gave him the impression of two distinct personalities; the orderly shelves, filled with accounting books and romance novels, seemed like Maddy, as did the knitted afghan that was folded up neatly on the floor, but the expensive sofa, wall-mounted plasma screen, and electronic putting mat did not.

In order to stop the room spinning, J.D. looked up at the ceiling. His neck felt tight; he remembered that he was still wearing his suit; he loosened his gold tie and undid the top two buttons of his shirt, but this did not make him feel any more comfortable. He gulped down the rest of his drink.

The snap of leather against skin, coming from the bedroom, caused him to look over; Maddy stood at her doorway. The light was on behind her, and in the darkness of the living room, she appeared in silhouette. J.D. recognized the shining braces and the outline formed by her hair and scarf, but the rest, from her bare shoulders and corseted chest down to her knee-high boots, belonged with an altogether different person.

Maddy slapped the riding crop against her thigh for a second time. "*Give* it to me."

J.D., who prided himself on being up for anything, fought to maintain his enthusiasm. He pushed himself up from the couch but fell back. Making a second, more forceful launch, he managed to stand.

"Don't you hold out," Maddy ordered, as he lurched across the room. "You can do whatever you like, but *give* it to me."

J.D. stopped in front of Maddy, where he could see her face more clearly; her eyes looked apprehensive. "Are you sure-?" He began to ask.

Maddy smacked him in the jaw, causing him to recoil in surprise. "I said *give* it to me!"

Even through the fog of drunkenness, J.D. perceived that the smack had more to do with her look of thinly masked fear than with adventurous foreplay. His mood had cooled.

"I'm-sorry-a-cantoo-this," he slurred.

Maddy dragged him forward, into a kiss. He tried to pull away, but it was like trying to pull a plastic bag out of a shop vacuum's hose: Maddy was practically gnawing on his mouth; he was forced to push her away with equal roughness.

"I can't," he said again, this time more clearly.

Maddy urgently unwrapped her scarf. "Take as much as you want."

J.D. did not understand.

Maddy leaned into him again but not for a kiss. Her head was turned to the side; she was offering something else.

J.D. retreated to the kitchenette and flipped one of the light switches; the living room light came on, and he saw that Maddy's neck and upper torso were covered with large, raised bites.

"What the hell are those?" he asked.

Maddy seemed confused by the question. "*You* know." She looked away, sheepishly.

"No, I don't know."

"Oh." Maddy appeared somehow hurt by his question. She flashed a bitter smile . "Well, I suppose I have a mosquito in the apartment."

"A mosquito?" J.D. brushed past her, into the bedroom. "Oh, yeah you do," he called back; the familiar coffin and vanity stood there, opposite her bed.

He returned to the living room, careening off of the door jamb as he did. "You and George are shacked up, huh?"

Maddy did not reply but glared at him.

"Lemme guess: you get help with rent, and he gets a hot meal."

"What's your point?" she asked coldly, snapping her crop on the last word for emphasis.

"He's using you for food!"

"Until I get what I need," Maddy acknowledged, through clenched braces. She moved closer. "If you've got a problem with it, then *you* give it to me."

"Give *what* to you?"

"Don't be coy. Tell me what it will take for you to share it."

J.D. had no idea what she was talking about. Then it came to him: he realized that the last half hour had been the result of a semantic misunderstanding that could have been avoided had either of them articulated the presumed common noun to which "it" referred.

"I'm not a vampire!" he yelled, resenting that it was necessary to point this out.

Maddy looked confused. "You forced Billy to promote you! You think I don't know what that means?"

"I didn't force him," J.D. replied. "He forced me!"

"Liar!" Maddy smiled, even though she was shaking. "That was *my* slot. Billy was giving it to *me*. There wasn't supposed to be some, asinine competition: the partners made him do that. He promised *me* the next slot! The *very next* one!"

"Tell that to your roommate." J.D. moved toward the door. "I'm going to call it a night."

Maddy followed him. Even as her face turned red, the smile remained, like some rictus on a demented clown. "You don't understand! Billy needs me! I'm the only one loyal to him! He told me so!"

"Goodnigh'Maddy," J.D. slurred, reaching for the doorknob. He turned around to tell her to feel better.

He froze.

Maddy had picked up the lemon knife from the countertop. There was a wild look in her eyes. Before he could move to stop her, she brought the blade down, jabbing it into her forearm again and again. "Take it!" She shoved the bleeding limb into his face. "Take it all, but *give it to me*! I'm his loyal servant! He needs me at his side!!"

J.D. fumbled behind him for the doorknob; he did not dare to take his eyes off of her. Finding the handle, he tugged the door open and backed out of the apartment. He pulled the door shut between them and staggered down the hall.

"GIVE IT TO ME!" muffled shrieks continued to hound. "GIVE IT TO ME!"

The alcohol was finally getting on top of J.D.; he fought back a wave of nausea as he stumbled out of the entryway and tottered out into what had become a lake-effect downpour.

Seeing a set of approaching headlights, he held out his hand, hoping the vehicle was a cab; it was, but it drove past.

J.D. lumbered along the sidewalk in the direction that he thought was home. He was getting soaked.

He passed a figure with a clear, bubble umbrella.

"Where-can-I-cash-the-brijlocal?" he asked.

The pedestrian averted her dark, sunken eyes and shook her head. J.D. stared at the scarf on her neck but forced himself to keep walking.

There was someone else up ahead: an older lady, hunched over with half a dozen grocery bags. J.D. was going to make the same inquiry of her, but as she neared, he saw that below her plastic rain bonnet she too wore a scarf.

"Tha's-bullshit," he muttered to himself.

The woman, hearing the remark, scurried past, breaking into a near jog.

"I-doh-makeup-the-rules!" he bellowed to the rain. "'Mmm-justryin-ta-survive-the-game!"

J.D. tried to stay focused on getting home, but when a young family walked by, the man carrying an umbrella and BrewMart shopping bag, and the woman cradling an infant, the couple's matching scarves and hopeless expressions were more than he could take.

"S'is-bullshit!" he spat, taking a few wavering steps along the curb before collapsing into the gutter with a splash. "BULLSHIT!"

Cars zoomed by, some honking, others accelerating as they swerved to avoid him, sending waves of dirty water on top of him.

He curled up and rolled over on his side, continuing to plead Not Guilty by Reason of Bullshit; his indignant chanting faded to a semi-conscious whisper.

He became vaguely aware of an automobile pulling over and shutting off its engine; he could hear a door opening and closing, followed by footsteps.

There was a brief dream, with black, buckle boots making small splashes in the rain:

"J.D.," Maddy was saying. "J.D.!"

He felt the smack on his cheek. "I said no, Maddy," he tried to say, but that earned him a second, harder blow across the jaw.

The face glaring down at him came into sharper focus; he saw that it was not Maddy's.

He wanted to tell Cerri he was sorry and to say he did care for her, but he remembered he would be torn apart the instant he said those things.

Instead, he told himself, "S'is-bullshit!"

"Okay, come on."

He was taken by the hands and dragged to his feet. He was too overcome to refuse being half-carried to the back seat, too exhausted to be embarrassed at being seen like this, and too drunk to care that he would soon be seen retching into a toilet.

"S'is-bullshit," he repeated as the backseat pulled away from the curb; he kept chanting the mantra, even after he forgot what he had meant by it.

CHAPTER 25

THE FIRST THING J.D. noticed upon waking was sunlight through fabric. A pair of short, brown curtains was drawn, attenuating the bright, late-morning blaze. Since he was not ready to move, he squinted into the diffused glow.

Muffled, raised voices provided an accompanying soundtrack to his view. "Why would you bring him here if that's what you think?" asked the gravelly one, forged by decades of cigarettes and public speaking; J.D. imagined an aging diva, standing backstage in a robe, knocking back an after-show drink.

"You didn't see the state he was in!" said the other, younger voice. "You don't know everything!"

J.D. recognized the second voice. He groaned at the humiliating recollection of being nursed through the night.

Petulant footsteps sounded below—heels against hardwood.

"Come back here, Child!" the gravelly voice commanded. "We're not finished!" but a door slammed, ending the argument.

In the ensuing silence, J.D. rallied his senses. He was on a soft bed, lying on his side and facing a window to his right. His stomach muscles hurt, as did his throat.

He concentrated on moving his legs, and after trying patiently for a minute, he got them to move. The mattress was spacious, probably a Queen; the feedback from his limbs indicated that he had been tucked into the left side; upon turning his head, he saw that this was the side facing into the room. Exposed wood trims, along the windows, door and baseboards, interrupted lavender-painted, plaster walls.

Turning to stare directly overhead, he saw that he was in a cozy alcove. The ceiling was textured and painted to resemble autumn leaves; the four bed posts, sculpted into trunks, ascended into the decorative trees.

J.D. propped himself up and noticed, strewn at the foot of the bed, a black nightgown and a pair of ladies underpants.

Glancing at the ground next to him, he saw his own clothes. They had been dried and folded, and cleaned. He lifted the flower-themed blanket and verified that he was, indeed, naked. This made him groan again.

He surveyed the rest of the room. A round, red rug, featuring a Celtic knot, adorned the darkened, plank floor. A full roll of bubble wrap sat in one corner; in another corner stood an end table, on top of which rested Cerri's straightjacket purse; there was an incense burner set up next to it; the stick of nag champa was lit, with ghostly, rising tendrils materializing from its smoldering tip.

There was a savory scent underneath the incense—a kitchen smell, out of place in the bedroom. Sniffing the air around him, J.D. drew closer to the bedside window. He lifted the curtain and saw, hanging against the pane, a long, thick braid of garlic.

J.D. put on his pants and shirt, which smelled faintly of lilac; he folded the blazer under his arm and then ventured out into the hallway.

He descended the stairs into a small but welcoming living room. Beyond the picture window, the untamed garden, with its long grass and tall sunflowers and rusting water pump, basked in the sun; the living room itself was in shade.

The old woman sat in an upholstered recliner, in front of a small television set. A game show rerun was on; the volume was turned down, giving the flamboyant emcee (bushy-eye-browed and mustachioed, in white, broad-lapelled tails and a blue, sparkling bow tie) a silent-film-comedian quality as he marched around the set, flailing his arms and hugging contestants.

J.D. approached his hostess, unsure what to say. In front of her, on a flimsy TV tray, he noticed the worn edges of what looked like Tarot cards protruding from under two unopened carry-out tins.

"Cerri's running errands," said the gravelly voice. "She asked me to pass along a message." The old woman turned her trembling head. She had long, white hair; there were a few streaks of red, which matched her lipstick. Beneath green wrinkled lids, stern eyes, toughened by years of pain, stared at J.D., making him uncomfortable; then the powdered face brightened. "Oh, yeah, I remember: I'm supposed to tell you 'Now, get out.'"

"I'm just leaving," J.D. said, hastily backtracking to the front door, which stood opposite the stairs. He tried to open it, but it was locked. The cylinder above the knob had a key in it instead of a handle. J.D. jiggled it, but the lock was stubborn. He tried simultaneously wrestling with the knob and grappling with the key but nothing happened. He felt himself being watched.

"Just a moment, Junior."

He stopped struggling and stood there, with his hands seemingly glued to the door's greening, brass hardware. He forced himself look back at the old woman. "Yes ma'am?"

"Over here, please."

J.D. made himself walk over to her.

"I need a favor," she said.

J.D. smiled, hoping that the grin would somehow mask his irritated sigh.

"Usually my shakes aren't this bad, but I didn't sleep. I don't know when Cerri will be back; I need you to feed me. That's not a problem, is it?"

"Uh, not at all," J.D. lied. Seeing he had no other choice, he pulled up a nearby folding chair, draped his jacket over the back and took up the plastic utensils from the TV tray. "What would you like to start with?"

The shaking face stared at him; he was not sure if the old woman heard him, but then, with mock impatience, she craned her neck toward the left-hand container. "The egg roll *always* comes first."

J.D. opened the tin and cut the appetizer into pieces. He worked in awkward silence, lifting a forkful to her mouth. She chewed the food slowly, with difficulty; J.D. averted his gaze, looking out onto the yard. The leaves had started to change colors. "Beautiful garden."

"Tell Cerri you like it," she told him between chews. "It's her touch."

"I will."

"I wish she would get out more," she said to herself. She followed J.D.'s admiring gaze over to the lawn. "She's such a worrier."

J.D. raised another forkful. The old woman returned her attention to him and scrutinized his taut face. "Why do you look like you just saw Santa Claus fuck a goat?"

J.D. chuckled, his jaw loosening. "I see where your daughter gets her personality."

"That girl doesn't know what she's talking about." The old woman shook her head. "You've been-" she started to say but then began again. "You're name's J.D.?"

"Yes ma'am."

"I'm not a ma'am; I'm Misses Morgan."

"Sorry. Misses Morgan."

"J.D., you've been around sickness before," Mrs. Morgan said.

"When I was little," J.D. offered quietly.

Mrs. Morgan accepted another bite. "Who was it?"

"My mom," he said casually. Feeling increasingly safe with the old woman, he volunteered, "I spent a summer taking care of her."

Mrs. Morgan chewed the last of the egg roll. "She died."

"Mmm-hmm." He nodded.

He opened the next tin and wound a length of lo mein noodles onto the fork. They sat in silence for the next several minutes, with him winding and slicing, and her thoughtfully chewing each forkful, looking intently at the tin.

"Were you there when it happened?" she asked gently.

"Oh, no," J.D. answered, dismissively. He began to wonder if she could read Chinese take-out the way fortune tellers read tea leaves. He withdrew into silence but saw that she was listening expectantly, waiting for more. He fed her another spindle of pasta. "I was out in the yard," he volunteered. "I mean, I could hear her. She was...She was calling for me."

The wrinkled eyes looked at him with concern.

"She knew where the medication was. No. Wait." J.D. hesitated; then he explained. "That's not what I mean: I mean I had to be out of there. It's like, all of a sudden I couldn't watch her like that anymore, so I...I just bolted up the block-"

"Any six-year old in that situation would feel the same," Mrs. Morgan interrupted.

"It's not like it's my fault," he continued, talking over her, but then he paused, registering what she had said. "I didn't tell you how old I was."

"What was wrong with her?"

"She had therapy-resistant asthma."

"What was the prognosis?" The gravelly voice had become stronger, almost sharp.

"She shouldn't have made it to forty." He looked into the compassionate eyes, and then said something that surprised and confused him. "I could have saved her." He said it matter-of-factly. Feeling his throat tighten, he chuckled and looked away.

"You sound like Icarus."

J.D. gave Mrs. Morgan a questioning look.

"I suppose," she sighed, "reading classical mythology would cut into your reality TV; let me give you the short version."

J.D. put down the fork.

"Icarus was a man who wanted to fly. His daddy made him a pair of giant wings of wax and feathers, and Icarus took to the skies. He was warned not to fly too high, but Icarus wasn't into limits."

When Mrs. Morgan said this, she gave J.D. a pointed, faintly amused look, like a teacher trying to scold a mischievous, favorite student. "He flew too close to the sun, and those man-made wings melted right off, and he plummeted to the earth. In the end, he didn't soar to greater heights than his parents; he didn't justify all the diapers he soiled as a baby; he just crashed and burned."

The amused eyes grew stern again. "*We* can't fly, J.D., and *we* can't cheat death, and everyone I know of who didn't learn to respect that—every which one—has eventually crashed and burned. We're human. Get over it."

This annoyed J.D.

On the surface, he did not like being told by a socially marginal invalid that he was less clever and less able than he needed to be; underneath that, he did not like that his lecturer might be legitimately prescient and, therefore, backed in her criticism by some higher, cosmic power; in his core, though, J.D. did not like that he knew she was right.

Hoping to charm his way out of the sermon, he flashed Mrs. Morgan his patented smile. "You're right: I'll need to take care of that 'get over it' thing." He stood up to put on his jacket.

The old woman reached out and grabbed his arm. Her grip was strong and steady; the shaking was gone. "You're not going to be able to succeed at your work, your *real* work, until you can do that."

No retort came to J.D., whose smile faltered.

"Go on. You've got things to do. I can feed myself now." Mrs. Morgan swiped up the fork and helped herself to another bite of lo mein.

J.D. shrugged into his blazer and returned to the door. He tried the key and knob; they turned cleanly. Pulling the door open, he hesitated. "So, did those noodles tell you I was six-?"

"GET GOING!"

"Yes, ma'am—sorry: Mrs. Morgan." J.D. scooted out of the house.

"And tell Cerri you like the garden!"

"Yes, Mrs. Morgan." He pulled the door shut.

CHAPTER 26

AMID LENGTHENING AFTERNOON SHADOWS, banks of sprinklers ticked and hissed, watering the cemetery lawn and darkening a few, prematurely-fallen leaves.

J.D. walked down the main path. He wore his black suit and tie, and with the addition of a pair of sunglasses and a bulging backpack, which he slung loosely over his shoulder, he looked like a stylish mourner-on-the-go.

His phone rang; he turned it off. He had already listened to eleven messages from George, each one a variation on the theme, "Where are you?"

Ignoring the pitted, granite headstones on either side of him, he made his way toward the brown brick building.

He had been inside once before, and as he pushed open the heavy, maple door, the stained glass and perfumed air brought a familiar, stifled feeling up from his stomach. The long, A-frame corridor and checker-tiled floor were exactly as he remembered them. The frayed runner, which ran the length of the walkway, was probably the same one from twelve years before. J.D. passed under the white plaster ceiling and exposed rafters. George had once likened this passage to the unending, vaulted hallway of Oz's throne room. Had there been a giant head waiting at the end to greet J.D., he would have preferred it; had he been tasked with killing a wicked witch, it would not have been a far cry from his actual purpose.

J.D. went through the far set of double doors and entered the parlor.

There were fewer than a dozen mourners. No subdued conversation took place; no soft words of comfort were offered; just shocked silence. One of the visitors, a young woman in a black skirt and brown, buttoned sweater—possibly a schoolmate of the deceased's—stood before the open casket, her shoulders heaving with noiseless sobs.

The coffin and skirted display table were located underneath the same, large, crucifix window where J.D. remembered having seen his mother. Sunlight, passing through trees, created shifting patterns on the stained glass, bathing polished pine and satin fabric in golden light.

On an easel, next to the foot of the coffin, a large memorial photo stood, capturing the deceased's unguarded, dimpled smile and sincere, squinting eyes. The script below read, simply:

Callie

J.D. lowered his head and discretely removed his sunglasses; he noticed the varicose veins of an overweight, middle-aged woman, who was sitting in an armchair by the doors. He looked up at the haggard face (eyes wide and vacant with despair) and knew that she was the girl's mother. Quickly, He looked away.

He sought out a chair in an unpopulated corner of the room, set down his bag, folded his hands across his lap, and waited. No one stayed for very long. The last to go was the mother. The funeral director, a third-rate-looking official (navy blazer, premature comb over, and large, out-of-date, rounded glasses) appeared and whispered into the bereft woman's ear. A young man who stood over her, resting a comforting hand on her shoulder, helped her up by the arm and escorted her out. She stumbled, nearly collapsing, but the son or nephew supported her.

The third-rate funeral director walked over to J.D. "I'm sorry, but we're closing."

"Could I please have five more minutes?" J.D. felt so miserable about what he was about to do that it played convincingly.

Signs of an interior struggle crept into the man's put-upon face, as if he had suddenly remembered his job description.

"Please," J.D. added. "It would mean a lot."

"Alright. But please just five minutes."

"Thank you."

The irritable man waddled out of the room, his shoulders swaying officiously from side to side.

J.D. got up and gently closed the double doors. He opened his backpack and verified its contents. The Roman Catholic Rites for Exorcism had been easy to find. The wooden stake, however, had taken some thought; J.D. had felt it could not be flimsy; ultimately he had settled on a leg from his couch; he had whittled the tip to a point with the old pocket knife. The holy water would have been simple to obtain, but J.D., who could not find an appropriate vial in the apartment, had decided for expediency's sake to use an empty Usquebaugh bottle. The sight of a young professional dipping a scotch decanter into the church font piqued the priest's displeasure (J.D. had apologetically explained, "It's for my friend: he's got a drinking problem. Will this help?" He had not waited for the answer).

Bringing the backpack over to the casket, J.D. took out the hardcopy of the prayer. He avoided looking at the body.

"'In the name of the Father and of the Son, and of the Holy Ghost...'"

He stopped, feeling self-conscious, and lowered the piece of paper. "I'm an atheist," he reminded himself, and the ridiculousness of an atheist vampire hunter hit him. He gathered up his bag and went to the door. He would find a therapist and work through whatever was causing him to break with reality; if it turned out to be Schizophrenia, then so be it: he would get on some meds. Whatever the case, he was not doing *this*. *This* was irrational *bullshit*.

He reached out to push the door and then thought, *Just one look over—she deserves that; then I can get out of here.*

He turned and went back and looked.

The amber rays from the window played softly over the restful face, warming the smooth skin and reddening the long, brown rosebud-adorned hair. The illusion of a peaceful nap was incomplete: the eyes and mouth had been unceremoniously sewn shut with black thread. The same stitches that were used to tease the face into tranquility were also in evidence on the neck, where J.D. could make out their outline in the high collar.

He reached over the sinewy, musical hands and grasped the collar. *If this were a movie*, he realized, *now would be the moment when those long fingers drop their bouquet and reach out to grab me.* Nothing of the sort happened. He pulled the fabric back and grimaced at what he saw. The throat had been deeply cut along one side, as though the girl had taken a razor to it. The stitched gash tore through, and concealed, George's swollen bite. Gently, J.D. straightened the collar. He saw a bulge in the pillow; he reached underneath. Someone had provided the deceased with a care package of travel-sized Hair #2 and Skin Tone #5 cosmetics.

J.D. straightened, no longer feeling silly.

He raised his printout again. "'In the name of the Father, and of the Son and of the Holy Ghost, Amen. Most glorious prince of the Heavenly armies, Saint Michael the archangel, defend us in our battle against the principalities and powers, against the rulers of this world of darkness-'"

The warm light was fading from the window, and he found himself squinting; once his eyes adjusted, he continued, "'-against the spirits of wickedness in the high places-'"

"Excuse me, sir?"

The funeral director, having apparently returned without J.D.'s hearing, had caught him in an awkward spot; J.D. tried to convince himself of this. He stared into the page, trying further to come up with a plausible explanation for why the funeral director would address him in a falsetto.

"H-how about a rose?" asked the disjointed voice, from the other side of the paper.

Slowly, J.D. lowered the prayer. There was, of course, no one else in the room.

Taking a cautious step back, he studied the face below him. Everything appeared the same as before, yet something was different. He leaned forward, just a bit, and scrutinized the mouth. The threads had loosened into small loops, tugging at the lips.

"For your lady?" the lips said.

"Holy fuck!" J.D. proclaimed, leaping back three feet and scampering toward the door.

"I'm sorry?" Quietly, the lips observed, "Wait, I can't—" Then they asked J.D., "What's going on?"

J.D. did not answer but shoved a hand into the backpack and fumbled around for the first available implement. He grasped the sharpened couch leg, but as he pulled it out it caught on the fabric. Clumsy with panic, J.D. yanked the stake, which tore a hole in the bag and became even more firmly snagged.

"Please say something," the voice entreated. "Are you there? Please?" She sounded just as scared as J.D.

He realized that her confusion might be a ruse, nevertheless he ceased wrestling with the bag and replied, "I don't really want a flower right now, ok?"

"I can't open my eyes."

J.D. pushed on the door, hoping to leave unnoticed, but a loose, pneumatic closer let out a sharp rattle.

"Please don't go," beseeched the voice.

J.D. could not help but feel compassion, and despite his best judgment he edged back over to the casket.

The dead head shook anxiously from side to side, as if aware of its claustrophobic environment. "I can't open-"

"I know, you can't open your eyes," J.D. morosely acknowledged. "Someone—" He thought about what to tell her. "Aw fuck," he said to himself. "Someone made it so you...can't really...open them."

"What do you mean?"

He let out a breath. "Sister, someone sewed them shut."

One of the hands went up to the face; the long fingers played over the eyes and mouth. "Why?" The lower lip quivered. "Why would anyone do that?"

"Because if...Probably they thought you were dead?"

The hands gripped the sides of the casket and awkwardly hoisted the upper torso into a sitting position. "Why would they think I was dead?"

J.D. sighed. "Because you *are*."

The brow furrowed in disbelief. For a moment the face looked like it was going to dispute his claim; then its look turned to horrified recollection, like that of a waking dreamer who has begun to remember an awful nightmare.

"No," the face pleaded, its look of dread giving way to desperate entreaty. "No! I'm going to college in August. I'm going to...I'm going to..."

J.D. stared at the carpet. "Not going to happen."

"Please no! I haven't...I-I haven't gotten anything done."

"I know you haven't."

"Oh no." The face broke down into the most terrible sobbing. "Jess...Mom...Oh God!" No tears streamed from the sutured eyes—only dried, red powder.

J.D. put a comforting arm over the cold back. "I'm sorry." He had not expected those two simple words to move him as they did; they acted upon him like two hairline cracks upon a massive dam. "I'm sorry," he managed to say one more time; he felt the dam buckle.

The two of them remained like this for a good few minutes—the wretched dead girl clutching her stomach, lamenting her life's hopes, and her reluctant exorcist covering his eyes, struggling to hold back a flood of long-disowned remorse.

The lips let out a final, drawn-out wail, and the head slumped down against its chest. There it stayed. The room had fallen to silence.

J.D. rubbed his eyes and looked over at the face.

When it spoke again, something in its voice had changed. "No, you're wrong. I have a future. Can't you hear it?" Slowly, the face, which now wore a preoccupied look, lifted. It tilted and listened to the air, intensely fascinated by something unseen. "Where is it coming from—that pounding? 'Bm-*bm*-bm-*bm*-bm-*bm*-bm-*bm*...?'" The voice trailed off, and the head craned toward J.D. Even though its eyes were closed, it seemed to be staring at his chest. Its expression hardened. "It's *you*."

"Please don't do this," J.D. begged. He drew back his hand and retreated toward the door. He felt a sudden, familiar chill.

"I'm so cold; so *empty*. You're so *warm*..." One of the hands reached out after him. "So *full*."

The threads grew taught as the mouth opened. A fang appeared; the proboscis tongue darted out from behind, searching for a way past the sewn, oral mesh. The formerly frightened and confused face bore malevolent yearning.

The dead girl issued a loud snarl—it sounded like the angry, drawn-out hiss of a large python.

"Ok," J.D. decided, backing up to the door and nudging it open with his shoulder. "I don't think I want to be here anymore."

"Come back."

"No," J.D. declined. "I'm going to go now."

He backed out of the parlor, allowing the door to rattle closed in front of him. He turned and half-ran toward the front entrance.

The funeral director was waiting for him. Perhaps curious about J.D.'s look of abject panic, he asked, "Is everything alright?"

"What's your refund policy?"

J.D. ignored the undertaker's confused expression and hurtled out of the building.

Accompanying his physical flight, there occurred within J.D. a retreat from adult reality. "I'm not gonna sit inside," he muttered as he stepped onto the path. "Just look at it out here."

He strolled along, in no particular hurry, and admired the beautiful, waning day around him—the sun sinking low into the trees, painting the lawn with red strips of light.

His dazed state kept him oblivious to the gasping funeral director, who staggered out of the building clutching his bleeding neck; J.D. remained unaware of the dead girl, who lurched up behind the mortician and clamped her hungry mouth over his jugular; J.D. did not hear him drop to the ground with a lifeless thud.

Instead, J.D. reassured himself, in a small voice, "She'll be fine. She just needs some rest."

What forced him back to reality was a sound from his past: a terrible, gasping mockery of human respiration, followed by the agonized, familiar entreaty, "Jamie...please come here!"

J.D. turned around and faced his pursuer.

She was gliding toward him, her pale, bare feet dangling a few inches above the ground. From a dozen yards away, she looked like a coughing, fairy princess. She held a hand upon her fitful chest. "Jaimie...Jaimie!"

"You don't call me that," J.D. warned.

She pulled the loosened threads from her eyes and opened them. They were black orbs, with tiny, glowing pin pricks of red that remained fixed on J.D. "Jaimie... Come quickly!"

It was more than an impression; it was a perfect mimicry—a faithful reproduction of J.D.'s dying mother, fashioned out of whole cloth. It was both offensive and beguiling.

Certain thoughts seem to cast powerful pulls upon the thinker, just as suns and black holes exert extreme gravitational forces upon nearby celestial bodies; a hurtful memory, if strong enough, can suck a vulnerable mind into its orbit. J.D. found himself in just such a circumstance. He knew that he needed to look away from the fledgling apparition's eyes, and yet, as he joined with his reawakened, obsessive undoing (running up the street, past the school, past the cinder path, trying this time to turn back to the house, caught up in relentless, desperate wish fulfillment), he feared that if he did look away, he would lose all memory of the most cherished person in his life and forget her forever.

What saved him was a thought that he had harbored for years but never been able to voice—not to his parents; not to his friends; not to himself: *I want to live, and She's NOT going to stop me.* It was a well-behaved child's taboo, and he was only able to disobey it, finally, because it was either do that or die.

Breaking eye contact, J.D. challenged, "You want me to take care of you?"

The hovering dead girl dropped all affectation of an asthmatic cough. She let out a frustrated shriek.

"Oh, I'll take care of you!" J.D. searched the ground around him. There was nothing that would save him, just grass, sprinkler hose, and asphalt. He looked up.

The dead girl stretched out her arms and launched herself at him. She was no longer floating gracefully but hurtling through the air, like a crazed witch on a rickety broom.

J.D. could not outrun her, but he ran anyway. He left the path and dodged between headstones. He instinctively followed one of the narrow strips of sunlight.

That did not stop her. She closed to within thirty feet... twenty feet...fifteen feet.

Something small gleamed in the light—something J.D. spotted on the ground, between two lawn sprinklers: a shiny connector, joining the two lengths of hose.

He dove for it. "You want your medicine?" he yelled, yanking one of the green, rubber ends loose from the cheap piece of plastic. He stuck his thumb over the opening to create a high-pressure stream and turned the hose on the dead girl.

The water had hit her full in the face, causing the cosmetics to rinse off in thick, flesh-colored rivulets.

She screamed.

What began to bubble underneath the dissolving makeup was the bruised, pale head of a one-week-old, ham-handedly embalmed corpse.

"Here's your medicine!" J.D. shouted as the convulsing body dropped onto the ground; it scrambled to regain its footing as it skidded up beside him. "Here's your fucking medicine!" he continued defiantly, using cathartic anger as a shield.

The corpse threw up its arms in a futile attempt to block out the sun, but the moment the skin tone washed off of the flailing limbs, they disintegrated.

"Here's your fff...!" J.D. tried to repeat. "Here's your fff...!" but his war cry failed him.

The thing that had once been an innocent girl gave a final, anguished howl.

The dam finally broke. "I'm so sorry." J.D. said it over and over, never once letting the hose stray from its target. He shuddered with uncontrolled sobs as Callie collapsed into a boiling, bloody, muddy mush.

After a few more moments of inundation, the water-logged mess settled. J.D. got himself up and reconnected the hose.

He walked across the lawn, to a newer section of the cemetery, and stood in front of one of the stones. He remained there, looking down at the grave until what he needed to do became clear.

CHAPTER 27

CERRI JAMMED HER TROWEL deep into the clay. She had been wrestling with the stubborn weed for weeks; first she had attempted to dislodge it with a standard weeding tool, but the root was too far down; next she tried dousing the tangle of leaves, stems and flowering tops with undiluted vinegar, but the rosette and its dandelions continued to thrive; then her mother cast a blessing over the garden, but that only seemed to make everything in the yard grow, including the weed. Much as Cerri did not like to gouge holes in her lawn, she had run out of patience.

Her trowel was in up to the hilt before it reached the yielding soil below the taproot. Cerri knew that if she attempted to pry the weed out, she would fail, and in all likelihood the trowel would bend. Instead, she dug a mote, circumscribing the taproot.

She had trenched three quarters of the way around it when the trowel stuck. She made an exploratory excavation along the line of resistance and discovered, to her chagrin, that the root had formed connecting tendrils, which in turn had sprung into satellite dandelions throughout the surrounding area.

She stared at the newly unearthed runners and surveyed the mess she had made in finding them. She picked up the partially-smoked joint and lighter that lay beside her, and she took a hit.

Cerri rarely left work before eight o'clock, but today she had decided, *Screw it*. She had planned to tend the garden as soon as she had gotten home from work, but when she saw the weed, which looked as defiant as ever, she continued into the house and pinched a modest helping of marijuana from her mother's dresser; then she went for a drive.

She tried to nudge the Focus past 100 mph, accelerating down a hill where she and her eleventh-grade classmates once executed high-speed cigarette handoffs. About halfway down, Cerri made eye contact with a traffic officer, who was nestled into a hidden driveway. Since she had no prior record, and since she fully took responsibility for her poor judgment, she was let off with a warning.

It had been years since the last time Cerri had smoked, and she had never driven while stoned. She had lately indulged in a lot of uncharacteristic behaviors, the most brazen of which had been the casual shagging of her date's friend in a public men's room.

Cerri exhaled slowly and shook her head into her palm. She was more astonished with herself than upset. She felt badly about hurting George, but the spontaneous, unreal quality of her tryst with J.D. made it feel like something that had happened in a dream; it drowned out protests of conscience, so that guilt registered as merely an uncomfortable background noise, like the buzz of an annoying insect.

Apart from the surrealistic nature of that night, there was another reason that Cerri accepted her actions: they kept her from going crazy. She had reached the end of her tether. Her world was crumbling around her, and no one could do a thing about it.

Her ailing mother had asked her to apply to BrewCorp, and she had dutifully obeyed, for what else could she do? Her town was dying an unnatural death, and all of the traditional sabbats and protective circles had stopped working, everyone in the flock knew it.

The company, Middlestop's latest and greatest, tax-abated hope for commercial revitalization—and which no one had ever heard of until the first store opened, less than a year before—gave off thick waves of terrible mojo.

The ethereal stink could have been coming from a disgruntled employee, perhaps a clinical narcissist, who was indulging in black spells—Cerri's mother would speak with the neighboring covens about whether any unstable practitioners had recently been thrown out—or possibly it was from a thrill-seeking executive who had carried a flirtation with Satanism to criminal extremes. Someone was playing with fire, with intent, and it would only be a matter of time before it rebounded against the perpetrator.

Cerri had reluctantly agreed to watch over her new workplace and to report any occurrences that were, as her mother put it, "left-handed." The paralegal job had turned out to be an odious one, requiring Cerri to proofread thousands of pages of toxic paperwork: false environmental disclosures; statements of eminent domain, targeted at stable school districts; blank building inspection forms, pre-signed by municipal public officials (all printed in tiny, 7-point font). She had left her adjunct teaching position at The Middlestop Art Institute for this; she had *had* to do so: she was her mother's daughter.

Cerri exhaled and took another hit. *I'm a maiden, and she's stuck me into the role of a crone.* She was being more open with herself than she might have been had she been more sober.

She had known her mother's friends and flock since she was little; she regarded them as an extended family, but where they, and her mother, saw a future leader, she only saw the steward of a failing, marginalized community.

Cerri set down her joint and lighter and pulled her trowel loose, laying it down next to them. She had lost the will to deal with the weed; it was as entrenched as every other force in her life. She stared into the sprawling ganglia of green stems and looked back over the past two years, seeking some insight that might restore her spirit.

She searched back and forth through her time with Brew-Corp, but those memories yielded no healing enlightenments. She had become privy to sensitive information: confidential details of capital expenditures, build-out blueprints for new stores, personal property expense books. The internal documents showed operating expenses approaching two hundred percent of gross income, private stockpiles of medical apparatus that had nothing to do with retail operations, and a syndicate of silent, overseas partners who paid no taxes.

The apparent fraud was ambitious but man-made; it was not why she was there.

Would reporting it have made me feel better? She wondered but concluded that it would not; no one seemed to support her going to the authorities, and as her boss warned, she would surely have gotten innocent people fired.

Her mother's assignment seemed pointless.

It hasn't been pointless, she reminded herself. Although she had never seen anything unusual at work, her job did, indirectly, bring her face-to-face with something left-handed in the extreme.

It had happened over the summer, when Cerri was cooling off in her backyard, following an evening run: she saw George walking up the driveway. He was dressed like Sytry, or Amon, or another of the aging frat boys who ran the company.

She did not even recognize him at first; then he took off his sunglasses and spoke: he happened to be in the neighborhood; was she interested in having dinner with him and, perhaps, catching a movie? His manner was oddly formal, and it made her wonder if he had found out about her and J.D. (no, it was not that; something else was not right: his recent promotion? That was sure to be messing with his head, but that did not account for why the hairs on her neck were standing up).

She tried making polite excuses; George interrupted her, telling her flatly that he wanted her; he did not say it seductively but wistfully, almost hopelessly. She gently replied that she did not feel the same.

That was when it happened: George rose into the air and drew back his lips, brandishing...whatever the hell that thing was.

He hissed that he could make her feel or do whatever he wanted; he told her that when he was done he would drink the soul out of her; but then, all of a sudden, he seemed confused; he returned to the ground, looking ashamed. He covered his face and ran.

Cerri had seen extraordinary things during her life: one time, a congregant with congestive heart failure attended a healing esbat and, two days later, he received a clean bill of health from his baffled physician; another time, a lady suffering from years of spousal abuse returned home from a protective circle to find that her husband had moved out; there was a note from him, agreeing to separate. Never, though, had Cerri, or her mother, or anyone else in their religious community, encountered anything like the physical phenomenon that George had just flaunted; the existence of a vampire had never entered the flock's wildest speculations.

Cerri's mother and the elders set to work: they organized protest rallies, which were held near the entrance to the headquarters building; they burned incense and made invocations, but these were largely symbolic acts. Cerri caught one of the demonstrations while coming to work, and it was like watching volunteer firefighters throw buckets of water at a nuclear blast.

Cerri searched for a more positive memory. The only one that she could come up with was her fleshly lark with J.D.

Her previous partners had each been shy, decent, respectful men, whose common shortcoming she was able to overlook; in J.D., she experienced the missing trait in its adventurous fullness. As obnoxious as he was, he had hit on her with a refreshing cheek that got Cerri feeling, at least for a few hours, as if she had been sprung from prison.

He was just a cute boy, out of college, who was offering a chance to let off steam—Cerri had no illusions about that. Yet, when she learned about his involvement with the company's pipeline, she felt betrayed.

Grudgingly, she asked herself what, after one evening, such a young man could possibly have meant to her; the answer surprised her: leadership; not the kind that her mother and the elders were wielding of late.

J.D. possessed an infectious, audacious...something. The Yiddish word for it (a Hungarian aunt on Cerri's father's side had been a fluent speaker) was *chutzpah*. J.D.'s roguish style, which Cerri noted many around him lacked, compelled people to respond to him. This was true at the office as well as happy hour. No matter how vehemently they aired their resentments about him when he was out of ear shot, people always showed up for J.D.; they could not seem to help it; they were under his spell.

Cerri was forced to acknowledge that, in the aftermath of George's miraculous and terrifying display, part of her had hoped that J.D. would be the one to do something—to get people to stand up and accept that—What? Fantastical parasites were bleeding them to death?

The admission made her feel foolish, all the more so since her impish beacon of hope had given himself over to the leeches, and had done it as casually as she had given herself to him.

A shadow appeared over the weed, and Cerri looked up.

Well, speak of the devil.

CHAPTER 28

J.D. SAW CERRI AS soon as he turned onto her block. She was sitting in her yard, legs folded under her, wearing a wide-brimmed hat to shade her eyes from the last of the sun.

Previously, he would not have given the hat a second thought, especially since he wore sunglasses for the same purpose; nevertheless, after what he had just seen, he opted to pause three houses down to assess her behavior.

She looked like she was having a very serious, telepathic conversation with one of her dandelions. Her expression made it seem as if the weed had been caught lying about being a prize orchid.

J.D. concluded that she was not undead, just weird. He walked up to her. His shadow roused her from the presumed confrontation, and she squinted up at him.

"I need your help," he said.

Cerri nodded, but he could not tell if it was to him or to herself. She gathered up her trowel and personal effects, along with an unemptied watering can, which was custom-sculpted to resemble the anguished, wavy subject of Edvard Munch's *The Scream*; she withdrew to the house.

J.D. tried to follow her inside, but she pulled the screen

shut between them and slammed the front door. He heard the lock turn.

"We work for vampires," he called after her. "I know you know—you and your mom."

The deadbolt retracted, and Cerri opened the door. "Could you be more specific?"

"Ok: our company is literally run by a bunch of undead, bloodsucking assholes; they see our city as a big frappucino, and I handed them the straw."

She stepped back outside.

"Your mom's a witch, right? A good witch? What do you call it? Wiccan?" J.D. lowered his voice. "Cerri, I have, conscientiously, and with meticulous attention to detail, completely fucked up. Is there anything—*anything*—I can do about it?"

In the next instant, J.D. found himself doused with water, which poured from the watering can's screaming mouth/spout and over the top of the hand-cradled head/tank.

"What-?" he asked, too surprised to articulate a specific question.

Cerri set down the can and held up a compact mirror. She opened it and stared into the glass; he saw that she was looking at him. After several seconds of scrutiny, she lowered it.

"You thought I was-? I'm *not* one of them!"

"You sure about that? When's the last time you took a good look at yourself?" She held up the mirror again and turned it toward him.

He saw a dripping wet suit, tie and sunglasses; they so dominated the reflection that his face and neck might just as well have been invisible; he pushed the mirror away.

"And what tipped you off?" she asked. "Was it the blood in your coffee? Or did you pick up on something subtle, like your friend flying first class without a plane ticket?"

J.D. used a palm to squeegee his head. "Why did you bring me into your house last night? Why would you do that?"

"You know," Cerri offered, narrowing her eyes, "you might want to rethink being the voice of caution; you haven't really got the hang of it."

J.D. looked down and, reluctantly, nodded.

"So, what are you saying? You want to take responsibility for your part?"

"Yes, I *am*. I *do*."

She looked out on the yard and shook her head; then, acquiescing to some private instruction, she turned back to him. "Let's go."

CHAPTER 29

CERRI DROVE ALONG WINDING state routes and country roads as J.D. looked out of the passenger window, watching dusk settle over passing barns and hilly fields. Neither one spoke.

After forty-five minutes, they turned onto a long, hidden, dirt driveway, at the end of which stood a well-kept, white farmhouse. Parked cars of various makes, years and conditions, filled the lawn; Cerri drove in among the assortment of automobiles and found a spot.

J.D. followed her past the house, behind a peeling red barn with a faded World War II sign—a serviceman smiling out over his tin coffee mug—and into a corn field. The tall, brown plants parted with a dry crackling noise as they pushed through row after row.

A narrow path had been cut between stalks; they rounded the first turn and found a man blocking their way. He wore a black suit and tie. For a moment J.D. thought that BrewCorp had sprung some sort of trap; then he saw that the man wore an earpiece.

"Identification," the affectless man demanded.

Cerri pointed at her face. "Ok, this is me." She pointed at J.D. "That's him."

She moved to pass the man, but he held up his palm.

"J.D.'s fine," Cerri told him.

The palm stayed up. "How did you make that assessment?"

Cerri puckered her lips and made a loud smacking sound. "With water and a reflection. How did you get your job?" She grabbed J.D.'s hand and squeezed by.

"Ok," the man declared behind them. "You may proceed."

"Prohhh-ceeding," Cerri called back, exaggerating his monotone inflection.

There was a second turn, followed by a long, straight stretch. Slow, rhythmic drumming sounded up ahead. J.D. smelled burning incense.

The path opened onto a large, round clearing.

Dozens of people stood in a large circle. The bonfire beyond made it difficult for J.D. to see anyone clearly, but he glimpsed t-shirts and jeans, delicate headdresses and velvet gowns, flannel shirts and sports caps, and a few cloaks and pointed hats. Within the circle, a group of percussionists beat djembes and cowbells while a robed man wearing antlers bounced around the perimeter; he waved aloft a burning sage smudge, leaving a trail of pungent smoke.

At the exact center knelt a young woman, her head swaying with the music. A tall, cloaked figure stood over her, partially blocking J.D.'s view; even so, he could see that the young woman was practically naked. She wore only a pair of colorful wings, fastened to her arms with leather straps, and a large, white feather, secured to a narrow, gold band on her head. In one hand, she held a staff with an animal head; in the other, she grasped what looked like an Egyptian ankh key.

Behind her stood a large tree stump with moss-covered sides; its wide, perfectly flat top had been painted with a green, knotted pentacle and served as a staging table for an array of unusual, but recognizable, items: there was a small, cast-iron cauldron, suspended by three legs over lit votive candles; there was a twig with a small, elongated, clear crystal jammed into one end; in addition, there was a silver cup, filled with pale blue moonstones, a small, double-edged knife, an assortment of tiny aromatherapy jars, each with its own, handwritten label, and there was a pair of muddy, sculpted candles—one of them resembling the man with the antlers and the other, a woman holding a sickle moon in her raised hands. Four, thick candles, two black and two white, bordered the makeshift altar, with a fifth, gold candle, larger than the others, placed in the middle.

"I have not sinned," the entire group recited, "I have not done violence; I have not killed; I have not taken property or food that was not mine"—J.D. noticed that Cerri was listening carefully to the chant and staring in bewilderment at the young, winged participant—"I have not lied; I have not cursed; I have not broken the vows of marriage or caused another to break the vows of marriage; I have not gossiped at another's expense; I have not pried into what was none of my concern..."

"You have got to be kidding," Cerri remarked softly, shaking her head—it seemed to J.D. that she did that a lot. She looked at him uncertainly for a moment. "Look, this is going to get weird."

"Think so?"

"Just stay here and don't say anything."

She walked over to the circle and quietly got the attention of the man with the antlers. There was a brief, inaudible exchange between them; the man went to the tree stump; he returned brandishing the small knife; he pointed it at her and traced an outline in the air. She entered the circle and accompanied the man over to his tall, cloaked counterpart; the three of them quietly held a heated conference. What few words J.D. could make out ("skyclad," "may-ut," or "muh-at," "channel trained") did not make any sense. The hooded figure broke off the discussion and nodded to the kneeling, winged participant; the young woman stood up and removed her scant costume, holding it out to Cerri. Cerri slid out of her skirt and unbuttoned her top.

J.D. realized he was staring; he shifted his gaze over to the tall, hooded figure, but she was disrobing as well; J.D. recognized her, and at that moment, to his queasy surprise, he grasped that instead of gawking at Cerri he was gawking at her mother. The old woman moved with such a steady, graceful fluidity that J.D. could scarcely believe she was the trembling invalid to whom he had, that morning, fed Chinese takeout.

Others in the circle followed Mrs. Morgan's example and got undressed.

J.D. did not believe in ceremonial magic, divine intervention, telekinesis or any of the other dozens of names given to action at a distance, but then again he had never believed in vampires; moreover, standing, gaping at Cerri as she literally bared all, had made him feel like some Roman senator at a pleasure palace, voyeuristically enjoying the spectacle of a slave orgy. J.D. took off his clothes.

Setting them down on a yellowing patch of grass, J.D. approached the circle. The night was mild and the bonfire warm. The smell of cloves, perhaps from the steaming cauldron, mingled with the sage.

Cerri, who had put on the wings and feather, looked up and saw him. She made a questioning face at her mother.

Mrs. Morgan looked from her daughter to J.D. She turned to the antlered man and nodded. "Cut him in."

The man walked up to J.D. and sliced an invisible arch, much as he had done for Cerri. The two nearest participants in the circle made a space for J.D., who, with a curt nod of thanks to each, stepped in between them.

As he glanced around, he recognized faces from his daily bus commute. Another of George's required reading assignments came back to him: *Young Goodman Brown*. In ninth grade, George and J.D.'s 19th Century Literature class had read Nathaniel Hawthorne's short story, in which a God-fearing man discovered his upstanding neighbors and their sworn Indian enemies holding a witch's Sabbath. The surreal tale had given George an epiphany that all schooling and parenting was a literal conspiracy, and he decided he would no longer play the fool; for the remainder of that school year, George had responded to all adults by declaring, "Oh, I know what's going on," winking, and walking away. The short story did not affect J.D. as much. He could not identify with its young protagonist, whom he saw as a laughable, ineffectual chump; still, the idea of signing two, mutually exclusive social contracts—one for sunlit town squares and another for moonlit woods—had spooked him.

He wondered if each person standing with him out in the middle of the corn was someone entirely different back in town.

No recognizable deacons or high secular officials here, he observed, just a bunch of socially conscious misfits with nothing more sinister to hide than body-fat percentages, SAT scores, and convention costumes. Nobody seemed to be violating any public trust. *What about self-trust?* he thought. *Is that what I'm doing here? Betraying myself?*

For J.D., that trust had always meant rational, goal oriented thought: *You're not getting paid enough? Don't bitch about it; learn new skills, and get a promotion. You want to lose weight? Don't wish for it while blowing out your birthday candles; take a pass on the cake. You got a speeding ticket? Don't blame it on a municipal conspiracy to increase revenues; drive slower—or learn how to talk to traffic officers.* Reason was how he got on in the world. He was not born with it; he learned it, exercised it, and made himself good at it, and in return he gained mastery over his life.

On more than one scotch-and-cigar-infused occasion, George had challenged him about his philosophy, but J.D. refused to concede that life could be influenced by anything like luck or fate ("Spent six months training for the promotion, then your company suddenly goes belly-up? Random occurrence; shit happens; polish your resume, and hit the pavement...Genetically predisposed to be overweight? Too bad, but still random...Got pulled over because the dealership frame covered a tiny piece of your registration sticker? Ok, cop's acting like a dick, but still he's going to ticket someone; it just happens to be you; random shit; cost of doing business in an impersonal universe.").

One time, George had countered, "And if all three happen to the same person on the same day?"

J.D. had never answered. Although he could see that such a coincidence was totally random, he knew in his heart that the person in question could not.

Now he stood in the shoes of that individual. There, in a pagan circle, he stood: a rational atheist, who had taken off his clothes and was going to cast a spell to get rid of vampires.

He stood there having reached the limits of what pure reason could do for him: it might get him a stimulating, well-paying job at one of the Top 10 Most Evil Places to Work; it might eventually provide him with a scientific basis for what he had seen at BrewCorp (perhaps he had suffered a cerebral hemorrhage five months earlier and had been hallucinating ever since); but reason alone could never free him from the nightmarish conviction that his world had suddenly, incomprehensibly *gone bad*.

He began to see how his sensible, goal-oriented thinking, which had pried opened so many doors with teachers, girls, and employers, could, when taken to its extreme, inspire his best friend to betray himself.

J.D., unlike George, had grasped human duality from an early age: some behaviors got him smiles and compliments; others got him what he wanted, and the two outcomes rarely lined up; that was life. He had always been comfortable with that dichotomy, and was not one to try and reconcile it; he saw no value in doing so (George, who had tried to reconcile it every second of every day, had filled his life—his natural life—with hesitation and insecurity); now, however, J.D. felt the need to reconcile himself, and he felt it so strongly that he was going to participate in a magical ritual; if nothing else, it would give him something to do, thereby lessening his feelings of help-lessness. Given the completely irrational circumstances, this, he told himself, was a perfectly rational course.

The drumming ceased.

Mrs. Morgan addressed the circle. "We're here because we care about this place; we believe something has turned. We have all seen or felt things we're not comfortable talking about: left-handed things that carry with them the staleness of rotten intentions.

"We call upon the Goddess to send those manifestations back to the place whence they came! We invoke her as Ma'at, the bringer of order and justice to help us to restore the nat-ural balance."

Leading with one shoulder and then the other, Mrs. Morgan moved slowly, deliberately, around the circle.

The drumming resumed.

"'I have not been angry without justification,'" she said; voice after voice joined her in the recitation. "'I have not polluted my mind or body; I have not spread fear or intimidation; I have not ignored truthful words...'"

The participants began to undulate as well; the circle began to turn. "'I have not sowed strife; I have not acted recklessly; I have not worked black witchcraft...'"

J.D. counted forty-two such declarations. After the last, the drumming became louder and faster, the dancing looser. Whoops and cries broke out.

The mix of noises reminded him of a Halloween sound effects CD he once borrowed from the library; the disc (canned cackles and badly synthesized drums), along with a couple of old paintings that J.D. and George saw during a grade-school museum visit (*Inquisitive Minds: Art of the Counter-Reformation in Southern Europe, On Exhibit Winter 2003*), comprised the entirety of J.D.'s education on Wiccan practices. Since the real thing did not seem to involve corpse desecration or child sacrifice, he let himself settle into the dance.

The circle picked up speed.

He noticed that Cerri, still kneeling within, had shut her eyes and was rolling her head and shoulders from side to side.

Drums and smoke and sage and people started blending together; J.D. realized he was becoming buzzed. There was a warmth in his core; it grew as he and the others moved, faster and faster.

The more he danced, the more he wanted to dance. For once, he felt free from competition with those around him; he felt like a boy, spinning and playing with other children. Even after what seemed like hours, he did not want it to end.

He glimpsed Cerri swaying in a pronounced, loose arc. Everything in the circle seemed to shimmer with a milky light, and her pale skin turned golden. She settled into perfect stillness. A pair of amber eyes opened. There was no trace of sarcasm on her face; it had become a mask of cold certainty. It was like a face on a statue, a face of a deity.

She stood. Her head turned toward the tree stump; the rest of her body followed, and she walked to the alter in four, long strides; her knees did not bend; her back stayed ramrod straight.

Mrs. Morgan and the antlered man came to her side.

The ankh key pointed to one of the aromatherapy jars. Mrs. Morgan took up the glass; she dribbled its contents into the cauldron until the ankh pointed to a second jar. She switched to that container; she poured until the ankh selected yet another of the vials. This went on until, after more than half of the jars had been used, Cerri lowered the ankh.

She turned her head, and her gaze found J.D.; the golden face followed him around the circle; she turned to Mrs. Morgan and said something; Mrs. Morgan nodded, bowing her head slightly, and gave some kind of reply.

The next moment, in an explosion of energy, Cerri led her mother and the other priest into a whirling frenzy around the cauldron. The circle was forced to speed up in order to keep pace with the three. The rapturous triangle raised its collective arms to the sky. It could have been a trick of firelight through smoke, or some sort of contact high from the group, but J.D. saw color after color appear, engulfing the trio in a cone of rainbow light; it was as if a giant prism, lit by the bonfire, had been placed around them.

They slowed and switched directions. The circle did the same; the light abruptly disappeared, and then Cerri, heaving, sank to one knee.

J.D. started toward her, but the participant to his right grabbed his shoulder tightly and gave him a warning head shake.

The man with the antlers fetched Cerri's cloak and draped it around her. He handed Mrs. Morgan the knife.

Mrs. Morgan picked up the wand from the tree stump and pointed it outward from the circle. "So mote it be."

"So mote it be," the circle responded.

Mrs. Morgan shifted a quarter turn to the right and again raised the wand. "So mote it be."

"So mote it be."

This was done for each of the four directions; then Mrs. Morgan held up the knife and walked a clockwise arc. "Our circle is released," she then declared. "Blessed be."

"Blessed be," the group replied.

As the antlered man brought Mrs. Morgan her robe, the circle disbanded; individuals and couples returned to their starting positions and gathered up clothes.

J.D. put on his shirt, pants, shoes and jacket; he stuffed his tie, underwear and socks into pockets and returned to where he had last seen Cerri; she was no longer there.

"J.D."

He turned around. Mrs. Morgan stood over the cauldron, dipping a vial into the mixture. It came up with an amber, metallic liquid (*Is the fire making it do that*, he wondered, *or did she mash in a bunch of lightning bugs?*).

She capped the vial and passed it to him. "Walk with me."

J.D. followed her into the corn maze. The man with the earpiece was still there, but he allowed them to pass without comment.

"Is he FBI?" J.D. asked as they rounded the turn.

Mrs. Morgan pursed her lips. "Yes and no."

"What does that mean?"

"It means federal agents don't publically set up sting operations against mythical, undead creatures; it means the FBI answers to congressional oversight committees." She gave him a sideways look. "Don't be dense."

J.D. recognized the parted corn through which Cerri and he had entered. Instead of stepping out of the maze here, Mrs. Morgan continued into more of the labyrinth, which she seemed to know cold.

"I just never pictured the FBI working with, uh..."

"Witches?" she supplied. "Who else do *you* know who can solve unsolved crimes?"

No light from the bonfire reached this part of the path, and J.D. momentarily lost his bearings; he pulled the vial out of his pocket; the effect was like activating a glow stick; Mrs. Morgan's impatient face became visible, waiting ten feet ahead. J.D. held up the vial. "What is this supposed to do?"

Mrs. Morgan turned and resumed her walk. "She didn't say."

"Who? Cerri?"

"Yes and no."

He caught up with her. "Ma'at?"

Mrs. Morgan grinned. "You're not as dumb as you look."

The maze let out on the side of the field facing away from the house. "What she told me," Mrs. Morgan said, "was that her spell was a two-parter. She cast the first half; the second requires an act of courage on your part." The old woman hesitated.

J.D. prompted, "Ok? And that would be...?"

"Getting your bosses, and all of their associates, to drink it."

He looked from her to the vial and gave a chuckle. "What am I supposed to do? Force it down their throats?"

"Don't be dense."

They rounded the edge of the field and moved toward the house.

J.D. tried to fathom what the old lady could possibly be suggesting.

It came to him. "Oh." He grasped not only what she wanted but why he had to be the one to do it: he was the only person with access to the pipeline. He thought about George. "Is it going to kill them?"

"I don't know, J.D.," Mrs. Morgan replied. "My coven never sends malice out into the universe—we don't tolerate that—but the manifest intention that concerns us here is not *ours*: most of it is your employers'.

"We've asked Ma'at to send it back to them because she's committed to justice, but she's a deity, you know? When you petition *that* kind of help, you don't get to sit down and have her initial all of your bylaws.

"And, by the way, in my entire life, I have *never* invited a goddess to take possession of a body. Jesus Christ..." She reached under her robe and pulled out an open pack of Salems. "I've been an ordained high priestess for over thirty years; I have cleaned bad houses—and I mean *bad*; I've located missing persons; I've resuscitated dead automobiles. I am *no* slouch, but this whole situation is way, way, *way*, out of my wheelhouse."

She placed a cigarette in her mouth and jutted it toward J.D. He looked back at her blankly; the cigarette wiggled up and down at him.

"Oh," he stammered, reaching into his pocket for his lighter.

"Do *not* tell my daughter." Mrs. Morgan eased the cigarette into the flame. She took two deep puffs and then threw down the cigarette, mashing it into the grass.

"You probably shouldn't smoke," J.D. said.

"Probably not."

They walked the rest of the way in silence.

At the steps to the front porch, Mrs. Morgan stopped.

"Here, you'll need some of this too." She reached into her robe; this time, she produced a small sheet of bubble wrap, which she pressed into his palm.

Thinking to protect the vial with it, he rolled it around the glass. The look of bewilderment from Mrs. Morgan caused him to stop. "Isn't this for the…?" he asked, weakly.

She slowly shook her head, her expression turning to disbelief. "It's for *Cerri*: you give it to *Cerri*, for crying out loud." She turned and continued up the steps. "She loves bubble wrap, J.D. Don't be dense."

THE MEETING WENT ON for hours. The veteran SWAT commander who ran it reminded J.D. of the character actor Bernie Casey—clean-shaven, short hair (unlike Casey's, the commander's was starting to gray), arched, unimpressed eyebrows, and a quiet, no-nonsense demeanor. Special Agent Warren began by asking J.D. for his story.

J.D. recounted all that he had seen and heard since going to work for BrewCorp; he described the highlights from his surveillance of George's bedroom; he showed the video that he had taken with his phone.

While the special agent watched the footage, he remained impassive, but once the video ended, he unwrapped the first of what turned out to be four chocolate bars and took a voracious, chewy bite. "So none of the customers was free to leave," he confirmed.

"None," J.D. replied.

"But probably none of them remembers." The commander paced around the dining room, absently running his hand along the white, Cape Cod wainscoting. He returned to the rustic table, where his eleven agents, including the officious fellow from the corn maze, were seated. "Except for you."

Obtaining a warrant for search and seizure inside Brew-Corp's headquarters would not, the SWAT team concluded, be the way to go: any paperwork citing a probable cause of "vampires," would be a career-ending non-starter, and three previous attempts to investigate more traditional allegations—that the company was engaging in financial fraud and domestic terrorism—had been quickly and quietly squashed from above.

The alternative would have to be a warrantless operation. The legal justification would be that the ongoing, alleged, danger to BrewMart customers created a set of "exigent circumstances," which required an immediate intervention; even if the argument did not hold up in court, and evidence gathered during the operation was ruled inadmissible, BrewCorp's luxuriant feeding would still be disrupted and its evasive bookkeeping would come under greater public scrutiny.

The group turned to the problem of engaging superhuman, flying corpses. The easiest detail to work out had been the signal: J.D. would walk out of the headquarters' front entrance, and, if successful in his task, he would light a cigarette. What should happen after became the topic of lengthy discussion.

A municipal floor plan of BrewCorp's headquarters was spread out upon the table. J.D. provided a verbal tour of the building, in which he confirmed or corrected every single, mapped detail. He answered technical questions (Fire controls? A master station in the main lobby, redundant consoles and heat-resistant automatic doors on every floor. Stairwells? Accessible from the first floor up); he also responded to queries about the owner-occupants (Coffee breaks? The whole group took them, each morning at 10 a.m., like clockwork. Typical movements? Confined to the top floor).

By degrees, fewer questions were asked and more assertions made ("Sir, it's safer for the informant if we go in through the loading dock; we can get anywhere from there in under a minute.").

J.D. had no idea what the emerging plan was, just that it would go into effect upon, as the commander put it, "delivery of the package."

Mrs. Morgan must have sensed J.D.'s concern; she cut off one of the agents, Jennings, who was advocating remotely shutting the fire doors and locking out the consoles. The agent claimed that his idea gave the team complete control over the building. The other agents stood and stretched; it felt as though they were getting ready to adjourn. Mrs. Morgan irritably reminded them that employees were a potential food source and that shutting the fire doors would trap pray with predator.

Another agent, Castillo, backed up Jennings: J.D.'s signal would confirm that the targets had been rendered harmless. Mrs. Morgan, her daughter, and the man who had worn the ant-lers, all responded with loud, cautioning protests. Mrs. Morgan interpreted the cacophony for the two agents: the effects of Ma'at's oil, though presumably powerful, were unknown; their timing, uncertain; the plan could rely upon the targets' con-suming the potion, but not upon any particular result.

Inertia descended. It hung in the air as discussion under-went several more approach-avoidance cycles. From around the table came exasperated pronouncements: the physical risk, to agent and civilian alike, could not be adequately managed. There was talk of postponing the operation.

"'Turning and turning in the widening gyre / The falcon cannot hear the falconer,'" Mrs. Morgan recited, and the room grew silent:

"Things fall apart; the centre cannot hold;
Mere anarchy is loosed upon the world,
The blood-dimmed tide is loosed, and everywhere
The ceremony of innocence is drowned.
The best lack all conviction, while the worst
Are full of passionate intensity."

She repeated, "'The best lack all conviction, while the worst / Are full of passionate intensity,'" and looked around. "What are we waiting for? Certainty? That's going to be long wait. "

No one spoke.

It was J.D. who broke the silence. "Look, I think I should just hand my phone over to one of the networks."

"How do you prove it isn't fake when BrewCorp comes after you for libel?" Warren challenged. "You might land a reality TV show after that, but you're a joke.

"And supposing someone does take it seriously. The DOJ starts to investigate; BrewCorp suppresses it: they submit their copy of the customer confidentiality agreement, the one with your signature on it, and they get a SLAPP order; then they come after you."

J.D. countered, "My video will still create a public outcry-"

"You can't win this war in the temple, kid," interrupted another agent, O'Neill. "Folks may be exhausted and sick, but they're getting their discounts."

Castillo shook his head. "Ed, man, that's bent."

"So, there are vampires," O'Neill stoically drawled. "So what? I fuel a lot of things that aren't good for me: climate change, income inequality, infotainment. You think everybody's going to suddenly take up arms? We didn't even do that against the Nazis!"

"Oh, here we go," interjected Castillo.

"It took FDR *years* to mobilize the public, and *he* had several distinct advantages that *you* do not: *he* had the power to create a wartime economy; *he* had *weekly* newsreels of London getting bombed into the Stone Age, which scared the *shit* out of everyone.

"What *you* have—*all* you have—is some Goth video that looks like it was staged by my fourteen-year-old and his friends and didn't even go viral."

Agent O'Neill's rant released the room's pent-up stress; laughter broke out.

Mrs. Morgan and Cerri did not join in; nor did J.D., though he did concede the point.

A second wind bolstered the group, and a viable plan took shape. Cellular and wireless communications would be jammed before infiltration occurred; upon attaining the lobby, the SWAT team would shut down the phone system and set off all fire sprinklers; that would trigger the evacuation of civilians, but not of the C.E.O. and his vice presidents, whose protective cosmetics would become thoroughly doused; agents outside of the building would impose a news blackout, turning away EMS responders and local media; agents inside would subdue the targets; in the event that a combatant remained resistant to conventional forms of restraint, the team was authorized to use weaponized garlic sprayers and silver-plated handcuffs.

The only question that remained was what to do about the uncounted others: the bloodsucking store patrons and basement technicians who never set foot inside of the headquarters. The best, imperfect answer, which the room was eventually forced to accept, was that the media blackout would, in theory, ensure that none of the others got tipped off and that the elixir would be imbibed by any devotee who normally enjoyed a morning cup of Gilded Roast.

The agents again stood, having apparently agreed not to discuss what would happen if the potion made no impact at all.

J.D., who was growing impatient with unspoken agreements, asked, "What's the backup plan?"

"The backup plan," replied Agent Warren, "is that, from tomorrow morning forward, we monitor police radio bands and respond to anything that sounds suspicious."

"So that's it, then?"

The commander walked up to J.D. "Based on the limited information available and the urgency of the circumstances, yes, that's it. Try not to second guess yourself."

Agent O'Neill added, "But *do* feel free to pray."

DURING THE RIDE HOME, J.D. tried to make conversation with Cerri ("So, that was something new"; "Are you okay?"); she responded with terse answers ("Mmm"; "Yep").

When the meeting ended, J.D. had overheard her trying to find someone else to take him home, but every time she located someone, her mother, who was across the room, had spontaneously called upon that person for some household chore ("Dillan, I need you to stay over and fix those foundation cracks, like you've been promising"). After the fifth time, Cerri had turned to J.D. with a chilly glance and taken out her keys.

As the car growled through downtown, J.D. thumbed through his emails, as though he was finishing a normal day.

This made Cerri crazy. "Why *did* you join the circle?"

"I didn't want you to have to go in there by yourself," J.D. told his email.

"There were eighty other people there."

"Yeah, but there's only one J.D. Pence."

"No, don't be cute. What were you thinking?"

J.D. put away his phone. "Look, I wanted to be there so you wouldn't be alone. You seemed like you were taking some huge thing on your shoulders-"

"See J.D., the thing is you don't get to be 'right there with me.' You couldn't be with me if I wanted you to, and I *so don't* want you to, and if you think about it, neither do you." She moved into the passing lane, signaling halfway through. "When this is over, you should have some fun. I'm serious: go someplace warm and hip; go tour the men's rooms of The Bahamas—send me a copy of the book, but get out of this place; it's just going to kill your wise-ass gleam."

J.D. felt that he was supposed to make an angry rebuttal—to tell Cerri that she had a martyr complex and that she had no idea of what he was about. He resisted the urge; he recognized, in Cerri's tirade, a familiar, responsible child left with a sick parent; from that point on, he understood that she was a kindred soul. There was nothing that he could say, so he set the bubble wrap in front of her, on top of the dashboard.

The bitter expression in the windshield settled into annoyance; Cerri reached forward and searched for an untouched bubble. There were only a few left, concentrated in one corner; one by one, she popped them. "Do you know what you're doing tomorrow?"

"Yes."

They pulled up next to his building.

"Keep some garlic spray handy, and leave your phone on."

"Ok." He got out of the car.

"But watch your behavior. Keep acting, you know…"

"Like a jerk?"

"I was going to say 'normal.'"

He nodded and went to his front door; she waited until it was open before pulling away.

CHAPTER 30

GEORGE COULD NOT GET the letters out of his head. All morning, as he leaned back, with his feet up on the desk and his phone pressed against his ear, he bore an onslaught of ghostly, handwritten notes, set down upon whatever stationery was nearest at hand. On each sheet of creased legal paper or frayed spiral notebook stock lay blessings, bestowed upon a young boy away at summer camp—away from home for his first time:

Everything is fine here. We miss you and can't wait to hear all about your adventures. Love, Grandma and Grandpa. (p.s. you are not to use the enclosed dollar for anything serious)...

Lots of stuff happening on the soap: Ronda and Rita just found out they're sisters! And Donovon's been kidnapped! Bubbie and I'll catch you up when you get home. Love, Mom...

Hope you are making lots of new friends and having a great time! Bet you can't wait to get back and catch up on Hebrew lessons (Ha ha. Just kidding), Love, Dad...

Aunt Sonia and I went to a costume party last weekend—your Aunt dressed as Cleopatra and I wore my gorilla costume. It made us think of you. Are we on for trick or treating this year? Uncle Jeff...

Although many of the correspondents were now long gone, their affectionate words shined brightly behind George's lens-shielded eyes; each remembered sentiment seared like a ray of direct sunlight.

The high price of George's promotion did not come as a surprise to him, but the mercurial form of payment did; on some days it took the shape of a restless, gnawing boredom; on others it congealed into the panic-filled certainty that utter annihilation awaited just moments away. Today's manifestation was the sharpest so far, for it cut through his most hardened, indispensable, rationalizations.

After he had overheard J.D. and Cerri in the men's room, what hit him was the crushing realization that any place the world held for him—socially, professionally, romantically—had been an illusion: *That,* he saw, had been school, but *this* was life. In the bitter hours that followed, he had told himself hurtful things like, *I'm just a piece of kosher meat, a replacement for dead relatives, lost in pogroms and concentration camps.*

Was it at all true? Who can say? Every living person shoulders the weight of history in some fashion, and no one—not even Mrs. Morgan—has the perfect magic formula for mending a broken heart.

I had no say in the hand I was dealt, George had sworn to himself when he grabbed the vice presidency, *but I'll be Goddamned if that's the hand I'm going to play.*

When his dying soul had made its anguished protests, he had stifled them by divesting himself of history, discarding photographs, home videos, and any other keepsakes—including his treasured books. This morning, however, history refused to be denied. George could not help but feel genuine love in the old words of his parents and grandparents; he could not help but beseech, *What have I done?*

A trickle of desiccated powder ran down one of the gaunt cheeks. Shutting his eyes, George wiped away the abrasive, red sand and swiveled his chair around. Fumbling blindly across his desk, he clasped up his mug and took a long, trembling drink. The Gilded Roast dulled his heartsickness, but it did not stop the parade of sensory images. Trying to take his mind off of them, he concentrated on the partition across from him.

On the other side of the glass, in front of the coffee workstation, sat his old friend, who was stealing nervous glances out into the lobby. George followed J.D.'s gaze. Sytry, Amon, and Bunet were standing outside, chatting. Hall appeared next to the group, perhaps to iron out a last-minute detail ahead of the 10 o'clock meeting. J.D. seemed to be splitting his attention between the four executives in the lobby, the desk drawer in front of him, and something taking place outside the window on his left.

Looking out of his own window, George saw that the ground delivery van was pulling up to the building, as it did every morning—though usually closer to noon.

He returned his attention to the partition. J.D. was turning off his display and peering into the screen, holding his head oddly close. George realized that J.D. was trying to spy on him.

He leaned back in his chair and returned his feet to the desktop. He gazed at his ceiling tiles and occasionally nodded into his receiver. Even with the cosmetic lenses, his peripheral vision afforded him an unnaturally good view of his voyeur; he easily discerned the pocketing of both the security key (silver, with red, color-coded bulb and tiny, perfectly round indentations for copy prevention) and the folded pump schematic (turned to page 27, *Command Sets, Cont'd*).

The four executives outside dispersed. J.D. walked out of his office.

George ended his non-existent phone call.

J.D. KEPT HIS HEAD high, holding his gaze just above eye-level as he strode through the floor: he was on-task, and not to be interrupted.

Sytry stood in front of him, blocking his way; J.D. tried to avoid making eye contact, but the vice president was staring at him, obviously expecting to get his attention. "The meeting's at ten," Sytry said.

J.D. looked at his watch. It was 9:50. "I won't be late," he assured, walking past.

"This is your first executive briefing, Pence." Sytry's eyes tracked J.D. "It would be good to get there a few minutes early."

"Okay, not a problem." Pretending to ignore his superior's unyielding gaze, J.D. continued across the open space.

When he got to the elevator and pressed the button (there was only one; a small placard beneath wryly reported, *There's Nowhere to Go but Down*) he made himself stare into the etched, stainless steel doors in front of him, resisting the urge to turn his head. The doors parted silently, with no stylish bell or ding to announce the elevator's arrival. The car was empty.

J.D. stepped in and pressed *L*, his safest choice in the event others joined him. In the brief delay before the doors shut, he looked out. Sytry remained in the middle of the floor, looking at him with a mixture of incredulity and puzzlement.

Then J.D. was alone and descending.

The car stopped on 3; Mark Amon stepped in. Seeing the *L* already lit, he pushed it anyway and twisted his neck-head into a sidewise glance. "Where are you going?"

J.D. was prepared for this. "I need to place a personal call; my reception's spotty indoors." He searched his pockets, making a show of trying to find his phone. The performance continued as the doors opened and Amon stepped out; then J.D. reached for the top button. "Left it upstairs."

The receding vice president did not seem to care. "Briefing's in five minutes. Wait until after."

"That's what I'm going to do," J.D. replied, wishing he had instead taken the fire escape steps. As soon as the doors closed, he dropped his hand down below *L*, and pressed *B1*. The doors opened onto the underground hallway. He ran down it.

Even though J.D. had realized he would be getting his first glimpse of the pump's normal operation, he was no less astonished, upon unlocking and opening the security door, to find bright red bands flowing through his delivery lines.

"Are you fucking kidding me," he chuckled, in spite of himself, for he saw that he had unknowingly fulfilled one of his boyhood fantasies and created a villain's lair. The central mechanism's steady, palpable throbbing made the pump's not-so-subtle cardiovascular metaphor all the more glaring. This room was no longer something from a Terry Gilliam film; it was something out of a cliché-ridden summer block-buster.

There was no time to dwell upon the absurd; J.D. scurried up a short flight of stairs and onto a platform that hugged the face of the machine. Among the high banks of cluttered instruments, he located a metal bubble, a miniature version of the domed hatch that one would see on top of an old army tank. There was no obvious way to open it.

Reaching into his inner vest pocket, he took out his operating manual and held it up to the light. He squinted at the numbered diagram and then flipped one of the switches in front of him; an indicator flag went from red to green. Referring back to the paper, he looked up a keypad sequence.

A familiar wave of hopelessness hit him; he lowered the operating manual. George was standing beside him. J.D. gave a start. "You scared me."

"I thought you didn't get scared," George said vaguely accusingly, as if confronting a new employee for lying on his job application.

J.D. frowned at the door across from him, which had just sealed shut.

"That closes too slowly," George pointed out.

"I'll tweak it," J.D. acknowledged.

"I saw you take your key."

"Yeah. It's nothing serious-"

"Actually, when you make an unannounced trip down here, it *is* serious."

J.D. racked his mind for a plausible excuse. He noticed the empty mug in George's hand; the manicured thumb was pressing down just a bit too hard on the white, porcelain handle. "I need this kept between us," he confided. "Do you have any idea how much money we would save the company by centrally heating the, uh, product?"

George stared at him blankly.

"Let me show you something." J.D. reached past George, to where the command keypad was located; he punched in the sequence. With a crisp click, the hatch sprung open.

George's expression changed. He leaned toward the opening and took a deep sniff.

"Knock yourself out," J.D. invited, nodding at the quivering mug.

George looked uncertainly from the hatchway to J.D., but he shoved his mug through the hatch; it came out overflowing with red. J.D. tried to maintain a confident grin, but it faltered as George took his first bloody gulp.

The vice president let out a yelp and reached up between his eyes. "Ice cream headache from Hell," he managed, massaging his forehead.

"Yeah." J.D. tried to ignore the dripping ring around his friend's mouth. "That's because we keep it refrigerated until the individual brewers heat it up."

George shook his head. "Fuck it." He thrust his mug through the hatchway again.

"What ever happened with Hall? Did he cut you off?"

George slurped down his second helping. Once the coldness abated, he replied, "He's got an idea. Wanted to know if I thought you were the guy."

"For what?"

"He'll tell you at the briefing." George lowered the mug. He used his lapel handkerchief to wipe his chin; all that did was smear the mess onto the white fabric. "Ok, go on, I'm listening."

"Look, central heating means cheaper, energy efficient brewers," J.D. improvised. "We'd save thousands on utilities and jump ahead in the cap and trade market. Think about it: the old man will never cut you off again."

The frown that played across George's eyes and mouth was one J.D. knew well, but he had rarely seen it since his friend had seized the vice presidency: it was an introverted, conflicted convulsion, which broadcast: *I need what you're offering, but is it real? And if it's real, will I share in it or get screwed again, like always?* The frown deepened; George rested a hand on the metal plating next to him. "How would you heat this?"

J.D.'s smile came naturally this time. "Come on, Bro, give me some credit. I'll make it work."

"When can I see something polished put together?"

"The sooner I finish down here, the sooner you get your pitch."

"Ok." The frown disappeared. George levitated over the platform and, clearing the railing, glided down to the door. He turned the handle and paused, turning back to J.D. "You know, lately I keep getting these crazy-vivid memories. I just now had this flash of our first poker game—Rich accusing me of cheating and giving me the shiner..."

"I beat the shit out of him," J.D. remembered.

They both laughed.

"God, the way you worked that hustle," George remembered. "It was beautiful!"

J.D. did not know what to say; he quietly replied, "I've always looked out for you, Bro...I mean, I've tried to."

"You know what you are?" George said, without bitterness. "You're the eye of a hurricane: everywhere you walk, it's seventy-five and sunny. The whole time I was walking next you? Trying to keep up? I was just stuck out in the storm." He opened the door and looked at his watch. "Oh, shit. I'll see you up there."

George launched himself down the hallway—a mediocre, over-caffeinated superhero, who upon crashing into a railing, issued an indignant curse and then ascended the fire escape shaft.

J.D. waited for the security door to completely re-close. Once it did, he took out his vial and emptied it into the hatchway.

The elevator, he discovered moments later, was in use, and since he did not want to be spotted creeping out of an unfrequented stairwell, he gave up an additional two minutes waiting for the doors to open. He then stepped in, pushed L, and repeatedly pressed the *door close* button. He took out his lighter and checked the time; it was 9:58. When he reached the lobby, he took out one of Mrs. Morgan's Salems and jammed it into his mouth.

The van was idling at the curb, just outside. J.D. strode toward the main entrance, and the glass doors slid open.

A cold hand gripped his shoulder and spun him around. "Let's go," Amon said, his thick fingers steering J.D. back toward the elevator. "You can smoke and make calls after the briefing."

CHAPTER 31

UPON WALKING INTO THE C.E.O.'s office, J.D. saw, to his relief, that he was not the only one late for the meeting: there was no sign of George, nor of the C.F.O., nor the Marketing Director. Sytry was there, sitting in an old yellow sofa, drumming his fingers on the armrest; across from him sat Duke Bunet, perfectly upright with his palms resting on his knees. The C.E.O. stood in front of an old-school brewer, filling the last of three mugs.

"Have a seat." Amon gestured to one of two antique armchairs, between the sofas and the desk. J.D. sat. He tried not to visibly shiver. Amon shut the door and stood quietly, which caused J.D. to wonder if the others would be joining them at all.

Hall passed two filled mugs to Sytry and Bunet and kept the third for himself. "We're on a tight schedule, Mark," he told Amon. "Do you mind holding off?"

"I grabbed a little something earlier," Amon replied. J.D. looked back and saw the pitbull eyes staring down at him.

"Alright, let's get started." Hall stepped behind his desk. He reached down and lifted up an orange, plastic bucket, which he set down upon the antique cherry wood. "When BrewCorp first came to Inini Falls, we were offered a 10-year tax abatement; I declined it. We pay all of our municipal taxes, on top of which, we contribute generously to local campaigns. Do you know why that is?"

J.D. saw that Hall was addressing him. "No, I don't."

Hall raised his mug high over the bucket and turned it upside down, letting all of his Gilded Roast empty. "It's so that if a group of New Age socialists tries to bring the FBI down on us, we know in advance."

Sytry and Bunet stood, approached the bucket, and emptied their drinks.

Hall sat down. "What does it do? This contaminant of yours?"

Well played, Bro, J.D. thought. *Well played.* In spite of all that had soured between him and George, it still stung to discover that his oldest friend had set him up. He met Hall's gaze in silence.

Hall looked bewildered. "Why do you think that attacking this company will solve the problem?"

"It won't, Pence," Sytry assured, as he and Bunet returned to their seats.

"Son, you're suffering some kind of hero complex," Hall insisted. "You're letting your ego run wild just when you need to keep your head on most.

"Think what you're about to do: that SWAT team will get massacred; there will be panic; people will *die* for Chrissake. You don't seem to want to recognize those facts."

J.D.'s resolve waivered. He realized that he was like a pre-adolescent who insisted Santa Claus was real, and Hall was like the parent, reminding him that he was too old for make-believe.

"What is this really about with you?" Hall asked. "It's *not* about safeguarding the public." Notwithstanding his exasperation, he spoke with an unflappable modulation; his demeanor betrayed, at worst, mild annoyance that a subordinate could not grasp the obvious. The C.E.O. turned to his vice presidents, perhaps hoping that J.D. would, in the meantime, sort himself out. "Alright, let's assume it's down to the four of us."

Bunet was the first to speak. "Fewer mouths for the tit," he confidently professed.

Sytry countered, "We don't know what this contaminant does. Maybe it does something other than kill, and after the other V.P.s drink it, they're willing to take plea deals."

"Nothing can make *us* talk," Bunet boasted.

Sytry gave his colleague an impatient look. "What about the *old* us, Duke? Could something make *them* talk?"

Bunet opened his mouth, but unable to come up with an argument, he shut it.

"The *old* us?" Amon interjected. "That would be a fate worse than death."

The three vice presidents snickered, but Hall was not laughing. He asked Sytry, "Are you going to be able to manage this or not?"

Sytry sobered. "I need a day to clean up, then anyone can come in and look. The main thing is that van: my intel is those guys are rogue and dark; their regional Operations Manager is 45 minutes away. Now, we have *other* people *closer*, but then we're talking casualties." He shot J.D. a scolding glance and warned, "You'd be doing your friends out there a big favor by calling them off."

J.D. got up.

"Sit down," Amon ordered, but the C.E.O. held up a silencing palm.

"You got me, Billy," J.D. admitted. "I have an ego, it's true. But here's the thing: since you're so concerned about protecting everyone, why aren't *you* drinking? What is *that* really about? I mean, since your lifestyle is such a heavy burden…"

Incredulity appeared in the leathery eyes. "Is that a joke?" Hall asked. "Suppose, for argument's sake, you've taken out every single one of our customers today. What are you going to do about our overseas partners, for starters?" The C.E.O. leaned back in his chair, holding his hands out in front of him and moving them up and down for emphasis. "I'm negotiating with them to drop the old ways and adopt your system—introduce it into their own communities. You think they're going to do that for just anyone?" Little, gold mugs on his cuffs clinked against the edge of the desk. He curled his hands back toward his chest. "They know and trust *me*. *I'm* the only one who can make that happen. What do you imagine they'll do when they find out I've been shut down? Go on a vegan cleanse-?"

"No, no, no, Billy," J.D. interrupted, shaking his head. "You've been tackling your…we'll call it your change management problem, for what? Decades? Centuries? What do you have to show for all that time?" He paused, but no one jumped in. He looked around the room. None of the vice presidents liked what he was saying, yet all three were listening. He turned back to the C.E.O., whose untroubled veneer had shifted; in its place appeared the resentful look of a man who had expected to be thrown a birthday party but had instead found that he was being put on trial. J.D. acknowledged, "Compared to mass murder, then, yeah, ok: technically, you've made some headway. But that's a pretty low bar, don't you think? I mean, who are you to use people that way in the first place? You are literally sucking the life out of my city. What gives you the right?"

The C.E.O. spoke slowly, enunciating each word. "Unlike you and your friend, George, I *earned* my right to lead, and I made sacrifices to do it." The wrinkled mouth twitched. "You allege that I'm making everyone sick. Am I dragging them into our stores? Am I forcing them to apply for the discount?"

"Oh, come on, man!" J.D. cried. "I got myself one of those discounts; I had no idea what was going to happen on the other side of that door! Those people don't know what they're *doing!*"

Hall did not reply right away. He seemed to be struggling with a new, abstract concept. "'Don't know what they're *doing*?" He stood and examined J.D.'s face; his head shifted slightly, as if he were noticing, for the first time, an enormous, alarming mole. "'Don't know what they're *doing*?"

The C.E.O. came around his desk and stood face to face with J.D. "Those are grown *people*. You're a grown *man*. What kind of chickenshit is *this*?" His chapped lips curled up on one side. "Why, you...you all expect to be excused from every one of your bad decisions, is that it? Every home you can't afford? Every kid you didn't plan on? Every pet you can't take care of? Every loan agreement you can't be bothered to read through?"

Hall's eyes widened. "You know what? You disgust me—*all* of you spoiled ingrates!" He shrieked into J.D.'s face, "I *pay* for my mistakes! I gave up family! I gave up friends! I gave up breathing! *Breathing*, you little prick! *That's* what gives me the right! I made tough choices and raised myself up, out of the goddam riffraff!"

Wrestling his voice under control, the C.E.O. drew in closer to J.D. "Now listen to me very carefully. Whatever your reasons, you have opened a can of worms today and made a big mistake; you can either fix it, or you can turn your back and let all Hell break loose. What's it going to be?"

J.D. looked at the C.E.O.'s vacated chair and noted the darkened glass behind it. Perhaps he could send a signal to the van below; he would need to position himself. Regardless, his mind was made up. "I'll take my chances with the riffraff."

He turned to leave, and was glad that neither Hall nor any of the others reacted to his hands sliding into his trouser pockets. He was not surprised to find Amon blocking the door; he did not expect to be allowed out of the office. His left-pocket hand found the SWAT-issued, pressurized garlic sprayer.

"You think you can two-step your way around all the consequences, do you?" The C.E.O.'s voice caused J.D. to look back; the weather-beaten mouth had straightened, and the commanding eyes had lost their warm crinkle. Hall looked down his nose, as if examining a small insect. "Fine. Let's see you prove it." Hall looked over J.D.'s shoulder and called out, "Mark, why don't you get us set up for lunch?"

J.D. yanked out his sprayer, but his surprised hands dropped the canister as the ground fell away beneath him. Claws, which had wrapped themselves around his throat, kept him from crying out. He looked up, but all he could see were nearby ceiling panels.

An upside-down face appeared; it looked like it belonged to a giant Anglerfish. "I wissed why worning cowwee wecause o'you," the thing grumbled, its long, spike teeth garbling half the consonants; J.D. realized it was Amon. The transformed vice president twisted J.D. around to face him. "Now, I'ne starwing."

J.D. looked down; six feet below, Sytry and Bunet removed a roll of heavy plastic from a cabinet and unrolled a long, clear sheet across the desk and floor. Something was happening to their faces, but it was hard to see because they were both looking down.

The C.E.O. was looking up; his mouth, like Amon's, had grown impossibly wide, forced into a sardonic grin by rows of elongating, white tines; he stood at his desk, pulling a large, stained bib out from a drawer and fastening it to his neck.

This, J.D. realized, promised to be neither quick nor pain-less. Looking back up, he found nothing he could use to get free, only the maw of his grouchy captor and the surrounding, coffered ceiling. He tried to wriggle out of the chokehold, but it was no use; his vision began to darken.

Wow, I can see all the blood vessels in my eyes, J.D. noted, fascinated in spite of his circumstances. *They're right there, superimposed over Amon's head and one of my sprinklers. Oh wait. Sprinklers.*"

Sure enough, a fire sprinkler hung from the intersection of four coffers, just behind Amon's head.

J.D. realized that his right hand was still in his pocket; he pulled it out.

A flicking noise behind Amon caused him to turn. He was just in time to see the flame from the outstretched lighter melt the metal fuse. Simultaneously, all of the sprinklers in the room went off. The hovering vice president, who was surprised (and who, along with his colleagues, was temporarily blinded by the cosmetics running into his eyes), lost his grip.

J.D. landed hard on the desk; he rolled himself across the plastic-covered blotter and tumbled onto the floor.

He jumped to his feet.

Sytry went for his throat, but J.D. evaded the vice president's fumbling, slippery claws.

Beside J.D. sat Hall's heavy chair. He grasped it by the padded armrests, heaved it up, wheels out, and rammed it at the window. There was an explosion of glass, and sunlight poured into the room.

Hall, Sytry and Bunet cowered off to one side, pinned against a shaded patch of wall, their suits newly pinstriped with thick, flesh-colored streaks; they had shrunk back there the instant they realized what J.D. was going to do.

Amon, who had been hovering directly in front of the window, was not as fortunate; he burst into flames, and plunged to the sunlit floor. He crawled, snarling and whining, toward his colleagues, but his head and limbs, and finally his whole torso, collapsed into a trail of well-accoutered mud.

Through the window's gaping hole, J.D. could see the van below. There was no time for him to wait for doors to open and SWAT agents to clamor out: Hall was trying to lower the shutters; the C.E.O. tugged at the cord, pulling it this way and that (becoming a vampire did not, despite its many perks, appear to grant any special mastery over unruly window blinds).

J.D. rounded the far side of the desk and located his garlic sprayer: it was lying underneath the plastic; he pulled back the thick sheet and retrieved the canister.

He ran to the door; the knob would not turn.

Behind him came a soft sliding noise, like a fine saw moving slowly across soft wood; the room darkened as the blinds lowered; they came down halfway and became stuck, leaving the door in sun. Hall raised the shade slightly and worked the cord again.

J.D. turned the knob the other way; the door opened. He bolted out of the suite, through the reception room (no sign of Maddy, who was rumored to be taking some personal time), past the coffee cup fountain, and past the rows of offices.

CHAPTER 32

SPRINKLERS INUNDATED J.D. FROM all directions. As he ran through the floor, he noticed some of the secretaries scurrying toward the elevators and stairs; others continued to work, some holding soggy folders and papers over their heads and trying to ignore the monotone blare of the building-wide fire alarm.

J.D. saw John Fourneus, one of the meeting's absentees, standing on top of his desk, twisting and crushing nearby ceiling sprinklers with one hand and keeping his raised mug level with the other; underneath the desk, Mike Ballum, another absentee, huddled, enjoying a cup of his own.

Somewhere behind J.D., someone cried out, "Holy shit!"

Risking a look back, he saw Hall, Bunet and Sytry rocketing past Sytry's secretary, who had unleashed the expletive on the phone. Her surprise at seeing three superiors looking like fang-toothed monsters, and defying gravity, was understandable; nevertheless, she informed her caller, "I can't tell you; we signed a confidentiality agreement."

J.D. raced toward the fire escape, overtaking other fleeing employees; he felt his back grow colder.

He scrambled through the door but slipped, feet-first, falling—nearly careening—off of the landing: the stairwell sprinklers had made the polished concrete utterly slick. J.D. improvised the quickest descent that he imagined he could survive: he straightened his body and cradled the back of his head in his hands (one made into a fist, clutching the garlic sprayer, the other an open palm); he back-surfed down the first half flight of steps and sailed across the landing below, slamming into a wall.

The door above opened, and he heard footsteps, accompanied by the murmurs of confused BrewCorp employees.

A growling voice ordered, "Get wack to work—*all* o'you!" The commotion ceased, and the footsteps hastily retreated. The door closed.

J.D. heard two new sets of footsteps: measured splashes, unimpeded by slippery concrete. He launched himself down the next set of steps and crashed into another wall.

For five stories, J.D. used himself as a human pinball; throughout the unrelenting ride, wetness, dimness, coldness, and closeness all did their work, and by the time his soggy shoes skated across the ground floor landing, he had become clumsy with panic.

He tried to stand, but his soles had no traction—they might as well have been roller blades. He tried pushing himself closer to the exit door, but even his frenzied hands seemed to lack the necessary purchase. The more his palms slipped around the landing's frictionless surface, the more desperate he grew.

As he inched toward the door's push-bar, he looked up, seeking assurance that he was not about to be torn to pieces. What he should have done instead, he realized, was gone straight for the push-bar, but it was too late: Hall and Bunet were standing over him.

The C.E.O.'s outstretched claws grabbed J.D. by the neck, which was already raw from Amon's grip; it felt like being stung by five large wasps. "How dare you!" the rotted monster-head

demanded. "You little wastard, *I* an the highest! How dare you dewhy wee!"

J.D. lifted his garlic canister and sprayed Hall square in the face. A plume of red steam blossomed forth. The C.E.O. howled and let go, throwing up his arms as a shield and blindly knocking Bunet out of the way; he withdrew to an overhead sprinkler and stood under the water, indignantly shaking his fists at J.D., waiting for the garlic to rinse off.

J.D. lurched for the push-bar but missed and accidently propelled himself off of the unyielding door, across the landing, and down the next half flight. This unintended maneuver, which slipped him into a face-down position, inflicted new beatings, mostly on his knees, testicles, and stomach.

Sliding across the next half-landing, J.D. rearranged his body face-up and pushed himself down what he prayed would be his last set of steps. Since he was below ground, he would no longer have any direct route out of the building. His only hope was that an elevator might be waiting on B1. He coasted into the middle of the B1 landing and bumped into something; he pushed off of it with his feet and glided back to the railing. Grabbing the metal support next to his head, J.D. pulled himself up into a crouch and wiped the water out of his eyes; he squinted at the obstacle.

It was Sytry. The vice president had somehow gotten ahead of him and was blocking the door. Sytry took a step toward J.D. but stopped; he looked up.

J.D. could hear it as well: muffled shouting and gunfire, reverberating throughout the stairwell.

Sytry's hesitation gave him just enough time to climb over the railing. Since the building foundation was the next floor down, and since there were really no other options left, he dropped into the stairwell core.

His ankle hit hard, and he rolled onto his side. He had landed in complete darkness, on the lowest level of the building. The only other time he had been down here had been during the installation of the pump. Nearly all of the fluorescent lights, which worked during that previous visit, had since shorted.

J.D. surmised that his punch list request for high-efficiency T8 ballasts and bulbs had gone partially ignored. Indeed, during the construction, he had noticed a stockpile of obsolete, T12 bulbs, stacked in the contractor's work area; he was now glad that he had been too busy at the time to say anything: the older tubes had apparently been used with the new fixtures, and as a result they now offered J.D. the potential cover of darkness.

The moment J.D. looked up into the stairwell, however, he lost hope: one by one, three pairs of fiery eyes appeared, with grinning, red tines glistening beneath each; one of the jack-o-lantern faces was staring straight at him. It drifted out, into the stairwell core. The other two faces stayed put and looked up; the sounds of fighting were getting louder.

"I should take care o'that," Bunet's voice whispered.

"Go," growled the hovering face. "And, Duke? We're deh... we're deh...deh..." He seemed to be having trouble forming his P's. "We're counting on you."

One face shot up, out of sight.

"Dick," said the face hovering in the stairwell, "you're with we."

"Willy, there's no woint, anywore. We should get out o'here."

"I SAID *YOU'RE WITH WE!*"

The remaining face hesitated a moment but then floated over to its twin. The two jack-o-lanterns descended toward J.D.

He looked around. A solitary flickering tube illuminated the far end of a hallway. He understood why the contractor had elected to short change him here: there was nothing worth seeing—just a fire door and console, installed to protect the pump room above, and a dead-end hallway that terminated in a spare janitorial closet.

The blinking fixture disappeared behind the lowering fire door.

J.D. used his feet to feel around in the darkness; he found the bottom step and pushed off of it, sliding himself toward the dwindling light. He skidded onto the hallway floor and came to a stop; the concrete had become rougher. He tried to stand and found that his grip had improved. Favoring his ankle, which burned every time he put weight on it, he hobbled down the passage.

He glanced back. The floating eyes and maws were drifting into the hallway, a pair of faces and torsos resolving from the darkness. The C.E.O. and Sytry accelerated toward J.D.

He limped faster.

He turned and looked ahead; he was just in time to avoid crashing into the half-closed fire door. He ducked under it and lopsidedly ran to the janitor's closet. He took out his key ring and, ignoring the pump room key, grasped its smaller, silver brother, inserting it into the lock.

"Don't owen that, you little wastard!" Hall warned.

J.D. twisted the knob and yanked open the door. All of the executives had master keys, and therefore he could not barricade himself within; he merely hoped to find a broomstick or a mop, something with which he could defend himself.

There were no such supplies inside; what he found instead was so unexpected that he momentarily forgot he was being chased.

The collection was the work of either a museum curator or a pathological hoarder: there were mounds of soiled liberty pennies, phonograph cylinders (some melted, as if burned), dilapidated rocking horses (wood and horse hair, with glass eyes), varnished silverware, faded cans of food (Clark's Ox Tail Soup, Squaw Brand Choice Sifted Peas), and antique baby cribs.

In the midst of it all lay the most garish funerary display J.D. had ever seen: behind velvet ropes, a gold coffin rested upon an inclined slab, which propped it above the clutter; a large flag was wrapped around the bottom half (BrewCorp, in blue and green letters, set against an emerald background). There was no lid covering the garlanded casket. A president, king, or general should have been lying there, in state; it was empty, which was just as well: the missing deceased had obviously chosen such an ironic location for his grand repose in order to elude visitors.

"I said get away ruh why things!" boomed a voice from above.

J.D. looked up and saw Hall circling over him, like some airborne shark.

It was time, J.D. decided, to rethink his strategy. During his young life, he had pulled off a good many contrivances and gotten away clean; he did not like getting caught, and he definitely did not like being cornered by demons in the midst of a waking nightmare. It bothered him so much, he realized, that in trying to avoid it, he had lost his cool; the impulse to escape, though seemingly sensible, had actually been leading him closer to doom. No, he concluded, it was time to make a change. The recollection of a phone call, from months before, popped into his head: there had been that loud scuffle in the executive conference room—something about the brewer not working.

Sytry had now flown into the supply closet and was staring at the coffin. "Gold." He nodded bitterly, looking at Hall. "You gae yoursel gold."

"I'ne the C.E.O., Dick," Hall answered, a touch defensively.

"That why you slashed why trawel and entertainwent wudget?" Sytry accused. "You said, 'We all need to tighten our welts!'"

"Not now, Dick!"

A loud metallic rattle interrupted the quarrel, as the fire door met the floor.

Hall landed in front of J.D. and leered into his face. "Where's your entitlewent now, you uhwitty little shit?" he spat. "Now that you got yoursel good and stuck in here! With we!"

"You know, Billy," J.D. answered, "I don't think you really do deserve that gold coffin; you don't think strategically. The console that opens that door? It's on the other side. So actually, *you're* stuck in here with *me*." He looked up at Sytry. "*Both* of you."

The C.E.O. rolled out his sucker-tongue, which seemed to sniff at J.D.'s neck, but Sytry, who had fully grasped J.D.'s words, warned, "No, Willy! We watient; the weat will cuh to us!" His worried expression gave J.D. a glimmer of encouragement.

Hall ignored Sytry and reached for J.D.'s neck.

Sytry dove headlong toward his boss, tackling him. "Don't do it!" he admonished, struggling to pin Hall to the ground. "Just wait and let those Weds get the door owen, then we'll weast on the whole lot!"

J.D. backed away from the executives and edged around the coffin. He would have preferred to put more space between himself and them, but there was no time: Hall and Sytry had stopped struggling; they were watching him; he knew that this would be his last chance to act. He drew the empty vial from his pocket and smashed it against the coffin; the end broke off, leaving him holding a jagged edge. He drew back a shirt sleeve.

"What are you doing?" Hall demanded.

J.D. brought the glass down on his exposed forearm and let the slashed limb drop to his side.

CHAPTER 33

FROM UNDER HIS HIDING place, George watched Cerri lead armed men out of the elevator.

As soon as the sprinklers started, he had lodged himself between the inside front of a desk and the knees of an entranced secretary. He had seen Hall, Sytry and Bunet chase J.D. to the stairwell; he had observed Sytry pry open an elevator's doors and leap into the empty shaft; and he had watched the other two go into the stairwell.

His superiors' desperate behavior had made him anxious enough, but when he saw Cerri arrive with a SWAT team, he realized that everything was falling apart: Gilded Roast was no longer safe to drink, his hopes of finding cover from the sun and getting out of the building were dashed, and he was trapped, with a former dating prospect leading seven, armored, stake-wielding varsity athletes straight for him.

Things looked only marginally better when, at the last second, the detachment veered past, into Fourneus's office.

"What are you little, mortal, *fucks* going to do to me? Huh?" Fourneus dared, from on top his desk—he had disabled his sprinklers, and was touching up his makeup when the men had burst in on him. They drew what looked like pepper spray canisters.

Fourneus dropped his cosmetics jar and coffee mug (nothing spilling out, because the poor bastard had never been advised not to drink). He raised his arms and turned to face the window. It looked to George like he was planning to make a daytime flight.

One of the men, probably the leader, looked at the shattered mug on the desk. "Sir, do *not* try to fly!" It sounded more like personal advice than an order.

"I'm a BrewCorp V.P.," Fourneus proclaimed. "I can do whatever the *fuck* I please!" Fourneus launched himself through the window and flew. By George's estimation, he travelled ten feet; then his horizontal glide stalled into a nosedive, and his haughty exclamation became a frustrated yell; he fell out of view, and his yell, which after a series of short "No"s turned into a disbelieving scream, terminated with a distant thud.

Mike Ballum sprang from underneath the desk and tried to bite the SWAT leader's neck; a couple of agents forced him down and cuffed him, but he kept snapping at them with his mouthful of small, stupid teeth and sticking out his small, stupid tongue. He looked like some delusional idiot from a Blake Edwards comedy who belonged in a straightjacket.

So, it was true. George had hoped that Hall's concerns were groundless, that for once his fate was beyond J.D.'s control, but he saw that it was not.

He stared at his hands. Blackened patches of opaque cellophane, like the shrunken skin of a bog body, appeared where the sprinklers had hit; even the flesh that was still protected was wrinkling. Stress had this effect. What he needed was a small, guilt-free pick-me-up, but there would be no more of those—not now.

He heard a noise, a latch retracting. Cerri and the G-men, who were escorting Ballum to the C.E.O.'s office, were too far away to hear it; someone was quietly opening a door. He shifted to the other corner under the desk to see who it was. He recognized the bald head peering out from the stairwell. It was Duke Bunet, who opened the door wider and observed the receding SWAT team.

"Clear!" came a voice at the far end of the floor.

George shifted back to his original position. He saw a G-man emerge from the C.E.O.'s office and join his team.

"That means we've lost four targets," the SWAT leader said. "They might have been tipped off."

Cerri warned him, "They have J.D.!"

"*Oh, no...They have J.D.,*" George mocked under his breath. "*J.D., J.D., J.D.*" In spite of the need for silence, he could not stop himself; in a higher, softer tone, he whispered, "*They have George! They have George! They have George! They have G-!*" He shook his head in resignation. "Doesn't even have the right ring."

There was a blur, accompanied by a rush of wind: Bunet was hurtling through the air, toward the backs of the unsuspecting SWAT team members. The blur seemed to pass right through one of the men; there was a mess of purple sphagetti, and the man folded into two halves.

The group scattered; there was a shouting of commands.

Bunet reappeared in front of the C.E.O.'s office, hovering there, licking his claws.

The men sent streams of spray at him.

He was too fast; he accelerated back toward George. On the way there, he flew over another of the men, and the man's head disappeared; in its place sprang a pulsating fountain of red, from the neck up; the body dropped to its side.

George could no longer see Bunet, who must have flown somewhere behind him; Cerri was pointing somewhere above his hiding place, yelling, "Shoot the windows!"

The SWAT team drew their handguns and fired, but there was no shattering of glass. There was another burst of wind, and George realized they were shooting at Bunet, who must have swung around for another run. One of the men ran forward from the others and knelt, aiming his gun high.

Bunet swooped into view.

A shot rang out; Bunet flinched as if hit, but he did not slow down. He side swiped the shooter and sent him spinning; the gun fell, and the man staggered: his hands were gone.

"No! The windows!" Cerri demanded. "Shoot them out! Now!" She grabbed the fallen gun and pointed it at a row of clerestory windows, which ran along the wall above the offices; she fired.

Sparkling glass rained down, and sunlight poured into the middle of the floor.

Bunet had already blown past.

The SWAT leader followed Cerri's aim.

George thought, *She was never this sure of herself in Comparative Lit. So, getting picked up by J.D. in a public restroom is good for self-esteem.*

By now, the rest of the men were following Cerri's aim, shooting out window after window, but each time they were too late. George envied his colleague's speed. Bunet bore down upon the SWAT leader, who had so fully committed himself to Cerri's strategy that he had left himself no time or space to do anything else; his tactic had obviously failed, and now Bunet was about to bore through him.

The leader turned his head away, in apparent resignation, but then he fired off a round. The window immediately next to him blew out, and Bunet burst into flame; he slammed into the man, whom he knocked across the room, out of the sun.

ANDREW MONTLACK

The SWAT leader put Bunet into a headlock; the two of them cried out from the smoldering skin and fabric. One of the other agents blew out the window directly above the combusting wrestlers; that finished it.

George did not linger to watch Bunet's gruesome dissolution; the fact of it was sufficient to make him clamber over the secretary's lap and run for the stairwell. He had to do it now, while Cerri and the others were tending to their leader's burns; if he did not, he saw what they would do. The world was, truly this time, out to get him.

He opened the fire escape door and crept into the darkness. He had no plan for getting out of the building, nor for protecting his skin, which the overhead sprinklers had completely deprived of sunscreen; his only goal was avoidance.

There were shouts below. "Get me out of here, Ed!"

"Stay calm, I'm going to get you out."

"Before it comes back!"

A noise caused George to look up. There, in the ceiling, he saw them: bright red eyes and a smiling mouth, full of shiny metal. He heard the noise again: a deep, animal exhalation, like a horse snort. The eyes and mouth fell.

"Oh dear God! Not again!"

In order to see better, George removed his lenses, which no longer served any purpose. He looked down and saw a gray, featureless space, with no textures—just gray railings and gray figures. The only gradations came from glowing orbs that pulsated in each man's chest. Two frightened men were trying to fend off the assailant; one was lying across the landing, injured; the other was firing his sprayer into the air.

A door opened far below, and a third man entered. *Supply support*, George surmised, judging by the three extra canisters the man carried; he wore the same heavy riot gear, mask and helmet as his friends. *In fact*, George noted, *every inch of his skin is covered.*

George saw his means of escape. He would have to be quick and quiet. He rose a few inches off of the floor and floated down the steps.

CHAPTER 34

BLOOD RAN FREELY DOWN J.D.'s arm and dripped through his fingers. Hall let out a gasp; Sytry, who was still on top of the C.E.O., gasped as well. Their red eyes seemed to roll back in their heads and turn to black.

Hall rose up—or rather, he spun up; his body toppling Sytry as it whirled, both width wise and height wise. His proboscis lashed wildly back and forth. He flew at J.D. Even from a distance, J.D. could feel the suction; Hall's approaching feeder pulled the blood off of his arm in sinewy lines.

The C.E.O. slowed to a hover in front of him, but before the sucker could affix itself to the wound, Sytry pivoted into the air, as if propelled by an invisible catapult, and rammed into Hall, sending him crashing into a pile of photographic plates.

J.D. felt a new stabbing sensation in his arm; he looked down and screamed; Sytry's sucker had fastened itself to the wound; the vice president's razor teeth were poised over the surrounding flesh.

Sytry's maw snapped shut, and red spattered J.D. in the face. The evisceration should have caused J.D. excruciating pain, but it did not. Sytry's face jerked back ten feet. J.D. realized that his arm was still intact. Hall's head appeared behind Sytry's; the C.E.O. yanked him backwards, for a second time, and again Sytry's loosened proboscis flung a spray of red at J.D.

Hall dragged his claws across his lieutenant's face, spilling powder out of four long gashes.

J.D. felt himself pushed down by an invisible force, and Sytry, with Hall clinging onto him, rocketed into the air. The vice president smashed into the ceiling, back-first, and ground his C.E.O. into the concrete; Hall bit into Sytry's shoulder, and both of them fell; they separated just before hitting the ground, and Hall spit out a mawful of rotten meat.

The contest raged on and on, with one or the other titan checking his competitor at the last second. The room, and nearly everything in it, was getting torn apart. It was all J.D. could do to scoot himself into a corner and kick frantically whenever a grasping claw or ravenous maw came too.

The standoff ended with Hall body-slamming Sytry into a crib. The vice president's impact smashed the wooden antique to pieces. Sytry swiped up one of the splintered ballisters and flew at the C.E.O., driving it all the way through his chest. Hall dropped to the ground and landed on his side, at J.D.'s feet. His glowing eyes were closed, and his maw was slack.

Sytry looked uncertainly from the skewered C.E.O. to J.D., like a dog trying to choose between a car and a mailman. He landed in front of Hall's lifeless frame and eyed the implanted spear. He took a tentative step forward; then another, and then another. He was walking, literally, over his boss's dead body; he paused between the sprawled shins and worked up some phlegm. Sytry opened his maw to spit.

He never knew what hit him: Hall tilted into a standing position, grabbed the vice president's surprised face in both claws and clamped down on his neck.

J.D. watched Sytry's eyes dim, and his struggling limbs droop, and he felt the temperature plummet. A mechanical knocking, like an off-balance, over filled washing machine, boomed overhead. J.D. noticed that a coffee delivery pipe, which ran along the wall next to Hall, was frosting over.

What he could not see was the smoke billowing from his compressors; he could not see the blockage of flash-frozen product causing his pump to fail; he could not see store brewers sputtering and stopping; he could not see three distracted basement technicians pounding irritably on one of the intake tanks; and he could not see, amidst suddenly-lucid discount applicants, a groggy soccer mom yanking the needle from her arm, helping her little boy off of a slab, and concluding, "You know what? We don't really need a third, movie-optimized tablet today."

The C.E.O. released Sytry, who collapsed with a dull thud. "You wissed, Dick," he said, pulling the wood from his chest; indeed the hole, which was even now closing, was several inches to the right of Hall's heart.

J.D. saw something happening underneath the C.E.O.'s suit: Hall's shoulder blades seemed to be growing, straining against the gray, pinstriped fabric. There was a tearing sound, and two, translucent tubes, with pointy tips, appeared; they must have been razor-sharp, for they sliced a pair of slits as they pushed through the back of the jacket; once fully extended, they unfurled into narrow, veiny wings, each one as long as Hall was tall.

The C.E.O. hunched over. More appendages tore through the front of his suit. These did not unfold but lengthened into six, segmented legs. A pair of antennae burst from the top of his head.

Sytry groaned.

"I'ne sorry, Dick," the transformed C.E.O. told his incapacitated lieutenant, "You can't wossilly understand now, wut suhday you will: I'ne always acting in the cowany's west interest."

Hall turned himself around, his six, new, spindly legs clicking unevenly against the cluttered floor and making a sound like tap dancing. J.D. found himself looking into a pair of bright red, bulging insect eyes. He wanted to look away but could not move.

The "Hallsquito," as he now thought of his former employer, crawled toward him. The C.E.O.'s proboscis reared up, like an angry cobra preparing to strike at his neck, but it hesitated.

The red bulb-eyes narrowed, and the C.E.O. gazed deeply into J.D.'s face. What he saw there caused the appendage to withdraw. "You were right awout this one, though, Dick," the C.E.O. realized. "Wetter to let hin go." The insect eyes drew close to J.D. "Lye's got suhthing worse in store wor you, and I'ne going to enjoy watching."

Before J.D. could puzzle over the words, a rattle from the hallway announced that the fire door was reopening. The C.E.O. rearranged himself around to face the retracting metal; his wings fluttered, creating a stale, icy breeze.

Beyond the door stood a pair of black, spiked boots, flanked by two pairs of combat fatigues. There were spray canisters, long stakes, neck plates, and finally, goggles and helmets. Cerri stood between the agent operating the fire console and another man, whose gear was melted and singed in a number of places; there was no one else.

The wings beat faster; a deep buzzing filled the supply closet.

The man at the fire console uttered a loud curse. J.D. recognized the other agent: Commander Warren; he was the burnt man with the furrowed brow—the man who hopefully had a strategy for engaging a giant mosquito in an Armani suit.

"Ready countermeasures!" the commander ordered, his breath becoming visible. He knelt in front of the fire console and pulled out his long stake, bracing it against the floor. The other agent moved in front of Cerri and raised his spray canister.

The Hallsquito took off, kicking up a thick dust that smelled like a hundred years of buried cat piss. He flew toward the men, in a zig-zagging, flitting type of flight that made him nearly impossible to target.

The agent at the console released a high-powered stream; he managed to briefly hit the C.E.O.'s face, which ejected a cloud of smoke, but the Hallsquito darted out of the way and kept coming. The spray ceased, and the SWAT agent let out another curse; his canister had frosted over.

CHAPTER 35

THE HALLSQUITO CAME STRAIGHT at agent Warren. The commander closed his eyes and mouthed what had to be a prayer.

The C.E.O.'s maw opened wide, and his proboscis shot out.

Then he dropped out of flight. At first it looked like a feint, intended to dodge below the commander's stake, but then the C.E.O.'s wings began sizzling and pruning. They disintegrated into a pile of ash. Hall howled, skidding to a stop at Warren's feet. The spike teeth fell from the C.E.O.'s mouth, his eyes shrank, fading from bright red to an unexceptional blue, and his proboscis withered and crumbled. "What is this?" stammered a perfectly ordinary looking old man.

"Damn! Damn!" All eyes turned to Sytry, whose appearance also had reverted.

"Dick," Hall asked, impatiently, "what's going on?"

"What's going on is we're back in the riff raff," Sytry tonelessly reported. "That's what's going on."

"But I didn't drink today!"

"Really?" Sytry pointed at his neck, where a patch of pink new skin had formed.

"I didn't drink any of the Gilded Roast, and neither did you."

Sytry pulled a small, shiny cask from his inner pocket and unscrewed the cap. He turned it over; coffee poured out, onto the floor.

"Dick, what are you saying?" Hall looked even more confused than before. "You've been double dipping?"

"I thought you were bullshitting about the product being contaminated, hoping we would flush the pipeline so you could keep all the runoff for yourself."

Commander Warren nodded to his subordinate; the pair moved into the room. Cerri, who saw that J.D. was bleeding, went over and used her belt as a tourniquet.

"You've been double dipping?" Hall repeated, as Warren cuffed him. "How? It's not possible. All the dispensers have cut-offs."

Sytry, who was also getting cuffed, sighed. "Do you really think no one knows you hacked yours? Mark's doesn't cut off either; I convinced him to keep quiet about it. He was *not* a tough sell."

"Who else?" Hall demanded. "Who else is stealing from me?"

Sytry let out a humorless snort. "I'll give you a hint: they get all the blame, while you take the credit." Seeing that this did not jog the C.E.O.'s mind, he spelled out, "All of us, Billy—all of your people: Duke, Mike, John, G.L.

Hall looked on his lieutenant with disbelief. "Mike?"

"Yes, Mike."

The C.E.O. seemed to turn inward; when his stunned eyes refocused on the vice president, they looked emotionless. "I have nothing more to say, to any of you." He lifted the side of his head from the concrete floor and turned it the other way.

"I think maybe you already knew about G.L.," Sytry retorted, raising his voice. "Maybe that's why you instructed me to, quote, 'make an example of him, and be thorough about it.'"

Hall turned his head back. "I have no idea what you're talking about—and for Chrissake, Dick, button it until counsel gets here!"

CHAPTER 36

THE FAR END OF the parking lot was in chaos: firetrucks and ambulances, with stylish logos (*Inini Falls Emergency Services— Safety Is First*), were jackknifed at the main entrance, where hundreds of drenched employees were shuffling about and trying to use their phones; three news vehicles had converged behind the EMS trucks and vomited reporters, cameramen, and makeup assistants onto the pavement. The reporters were trying to talk to the first responders; the first responders were ignoring them and instead arguing with the perimeter SWAT team.

J.D. witnessed these initial, distant aftershocks from the rear loading dock, having followed the SWAT commander, his agent, and the two arrestees, out onto it. Cerri, who had insisted he keep his wound raised, placed his arm around her shoulder and supported his bad ankle while he peered around the edge of the building.

When J.D. turned around he saw two perimeter agents at the other end of the dock. They had apparently crept along the landscaped side of the building, where no vehicle could easily follow. One of them carried a first aid kit; he came straight over and began wrapping J.D.'s arm.

The other agent consulted a small piece of notebook paper. "All targets are accounted for, sir," he reported to Commander Warren. "We're holding two in the van. I've got three kills: Mr. Pence took out Amon in the C.E.O.'s office; you took out Bunet; and Fourneus"—he pointed to a spot behind him; the executive lay there, face-down, mushroomed against the asphault—"took himself out."

"Thank you, Castillo." The commander looked around the side of the building. "Let's bring the van back here for expedited extraction."

"On my way." The agent tore up the paper and began walking.

"Wait a minute," J.D. called after him.

"Hold it, Castillo," the commander seconded; the agent stopped and turned.

"What about George Unger?" J.D. asked.

Castillo nodded. "Got him in the stairwell. He's in our custody."

"Can I see him?"

"That'll do," Warren told Castillo, who disappeared around the corner. "There's no time," the commander told J.D. "As soon as those news crews see our van moving, they're going to forget all about the employees in front and follow it back here." The commander then instructed, "Before they *get* here, you and Ms. Morgan are going to run around that side"—he pointed after Castillo—"and when you reach the front entrance, you're going to mingle with the evacuees for a minute or so and then get into Ms. Morgan's car: you're just a couple of dazed, wet employees, going home to change into something dry.

"You will leave your own vehicle here, and *you*"—he turned to Cerri—"will drive him straight to your house. You will both remain there until you hear from me, personally. Is that clear?"

"Crystal," Cerri agreed.

J.D. wanted to press the commander; he wanted to see that George was alright; if he was being honest with himself, he probably wanted to tell his friend how sorry he was for the way things had worked out and to beg forgiveness, but he recognized the urgent need—for the sake of everyone involved in the operation—to get away quickly and anonymously. He unrolled his sleeve, so that it covered his bandage, and buttoned the cuff.

Reaching the front of the building, J.D. and Cerri waded into the center of the crowd, and away from any EMS uniforms. As they neared Cerri's car, they saw a fire marshal standing next to it; he was arguing with Agent Castillo.

"You're not hearing me," J.D. heard the impeccably-dressed city official insist. "We have to go in and check it out. Brew-Corp-" He lowered his voice and shared something that J.D. could not make out.

"For all of it?" Castillo asked. "Directly?" the SWAT agent looked astonished. "The radios? The vehicles? The uniforms?" He noticed J.D. and Cerri moving out of the official's line of site; he took a few steps back from Cerri's car.

The fire marshal shifted as well, while confirming, "Everything but payroll."

J.D. and Cerri snuck behind the fire marshal and climbed into the car; J.D. gave Castillo grateful smile.

"Do you have an eBay account?" the agent suggested to the fire marshal. "I'd get one." Castillo rubbed his eye as though clearing a speck of dirt. J.D. realized that he was winking at them.

FOR THREE DAYS AND nights, J.D. and Cerri remained seques-
tered in the Morgan home. The house was cozy under most
other circumstances, but under these ones it was stifling. Reek-
ing garlic wards, which Mrs. Morgan had strung throughout,
amplified the creepy sense that some nebulous, old-world
nightmare was waiting just outside, trying to pour in through
the cracks.

Television and the internet offered no diversions, since
J.D. and Cerri combed broadcast and web media at all hours
for local news of neck bitings and bizarre deaths. There were
no reports of strange casualties; there was no news of any
kind, other than a single, brief preview that aired on the first
afternoon ("Area BrewMart stores are dark after a mysterious
federal raid, story at six"); the story never ran—not at six; not
at ten; nor did anything run on any of the national or cable networks (a *Breaking News* banner interrupted one of the national
broadcasts, but it turned out that a teen rock star had been
sentenced for his third DUI).

On the fourth afternoon, Commander Warren came by
and informed them that they could get on with their lives. He
would not volunteer any specifics about the outcome of the
operation ("the less you know, the better"), but when pressed,
he assured J.D. of George's wellbeing: a preparatory facility for
informants would be doubling as a halfway house for recovering vampires (George and his bosses would, the commander
predicted, be allowed back into society as soon as they could
competently behave like empathetic human beings).

J.D. and Cerri, keen to celebrate their freedom, walked to
the pizza shop, but the aftermath of BrewCorp was everywhere; they could not go more than a block without hearing
hostile remarks about the anonymous whistleblower who had
just destroyed the town's economy.

By the end of the week, they noticed utility poles and bill-boards marked with the word *Coward*, in yellow spray-paint.

Hoping to find relief from the simmering anger, they drove out to the farm but found the barn's World War II rationing mural disfigured (the slogan above the cheerful, coffee-toast-ing serviceman now read, "*Wake Up, Drink a Cup, and Shut the Fuck Up*").

After another week, Cerri practically had to drag J.D. out of the house; she nagged, and comforted, and coaxed, and negotiated, and pulled, and even kicked. She did this calmly and brightly, the way a mother would with an anxious child on his first day of school.

When J.D. went out with her, she would stand with him at the unemployment office, or sit with him at the sec-ond-run movie house (popcorn, courtesy of Mrs. Morgan's 30-year-old, twist-knob microwave). Each time the inevita-ble, angry proclamation of civic traitorship was overheard, Cerri would take J.D.'s clenched hand or rub the back of his tensed neck.

SHE HELPED HIM MOVE his things out of the apartment. He rewired her basement and setup his computer and work-bench.

Mondays through Thursdays became job-hunting days; Friday evenings were for sabbat and circuit bending; Saturday nights were date nights, and Sundays were family dinners, during which Mrs. Morgan regularly suggested ways in which J.D. might mend bridges with his father.

Guilt and fear still intruded into J.D.'s thoughts, often without warning, but they gradually became less intense;

J.D. grew accustomed to them, the way a person walking far in the rain grows accustomed to soggy shoes.

He began to make room for other things.

CHAPTER 37

"I WANT TO SHOW you something." J.D. led Cerri over the property fence and into the clearing, where red and brown leaves rustled in the trees and blew up from the ground. The angry wind was typical of late October in Middlestop; the long Indian summer was not. "This is my favorite place in the world."

The dusk sky was still red enough to offer Cerri a good view of her surroundings. "Can I ask you something?"

J.D. raised his head, expectantly.

"Are you homeless?"

"Nice."

"I had to."

J.D. entered the grove and saw that construction fencing and torn earth had finally invaded the edges. He walked up to the Property of BrewCorp sign and kicked it; the wooden post snapped and toppled over, bringing down a section of the orange plastic with it. He stepped over.

Cerri followed him through a thicket of tall, wide trees, and into the central patch of earth; all that remained of the clubhouse was the carpeting, which had merged into the soil. "What's this?"

"Forget it."

"Come on, don't be that way. What is it?"

"So...when George and I were in fourth grade, this was our clubhouse."

For the first time in her life, Cerri had a giggling fit.

"Ok, we're done here." J.D. turned and walked out.

"I'm sorry." Cerri tried to stifle her laughter.

"You know, I've never told parents or girlfriends, or anybody, about this place."

"Ok. Come back. It's just sweet."

J.D., who could hear the smile in her voice, decided it was time to take the box out of his pocket and open it. The ring, according to Mrs. Morgan, had belonged to Cerri's great-great-grandmother. J.D. had been carrying it with him during the two weeks since he had picked it up from the jeweler. To pay for the new stone, he had accepted an offer of consulting work from Commander Warren, who was impressed with his handling of Hall and Sytry and was actively recruiting talent for a brand new division he dubbed "Natural Law Enforcement."

Cerri stopped smiling; her mouth hung open.

J.D. got down on one knee and held out the ring. "Cerridwen Morgan, will you please be my best friend for life?"

She did not say anything but gaped from the ring to J.D. A leaf landed in her hair.

His leg started to cramp.

"I gotta pee," she finally said.

"Right now?"

"Yep." She trudged back through the tree line, leaving J.D. kneeling there, in the middle of the clearing, looking like a ridiculous statue. He tried to remain that way until she returned.

He might have succeeded if it were not for the vibration in his pants. Getting to his feet, he took out his phone. *911* appeared on the display; it was Commander Warren. He took the call. "Hello?"

"Was any......man?" asked the garbled voice.

"Say again?"

"I've just...rived...afehouse; there's...inconsistent with...... Was.........man?"

"Can you hear me?" J.D. asked.

"...you hear me? Yes I can hear you. Can you hear me?"

"My reception's spotty. I can barely hear you."

"Was one of the...cutives...man? peat, was...executives... woman? Was one of...?"

"Was one of them a woman? No. No women. There were no women. Did you hear me?"

The call was dropped. J.D. checked the display; there was no reception, in spite of the fact that there were plenty of cell towers nearby. A shiver ran down his neck. "Cerri," he called, "I think we need to go."

There was no answer.

"Hey Cerri?" He started walking. He retraced their steps, crossing back over swirling leaves, back below swaying branches, back between venerable oak trunks. "Cerri?" He walked faster and faster.

He cleared the tree line and saw why she did not answer. It stood about twenty yards away, with its back to him: a mummified thing that wore tattered remnants of what had once been an expensive suit. Cerri was there, sinking into its tight embrace, her dazed head resting on one of the bony shoulders, and her pale neck straining under the pair of shriveled, gray lips.

J.D. burst into a run. He dashed over the collapsed fencing and swiped up the toppled signpost. He aimed the wooden tip at the back of the thing and let out a yell.

The thing was startled; it dropped Cerri to the ground and turned around. J.D. drove the sign into its heart. It gasped, its bloody proboscis retreating behind surprised lips, and its black eyes (dim, red pinprick pupils) turning white and hazel.

Waves of despair, natural and unnatural, washed over J.D. as he realized who it was. "No! No!!"

"What happened? What happened?" George asked, as if he had just been roughly wakened from a deep sleep.

"I-I-," J.D. stammered.

George tried to focus past the sign, which seemed to hover between his face and J.D.'s; his eyes followed the post down. "Oh, no. Not like this. Please, not like this."

"This can't be happening," J.D. insisted. "You're locked up. They caught you in the stairwell."

"That wasn't me," George said. "It was Maddy-" a convulsion shook his body; he seemed to recover. "Psycho bit me while I was in my box-" he seized again and hunched over. Whatever force had enabled George to stand, impaled on a five foot stake, and carry on a conversation, it was leaving him.

J.D. saw that George was going to collapse, and he caught him and laid him on his side.

Cerri sat up, dazed. "George?" She stood and began to go over to him but had to stop and crouch while her head cleared. George covered his face and tried to turn away from her, but the most movement his harpoon would allow was for him to look skyward.

"Don't let her look at me," he begged J.D.

J.D. went to Cerri's side, but she shook her head. "Go stay with him," she told him as she felt her throat. J.D. pulled her hand away and examined the wound. There was blood, but the bite was not deep.

ANDREW MONTLACK

"Is any of it his?" J.D. asked, not knowing what he would do if it was. "Did he make you drink anything?"

"No," George insisted, shaking his head. "I would never."

"No," Cerri reassured. She stood again, this time more steadily. "I'll just..." She looked from one to the other. "Yeah, I'm gonna go walk it off." She disappeared into the treeline.

"What did I do wrong?" George asked the stars.

J.D. sat beside him. "Nothing."

George shook his head. "I'm going to die." He started to shiver. He inclined his head up at the Property of BrewCorp sign. "I'm going to d-die as a s-sight gag."

"That's not your fault, it's mine," J.D. said; he meant it.

George looked from the protruding stake to J.D. "Don't take this the w-wrong way"—he paused to gasp, using his lungs for the first time in months—"but I d-don't think I sh-should have been f-friends with you."

J.D. nodded. "Do you wish you had it to do over?"

"No."

George's gray hands started to crumble; the same thing seemed to be happening under his flattening socks and trousers. "Oh no!" Soon, the trousers and sleeves had completely caved in, spilling ashes from every opening and creating a cloud of dust. "You have to tell my parents I'm Ok. M-Make something up."

"I'll say you embezzled from the company, ran off, and became the discount underwear king of South America. How's that?"

"Ok."

Quietly, helplessly, they watched George's torso flatten.

He told J.D., "I'm glad it was you."

J.D., who could think of nothing to say, nodded.

The remaining hair fell out of George's head, and his scalp peeled away. "Remember me, ok?"

It was hard for J.D. to get the words out; he tried to remain composed, but his quivering mouth refused to cooperate. "Always," he finally managed. "Always."

The sad and frightened eyes went, at last, and the ashes of George's face fell into his friend's lap. J.D. slouched over them, his stomach clenched to the point of pain, and watched them scatter.

From above, a soft voice promised, "I will too." He looked up. Cerri stood over him. She held out her hand. He took it and clasped it tightly.

EPILOGUE

"BEFORE WE START, I'D like to point out that our comptroller likes us," Mr. Barrel told his senior engineers. "He likes business; we have him to thank for today's food."

Applause erupted around the shiny conference table, where half-emptied martinis and scotches complimented dry-aged filets.

"It's time to deliver for him." Mr. Barrel tapped his laptop. The logo behind him (*Barrel & Barrel Development, LLC*) changed to a map of Greater Middlestop.

He got up from his seat at the head of the table and, with his laser pointer, traced the path of an animated overpass through several neighborhoods. "We need to demolish more than three dozen residences. There's going to be significant pushback, but we're a 'go.' Am I clear?"

There was a chorus of yesses.

Mr. Barrel looked unconvinced. "If anyone has a problem with this, and I'm talking about you, Pence, you socialist chickenshit"-he pointed at J.D., much to the other engineers' delight—"then now's the time."

J.D. ignored his colleagues' muffled snickers and silent smirks; he squinted at the map, following the path of the proposed highway. "Hey, wait a minute!" He jumped up from his seat and pointed at the screen. "That's my house!"

His performance met with approving laughter and more applause.

He opened his briefcase and began distributing a set of packets. "This is the digest of the new construction materials. The safety concerns are just more rhetorical bullshit from the community groups." J.D. held one of the packets out to Mr. Barrel, who with his typical impatience snatched it away, causing a protruding, heavy-grade staple to slice through J.D.'s thumb. He cursed under his breath. The cut was already bleeding onto the remaining packets. "Sorry, I'll be right back."

J.D. shoved his briefcase under one arm and, sucking the thumb, scurried out of the meeting. The men's room was just across the hall. J.D. set his briefcase down on the quartz countertop and pulled his wallet out of his back pocket. He opened it and removed a bandage.

As he struggled with the packaging, he became aware that the room was growing cold. Continuing to focus on the bandage, he casually announced, "You're under surveillance right now. Special agent Pence, Bureau of Natural Law Enforcement." For the benefit of the individual behind him, he nodded at the open wallet, where a shiny badge substantiated his claim. "My I.D."

J.D. parted the packaging, peeled the backing away from the bandage, and dressed his thumb. He looked in the mirror and was not surprised to see one of the firm's rising stars staring at his neck. He had been watching the junior partner—Marky to his peers and superiors, Mr. Marchokias to everyone else— ever since seeing plans for a series of turnkey, combination funeral homes and blood banks: Marchokias was listed as the architect of record.

"So, Marky," J.D. said, turning to face him, "you can't keep doing what you're doing. We can either administer an antidote, followed by six months of rehab and sensitivity training, or you can resist and end up in a coffin." Realizing that it had been a poor choice of words, he then added, "Uh...I mean permanently."

Marchokias's jaw and nose pushed forward from his irate face, and gray fur sprouted all over his skin.

J.D. turned toward the bank of bathroom stalls. "He's going public!"

Three of the doors swung inward, and Commander Warren and two of his agents came out with garlic sprayers raised. "On the ground, now!" the SWAT commander ordered.

The wolf-headed partner howled and drew back his ears, and an unseen force hurled Warren and his two lieutenants against the tile wall; all three were knocked unconscious.

Marchokias returned his attention to J.D.; he backed him into a corner. J.D. reached for his briefcase and clutched it to his chest, for dear life.

Marchokias howled, "I know about *youuu!* You think because you took down some candy-asses at BrewCorp you can take us *all?*" He forced J.D. back against the countertop. "What did you want to do with your little self? Before I tore it to pieces?"

J.D. tried to stay calm. "Build stuff."

"What stuff?"

There was a sound like a CO_2 cartridge going off; the wolf head shuddered, and Marchokias staggered back.

"Briefcases." J.D. lifted his finger off of the small button on the side of the attaché. The hidden projectile, which launched from a camouflaged hole in the front, had found its mark. During the past year, J.D. had been experimenting with various grades of wood. Cypress seemed to consistently work the best. Marchokias went within seconds, and the small stake clattered to the floor.

J.D., who was covered from head to toe in ash, spit several times, trying in vain to clear his mouth.

THE INVOICE HAD TO be filled out by hand, since J.D.'s rickety little desk did not come with a workstation (Commander Warren's way of keeping a low, interdepartmental profile).

He had worked sixty hours, made no arrests, and gotten only one kill. The department would consider that a success, since the overall objective had been met and the target neutralized, but to him it was a draw. He would get his modest hourly rate, plus a single bonus for dispatching Mr. Marchosas ($500/target); there would be no live capture bonus ($2000/target). Payment would cover his half of the mortgage, car lease, and groceries, with nothing left over for home improvement (with all of Cerri and his galvanized plumbing needing to be replaced, J.D., who was still covered in ash, resented not being able to get decent water pressure from the shower). There would at least be money for formula and diapers; J.D. had seen to that when he began using a checkbook register to keep track of his credit card purchases.

Life had become quite strange, and not just at work. There had been a kind of voluntary forfeiture—a surrender of wild, youthful aspirations and relationships in exchange for less familiar, mellower ones.

Recently, J.D. had gotten back in touch with his former poker mark, Rich, via social media. Rich, who had long since forgiven him, and had been a faithful member of his high school entourage, lived in Boston, making a six-figure entry-level salary as a junior hedge fund analyst (his brokerage was one of the vampire-free ones, according to the bureau's latest intelligence, although the urban tanks, power suits, and coffee did, briefly, raise some red flags).

What are you doing for wrk now? Rich had messaged, after reading that BrewCorp was being dismantled. When J.D. had replied with his cover story—that he was doing office temp work—Rich had written back, *In Middlestop??? What do they pay you?? Say it ain't so, Pence!!! LOL.*

J.D. had found that he did not like the way this response made him feel, and this had prompted him to ask himself why he kept up with Rich in the first place; he had decided not to reply.

He studied the three, framed pictures on his desktop. His mother, father, and wife and child seemed to study him in return.

J.D. signed the invoice and walked it to Commander Warren's desk, which was less wobbly than his own. Glancing down, he noticed a piece of cardboard wedged under one of the legs.

"Very good work," the commander said, and looked up from his notes. "Thank you, Pence."

The topic of compensation had come up a few weeks earlier, at a department meeting. The commander had responded by asking J.D. and the rest of the agents to stick together and have faith. If any other superior, in any other office had told J.D., "We're all in this together," he would have walked out and resumed his job search. In this case, though, he knew it was the truth.

"My pleasure," he replied.

THE GROUND HAD BEEN reseeded; declining trees had been chopped and removed, transforming the thicket into a natural colonnade that provided lawn seating for picnickers.

J.D. sat down at his usual spot.

He had still been preoccupied with household finances upon arriving at Unger Field (officially Middlestop Heights Field, but he had affixed his own placard while rebuilding the batting cage, and no one had yet removed it); an impromptu game had started, and the healthy turnout of community spectators gave his spirits a lift, as did the absence of construction fencing and equipment.

Puffing on his cigar, he removed the paper bag from his backpack, pulled the cork stopper out of the bottle inside, and poured two fingers of Usquebaugh onto the earth next to him; he poured himself a glass and made a quiet toast.

J.D. had barely gotten to enjoy his first sip when he spotted Cerri's flowing summer dress. She was striding towards him, and from her purposeful gait he knew that he was about to be given an assignment.

She kissed him first, at least. "They want us to submit drawings for the 4-season greenhouse."

"Where's the monster?" he asked.

"With my mom. Your dad came by with diapers when I was on the way out."

He was touched, but in no mood to show it. "When do you need the drawings?"

"Monday."

It was Friday.

"Dammit, Cerri." He had not seen her all week, and for the entire previous weekend, she and her mother had been fighting. "That's going to take all weekend to finish. If I'm going to be working on something, it should be billable."

Cerri said nothing but helped herself to a sip from his glass.

J.D. shook his head and asked himself, "Why am I doing this?"

"For all the free pussy?"

He ignored the joke. Silently, he reminded himself that he was doing it because he had to, even though his winning smile and rock star engineering skills did not impress any member of the startup's granola-crunch community; even though Cerri's meetings made him feel, for the first time in his life, out of place and socially awkward.

The botanical network had been her idea. She envisioned planting a naturopathic community garden in front of each abandoned BrewMart. Greater Middlestop's city councils, although traditionally loathe to practice regional cooperation with one another, had all been unanimously eager to find a use, any use, for their toxic, shared stock of the unwanted retail buildings. Within less than seventy two hours of approaching the local governments, Cerri had gotten three of them to grant thirteen variances and had become a local hero. The gardens had caught on with members of the coven, as well as with non-affiliated, socially conscious undergraduates and young professionals.

What had gotten the rest of Greater Middlestop's attention was black strap molasses. Cerri had given away her first successful batch at the gardens' harvest party, and from that point on, she had become, gradually, inundated with phone calls and emails: many of the party attendees' ailing friends and relatives found her syrup to be remarkably reinvigorating. J.D. had pointed out to her that, a) blackstrap molasses was an excellent source of dietary iron, and b) half of Greater Middlestop had probably become severely anemic. Thus, *Cerri & J.D.'s Miracle Cure for Middlestop Syndrome* was invented.

It was first offered at farmers' markets, but soon neighborhood groceries were asking for it. By November, Cerri was taking backorders; by December she had run out of stock. Her garden's yield of cane, the basic ingredient, had been thoroughly exhausted. In order to grow more, and to do so continuously, she would need climate-controlled greenhouses.

J.D. realized that Cerri was still waiting for his answer. He had evidently been holding his breath for the past minute, while quietly ruminating over the loss of the weekend. He forced himself to breathe, and wished his old friend had been there to snarkily point out the irony.

Being true to oneself would be neither fun nor easy—nor painless; that was one fact of life that George had grasped first.

J.D. poured two more fingers into the earth and turned back to Cerri. "I'll take care of it."

"I know," Cerri replied. She said it not defensively but with a smile.

They did not unpack their picnic dinner but instead nestled against one another, half-watching the game, and when it grew too dark to see well, they closed their eyes and listened for the cracking of a bat and the cheering of young friends.

The End

THANK YOU FOR READING!

I hope you enjoyed this story. *Drip* started out as a follow-up to an independent feature film I made, *The Devil's Filmmaker: BOHICA*. When financing for the screenplay didn't materialize, *Drip* became my first novel. It was a blast to write, and there are many more stories I hope to tell.

For a special look at the movie version that might have been, sign up on www.AndrewMontlack.com

Please leave a review on Amazon, Goodreads, or Loganberry Books! Honest reviews make independent authors become better writers and are crucial in helping our books find their readers. Your thoughts are greatly appreciated.